Praise for Lifε

'A **very enjoyable read**.' Marian Keyes

'*Life, Death and Cellos* **is a witty and irreverent musical romp**, full of characters I'd love to go for a pint with. I thoroughly enjoyed getting to know the Stockwell Park Orchestra and **can't wait for the next book in the series**.' Claire King, author of *The Night Rainbow*

'*Life, Death and Cellos* is **that rare thing – a funny music book**. Rogers knows the world intimately, and portrays it with warmth, accuracy and a poetic turn of phrase. Sharp, witty and richly entertaining.' Lev Parikian, author of *Why Do Birds Suddenly Disappear?*

'With its **retro humour bordering on farce**, this novel offers an escape into the turbulent (and bonkers) world of the orchestra.' Isabel Costello, author of *Paris Mon Amour*

'**Dodgy post-rehearsal curries, friendly insults between musicians, sacrosanct coffee-and-biscuit breaks, tedious committee meetings: welcome to the world of the amateur orchestra**. Throw in a stolen Stradivarius, an unexpected fatality and the odd illicit affair and you have Life, Death and Cellos, the first in a new series by Isabel Rogers.' Rebecca Franks, *BBC Music Magazine*

ISABEL ROGERS

THE
PRIZE
RACKET

THE *Stockwell Park Orchestra* SERIES, BOOK FOUR

This edition published in 2022 by Farrago,
an imprint of Duckworth Books Ltd
1 Golden Court, Richmond, TW9 1EU, United Kingdom

www.farragobooks.com

Print ISBN: 9781788423991
Ebook ISBN: 9781788424004

Stockwell Park Orchestra

Percussion

Tuba

Trombones

Trumpets

Bassoons

Oboes

Clarinets

Flutes

Violas

Cellos

Double basses

Conductor

Second violins

First violins

French horns

To Pearl's tea urn and custard cream stash...

Chapter 1

'That'll do for now,' said Eliot, laughing and putting his baton on his stand and running fingers through his hair. Sunbridge Academy's hall curtains absorbed the end of the final chord of Brahms's second symphony, adding it to the memory of Monday's school dinner. 'With any luck there'll be some coffee – I saw Pearl make a quick exit five minutes ago. Fair enough: it was her urn or those scales.'

David stood up from his fourth horn seat and called out over rising hubbub, 'I've had an interesting request come in – I'd like to see what you all think. Eliot, can I chat to you in the break?'

Charlie and Erin exchanged raised eyebrows at the front of the cellos, and looked up at Eliot, who shrugged and mouthed *'no idea.'*

The first coffee break of the first rehearsal of Stockwell Park Orchestra's new season erupted in its usual slow-motion stampede for the foyer doors, beyond which lay Pearl, her trusty urn, caffeine and biscuits. It was early September in south London: still muggy and close after the months-long summer heatwave. The orchestra had returned from its European tour, and were back to start a new term's rehearsals.

Nobody even smelled of canal water anymore, and the likelihood of any more unexpected dunkings was slim now they were back in south London.

'What's this, then?' Eliot asked David, as they moved out of the way of the oncoming coffee queue and stood by the foyer wall. 'Not another tour. Yet. Please. I'm not ready.'

'Wimp,' said Charlie, joining them, taking tentative sips of his scalding coffee. 'It was only your first. We can't have broken you. You need some of Ann's stamina.'

'Is that just another way of saying I'm old?' said Ann, walking towards them with Erin.

'No,' said Charlie. 'Not at all.' More definitely. 'We bow to your—'

'Oh, don't worry,' Ann said. 'I'm old enough not to care.'

'Come on, David,' said Erin. 'Tell us what's going to happen this year to distract us from our Christmas concert.'

'It won't be as exciting as last time,' muttered Charlie. 'I mean, Eliot will survive. Probably.'

Eliot made hushing, flapping motions at Charlie: whether it was to shut him up or waft away any lingering curse was unclear. 'David. I'm all ears.'

David cleared his throat. 'I've been approached by a poet, Gregory Knight, who wants to join us for a couple of months. A "residency", as he put it. I think he wants to use us to spark some kind of, um, artistic genesis.'

'Was that how he put it too?' said Charlie.

Ann snorted.

'Shut up, Charlie,' said Erin and Eliot together.

'It was, as a matter of fact,' said David. 'I've got his email, hang on.' He fished his phone out of a pocket. 'Yes, here – look… "mutually beneficial symbiosis … explore the creativity of cross-genre fertilisation … opening up possible echoes of the lost worlds of tuned bardic tradition …" – well, he goes on for a couple of paragraphs like that.'

'Tuned bardic tradition?' said Eliot faintly.

'God, he's not going to sing us ancient folk songs, is he?' said Ann.

'Bet you a fiver he brings a lute,' said Charlie.

'I don't think he wants us to do anything special,' said David. 'He just wants to listen. The point is, I thought it might be interesting. He's local. Done some festival work round here. And this wouldn't involve any extra work or – crucially – cost us anything.'

'Rafael will be delighted,' said Erin. Rafael was both second bassoon and orchestra treasurer. Everyone was slightly scared of him.

David smiled a tight, thin-lipped smile. 'Well, yes.'

Eliot grinned. 'I think it's a great idea.'

'Here we go,' said Charlie.

'No, no,' insisted Eliot. 'Since when have we ever tried something new and regretted it?' He held up his hands at the chorus of recent examples they shouted at him. 'Nonsense. They all turned out fine in the end. Let's invite this chap along. Poets are fairly harmless, surely?'

Whichever small literary god was drifting over Sunbridge Academy at that moment must have heard that, and laughed. A hollow, gauntlet-down sort of laugh.

With Eliot's backing, David got the go-ahead with a show of hands when they started the second half of the rehearsal, with only minor muttering from Charlie from the front cello desk underneath Eliot's right ear. David said he would invite Gregory the following week.

Chapter 2

In the pub after the rehearsal, Eliot was the focus of some forceful and, at times, drunkenly sweary questioning.

'What were you *thinking*?' said Charlie, talking through an ambitious mouthful of crisps. 'Can't we have one term of peace without inviting weirdos into our rehearsals?'

'Oi!' said Kayla from the other side of the table, where she was trying to fend off Carl's insistent crisp-pinching habit. 'If you hadn't invited weirdos in, I wouldn't be here.'

'You weren't the weirdo,' said Carl. He put his arm round her shoulders and planted a salt-and-vinegar-enhanced kiss on her cheek. 'It was those posh kids.'

A collective shudder ran around the table as they remembered the events of the previous spring, which had ended up with Kayla, the Head of Music at Sunbridge Academy, being persuaded to join the orchestra permanently, while the Headmaster of Oakdean College retreated behind his posh rhododendrons to rue the day he ever agreed to an exchange programme with state-school riff-raff.

Eliot picked some partially-chewed bits of Charlie's crisps off the front of his shirt and offered them back to Charlie, who declined. 'I can't help being a friendly guy. Maybe I'm destined to be the Mrs Bennet of this orchestra and arrange introductions to prospective matches. Take Carl. I got him a girlfriend.'

'Oi, again,' said Kayla, but looked as pleased as anyone could look while their trombone-playing man was trying to give them a soppy hug at the same time as waving a thumbs-up towards Eliot.

Eliot was unabashed, and third-pint-expansive. 'Maybe this is just the start? Maybe Erin will fall in love with this poet?'

'My turn to say "oi"!' said Erin.

'And mine,' muttered Charlie.

Ann shook her head into her beer and smiled.

'Apart from your shocking paternalistic view of things,' Erin continued, 'this smacks of poetic stereotyping. He might be married.'

Charlie, Ann, Carl and Eliot all stared at her pointedly.

'Remind me who our conductor was before Eliot turned up to save the day,' Carl asked nobody in particular, conversationally. Everyone sniggered, knowing full well their former – now disgraced – conductor's marriage hadn't stopped his affair with Erin. The affair had been mercifully brief. Erin learned fast.

She rolled her eyes and acknowledged the small amount of hypocrisy in her statement, but rallied to her point. 'Or gay. We don't know. We shouldn't assume.'

'You're right,' declared Eliot. 'But I hope he's young and dashing and ready to write sonnets for everyone. We could be immortalised.'

'Immortalised?' came a voice behind him. 'I know you spend a lot of time here, but I'd stop short of describing you as immortalised.'

The figure of Detective Inspector Noel Osmar had appeared without warning, as he always seemed to. He had rolled up his shirtsleeves and held a pint in one hand and a book in the other.

'Noel!' shouted everyone, and shuffled their chairs around to make room at the table for him.

'Thought I might find you here on the first Monday night of term,' Noel said, nodding amiably all round.

'Ever the detective,' said Charlie.

'Nice to see you,' said Eliot. 'Just finished work?'

'But you brought your book anyway,' said Erin. 'Good call. We can be boring.'

'No chance of that,' said Noel, sitting down. 'How is everyone? Good to be back home?'

'Eliot's trying to set Erin up with a poet neither of them have ever met,' said Kayla.

Noel blinked and took a long swallow of beer. 'I think, as always, I've arrived too late for any of you to make sense. Cheers.'

Noel spent the rest of the evening until closing time slowly and happily making his way down his pint, listening to musicians who were two or three drinks ahead of him bicker about whether poets would converse in iambic pentameters throughout orchestral rehearsals. It was a funny old life, he thought.

Chapter 3

The following Monday evening, Eliot started the orchestra's rehearsal with the second movement of the Brahms. Brahms had written his second symphony in the uncomplicatedly happy key of D major, although that description – as is so often the case – masks some key signature shenanigans in the middle. This second movement is marked *Adagio non troppo*: the get-out clause of composers. It is an instruction that avoids shouldering blame for any outcome – 'Slowly, but not too slowly, you fool. Don't *wallow*. Don't rush at it either – no, that's not right, you've ruined it now.' Depending on how the conductor is feeling, playing this symphony can take anything from forty minutes if they are in snappy form, to nearly an hour if they are just emerging from a particularly poignant break-up and can't afford therapy.

The second movement whacks in a key change to B major, which ramps up the sharp count from a comfortable two to a squint-inducing five. This means for five out of every seven notes you have to remember to raise them by a semitone: no mean feat for amateur musicians playing on a weekday evening, many of whom were rehearsing after a full day at work. And this was before the coffee break.

If the sudden sharp onset wasn't enough, the movement starts with a melody in the cellos written in the tenor clef: the clef of squeaky terror, where the music goes higher than cellos usually like to. Within five bars they are already two ledger lines above the stave, being implored to play it *poco forte espressivo* (a bit loud, with expression). Luckily, it is also one of Brahms's most banging 1877 tunes, so the sectional spirit usually rises to the task. By the time they hand over the melodic baton to the violins and flute and return to grumbling along on their bottom string, the tune has been effectively stamped 'cello approved' and everyone goes home happy.

Eliot turned to Erin and Charlie on the front desk before starting. 'Everyone OK? Do you need a sectional before this?'

'Nah, we'll be fine,' said Erin, glancing behind her. 'Ann must have played this – what? – about a million times.'

'Roughly,' called Ann from her preferred seat at the back of the section, just in front of Kayla playing double bass. Ann was a former pro, but very much enjoyed her current position of no responsibility, from where she could snark with abandon.

Carl chipped in from the trombones. 'Even we have to play *pianissimo*, so this had better be good.'

'Watch and learn,' said Charlie.

'Fighting talk,' said Eliot, laughing. 'Here we go then. In four.'

The eerie melancholy conjured by Brahms rose around them like a smoke machine switching on. With Erin's confident lead, the whole cello section sang together, despite some people falling off the odd sharp and wincing an apology at Eliot, who waved them through with benign sangfroid.

After the violins had their turn, Neema on first horn emerged into her solo from a held note – like a figure coming out of a forest into a clearing, making a listener suddenly aware of her presence but with the realisation she had already been there for some time, as if the trees had melted away around her. First doubled by Courtney on bassoon, she was then joined by Gwynneth on oboe, and then the flutes, and their melodies twined around each other like ivy climbing skyward. Even Brian's legendary wayward flute tuning seemed to fit. By the time the cellos re-entered with another phrase, the glorious woodwind and horn had completed a kind of mini chamber concert within the orchestra before the whole lot swerved into a different direction and mood. Brahms was very, *very* good at his job.

As Eliot brought the orchestra to a halt to work on some of the detail, there was a ripple of foot-shuffling throughout the players, as an appreciation for the superb efforts of all concerned. Exposed solo work can be nerve-wracking, and a brief foot-scrape from fellow musicians can make all the difference to morale.

'Hear hear,' said Eliot. 'Great stuff. Now, let's go back to letter A, where Neema comes in – and Gwynneth, when you and Courtney join her, we really need to get our ensemble tight, OK? Remember it's only *piano* to start with. We've got time to let it grow.'

As they worked through steadily, the hall door opened behind Eliot and a shortish man in his late forties walked in. He stopped just inside the door, closed his eyes, spread his hands out wide and inhaled, letting the music wash over him and – perhaps more importantly – letting onlookers *know* he was letting the music wash over him. He wore a beanie hat despite the mild evening, and had a bag strap slung diagonally over his chest, pushing his collarless shirt askew and rucking up several coils of beaded necklaces. His dishevelled jeans stopped slightly too short above the ankle to be a deliberate fashion statement, revealing odd socks and neon laces on his boots. It was as if a scarecrow had been transplanted into the school hall to lead an exercise in yoga and mindfulness.

'Aye aye,' whispered Charlie to Erin, leaning closer to her in their bars rest while the wind players were practising. 'It's the poet. Looks like he's sparking his artistic genesis as we speak.'

Erin glanced toward the door and smothered a giggle. A faint trace of patchouli began to drift over to the players.

Charlie was not the only player to notice. Eliot, with his back to the door, knew something was afoot from the darting glances of musicians who were supposed to be looking at him. An orchestra is just as good as a rear-view mirror, with an added prism of opinion. Even before he turned, Eliot knew it would be worth it.

At the next halt, he twisted round to greet the newcomer, who was still standing with outstretched arms and closed eyes. After a moment of silence, the man opened his eyes and reactivated his limbs from starfish mode.

'Hello,' said Eliot. 'You must be Gregory. Welcome to Stockwell Park Orchestra.'

Gregory took a huge inhalation through his nose, raised his face once more heavenward and closed his eyes, putting his hand over his heart in fervent thanks as he performed a small bow.

'Doesn't he talk?' said Charlie, under his breath. 'Bit odd, for a poet.'

'Maybe he mimes them?' said Ann.

'Poetry through the medium of modern dance,' said Erin.

'Maybe he's got the wrong evening class,' said Carl.

Eliot's lips twitched, and he mouthed *shh* at them before turning again to Gregory. 'Sit wherever you like. We're working on Brahms's second symphony at the moment. Slow movement. Got about half an hour before coffee break, so...' He trailed off, gesturing to the collection of chairs scattered about the edges of the hall.

The orchestra continued with Brahms. Gregory Knight walked to a point midway between the door and Eliot, putting his feet carefully directly in front of each other as if he were walking on a narrow beam. He may have thought it gave him the air of a fastidious cat, but actually it looked more as if he had been sent down a fashion catwalk after too many Bacardis. He came to a halt, lowered himself to the floor and stretched out on his back, with his arms in much the same position as before albeit on a different plane. After a moment, he lifted one buttock and wrestled his messenger bag out from underneath, sliding it around to his belly, where it rose and fell with his deep breaths. His eyes closed.

By this time, many of the players were in helpless giggles, and there were a few sudden unplanned squawks from the brass and wind as they fought to gain control. Even David, from his place as fourth horn, found himself sharing a smile across the hall with Ann, as the ghost of his tic, faithful companion during many stressful Stockwell Park Orchestra exploits, threatened to come back to life behind his eyebrow.

Chapter 4

Pearl was given her usual five minutes head start before the break to get the urn up to temp. She skirted around the supine Gregory with as wide a berth as she thought decorous, but he seemed unaware of her. Or indeed anything. When the music stopped and feet started to trundle past his head, he opened his eyes and watched them go past.

David loomed into his sightline. 'Hello, Gregory. I'm David – orchestra manager. We've emailed.'

'Hi, David,' said Gregory, from his place on the floor. 'Thank you for letting me sojourn with you. I can feel I'm going to draw great spirit from this residency.'

'That's marvellous. Um – would you like a coffee? Or tea? We're just having our break now.'

Gregory unpeeled himself from the floor and stood up. 'I would, thank you.'

They walked through to the foyer and joined the slowly-moving swirl of a queue for Pearl's refreshments, while Gregory outlined to David his vision for future work. David listened in silence. Carl's great height and bulk was ahead of them; he was standing with one arm draped around Kayla's shoulders.

'Tell you what, though,' Carl was saying, 'this poet fella is going to be good value.'

'If he doesn't get squashed in the custard cream stampede,' said Kayla. 'Never get between this orchestra and their biscuits. I've learned that much.'

David cleared his throat with enough projection that they both turned around. Gregory was still talking, oblivious. David eyed Carl with the air of a man who might have made a mistake but was hoping very much that he hadn't because the energy involved in backtracking had not been budgeted for.

Carl took pity on him and nodded at Gregory. 'Alright, pal? Sounds like you've got a whole lotta plans for yourself there.'

Gregory stopped directing his verbal stream at David and turned to Carl, swivelling his eyes up until they could fit Carl's head into view rather than his chest, which was at everyone else's normal eye level. 'I *have*. This is happening at a supremely exciting juxtaposition in my professional—'

'Going to stop you there, mate,' said Carl, following Kayla to stand in front of Pearl's table and dropping some change into her Tupperware pot. 'First things first. Thanks, Pearl. Magic.'

Pearl beamed at him and turned to Gregory with an enquiring smile. 'Tea or coffee? Milk and sugar are just up there.'

Gregory scanned the table, with its neat rows of disposable cups pre-dosed with instant coffee or a teabag. 'Tea, thank you.' He took the proffered cup and began to follow Carl. Pearl made a little fluttering sound and glanced at David, not knowing if Gregory was a VIP and was thus entitled to a Free Beverage, or if she should be requiring payment as per.

'Ah, yes,' said David. 'Gregory, we generally make a contribution to the cost of refreshments…?' He trailed off, his tone wending its way upwards so as not to cause offence – as is the British way.

'Oh. Well.' Gregory patted one side of his jeans pockets with his free hand. 'I'm afraid I haven't…'

'Never mind,' said David, putting in extra for his own to cover it. 'I may well have omitted to mention that in our email exchange. Perhaps next week?'

They both moved away, and Pearl nodded her thanks to David and turned her attention to the next person in line.

Carl and Kayla wandered over to join Erin, Charlie, Ann and Eliot.

'Do you know the poet is following you?' said Charlie to Carl.

'Looks like he's come out of his shell anyway,' said Erin.

Ann sipped her coffee and looked over.

'Now he's started talking, I don't think he can stop,' said Carl. 'He's on cruise control with extra vocab.'

'I thought poets were supposed to be socially awkward introverts,' said Kayla.

'Let's give him a chance,' said Eliot. 'Come on, here he comes. Be nice.'

Carl grimaced but turned his body slowly, like a lock gate, to invite David and Gregory into their circle.

'…and I'm going to use that research to recalibrate the nexus of my forthcoming sequence,' Gregory was saying to a rather glazed David.

'I sometimes wish my nexus could be recalibrated too,' said Charlie, nodding kindly. 'But the subs go through the roof.'

Gregory stared at him blankly.

'Sorry – Netflix,' said Charlie. 'I'm always getting them muddled up.'

Ann's face disappeared into her coffee cup.

'Gregory, this is Charlie, one of our cellists,' said David hurriedly, 'and you've met Eliot of course. And this is Ann, and Erin, also cellists. And Carl, trombone, and Kayla, bass.'

'I'm sure you'll get to know us all before long,' said Eliot.

Erin sneezed without warning, somehow managing to make it one of those tiny, quiet, internal ones, and also miraculously keeping her coffee cup stable.

'Bless you,' said Ann.

'I'm sure I will,' said Gregory to Eliot, bestowing on them all a wide smile. 'In fact, my aim in coming here is to—'

Erin sneezed again, twice. 'Sorry.'

'What is it this time, Sneeze Girl?' said Charlie. 'Honestly, if it's not lilies in posh schools, it's… oh.' He flicked his eyes toward Gregory and his patchouli aura.

'Actually, Eliot,' said David, seizing the opportunity of a pause in Gregory's delivery, 'I've had another email this week that might be of interest.'

'As interesting as the last one?' said Eliot.

'Surely not,' said Ann.

David pressed on. 'It was from a TV producer, wanting to sound us out about taking part in a new programme they're putting together. A kind of competition. Kind of like *Strictly Come Dancing*, only for musicians. At least, that's how he put it. He'd seen us all over social media last month in Bruges and wondered if we'd be up for it.'

'I'm not wearing a leotard for anyone,' said Carl.

'Oh, go on,' said Kayla, giggling. 'Not even in private?'

'I'm with you,' said Charlie to Carl. 'My thighs emerge into daylight for no man.'

'Shame,' said Erin. 'I could get used to the boys in spangles and glitter. What do you reckon, Ann?'

'I hope to god this isn't true,' she said, shaking her head and laughing. 'David? Come on.'

'I never mentioned spangles,' said David. 'I think it was more of a competition analogy he was using. Instead of individual celebs, he was talking about groups of amateur musicians – of all kinds. You know, from an orchestra to smaller ensembles.'

'What – all classical, you mean?' asked Eliot.

'No, I don't think so, necessarily,' said David. 'He said it was quite a broad base.'

'Carl's base *is* quite broad,' agreed Charlie.

Gregory was taking sips of his tea and following the conversation closely. He seemed to have a binary sort of communication setting: in or out. One hundred per cent in either direction.

Erin embarked on a whole set of mini sneezes. Charlie put his hand on Gregory's shoulder.

'You know who would be fascinated to hear about your nexus, mate?' he said, steering Gregory away from Erin and into the throng of musicians behind him. 'Maureen here.'

Maureen turned, her face puckered into her permanent scowl. 'Oh. You're the poet, aren't you?'

'I am,' said Gregory, nodding his greeting to Maureen and his thanks to Charlie, who was already melting away back to his friends.

Maureen, the orchestra's energy sink, turned her full attention to Gregory, who began to outline his options for recalibrating his nexus before she could pour cold water on the idea.

Charlie returned to Erin and gave her a thumbs-up. 'Maybe Maureen will act like an air filter and soak up his patchouli along with his bloody nexus drivel.'

'We can hope,' said Ann.

'Thank you,' said Erin.

'And I don't even feel sorry for either of them,' said Charlie, grinning.

Behind Charlie's back, Gregory had already sidled past Maureen towards Beatriz, who played first clarinet. Beatriz was young and beautiful, with dark hair that fell in a curtain of curls down her back. Maureen watched Gregory smile at Beatriz the way men never smiled at her, and the lines around her mouth deepened. It didn't occur to her to direct her antipathy toward Gregory rather than Beatriz.

Gregory leaned close to Beatriz and put an arm round her shoulder, intent on imparting insightful gems of wisdom. Beatriz froze – her eyes wide, her coffee cup raised to her lips – making all the lightning assessments young women must when faced with the distasteful attentions of an older man with tin-eared confidence in public. Maureen drank her coffee alone. Gregory's attention was, after all, a gift neither she nor Beatriz actually wanted.

Chapter 5

They returned to the Brahms for the second half of the rehearsal: this time focusing on the last movement. Gregory accompanied Beatriz right up to the violin seats on the edge of the orchestra's territory, beyond which he felt he could not go. As Beatriz picked her way through the string chairs, past the flutes to her place in the clarinets, Gregory watched her retreating back, her swinging hair catching the light. He had a pensive, satisfied expression as he turned and strode to his previous position halfway between the door and the orchestra.

Eliot, walking to his stand, passed Gregory settling himself onto the floor again like a huge, dry starfish.

'You might like this,' Eliot called down as he passed through the patchouli cloud, not slowing his walk. 'I guarantee it will make you grin.'

Gregory raised both thumbs.

Carl wandered back into the hall, and skirted Gregory wide on his way to the trombones. Sixteen-year-old Tracie Scott was just behind him. She was the newest trombone player, and the youngest musician in the whole orchestra, having been recruited two terms earlier as part of a community outreach programme that had rather spiralled into organised crime by mistake – but that is another story. Freshly home from stowing away on the orchestra's European tour, she was back to her old direct and unrepentant self. She was a pupil at Sunbridge Academy, and ate weekday lunches in this very hall.

She nudged Carl, jerking her head over at Gregory. 'Not bein' funny, but he don't wanna stay down there. Marshall Wright had an accident at dinnertime – one of his big ones – and they only mop the floors once a week.'

Carl snorted. 'Reckon he's laid down in worse places. Not our problem.'

They sat down and retrieved trombones out of their cases.

The fourth movement of the Brahms – the final one – was marked *allegro con spirito* (fast with spirit), but disguised its true nature by starting with strings in unison *sotto voce*, unwrapping each part away from each other like a fraying plait as it went on, still quietly, until the woodwind joined in and they all threaded themselves together in a new pattern. Gregory had closed his eyes again.

What Gregory didn't know was that after twenty-two bars of this benign pastoral dance, Brahms had given the orchestra one beat of total silence before letting rip with the timpani and most of the brass – crashing into this idyll with a boisterous *forte* capable of surprising the unwary listener. It is the aural equivalent of someone jumping out of the bushes yelling '*BOO!*'

Eliot raised his eyebrows at the orchestra in that beat of silence, grinning, and they responded with such a thunderclap of energy it jerked Gregory into an electrified bundle of limbs. The full force of Brahms in tumbling spate filled the hall and, after a few sudden *sforzandos* to kick-start them, the engine of violins and violas set up their quavers to push everything forward. Gregory sat up to watch, open-mouthed.

Pete, at the back of the viola section, shuffled forward on his chair and leaned closer to his music stand, his tongue creeping out from between his lips as he valiantly scrubbed with the rest of the upper strings. For twenty-two bars the violas belted out wall-to-wall quavers, without rests, at a blanket *fortissimo*. It was supposed to be played on two strings at the same time – double-stopped, to give it its technical term – but Pete only ever defaulted to the lower note of the pair, even though his outer seat on the desk meant he should take the upper note if they split. There was only so much he could give. It is to Brahms's credit that he had designed this passage with such intrinsic energy, the whole viola section kept going as one synchronised component. When it all calmed down a bit, Pete shifted back again in his chair and resettled his viola under his chin, exchanging a brief relieved smile with Pearl. Making it through such passages together are the foundations of a desk partnership.

Gregory remained upright, gazing at the musicians. He stared at Beatriz, though he couldn't pick out her notes in the texture of the full orchestral sound. He found it thrilling that Beatriz kept looking up from her music to stare right at him with intensity, not realising his position behind Eliot made it easy to mistake the direction of her gaze.

Eliot called a halt a bit further into the movement. 'Great work. Can we just hear the strings at letter D?'

'Uh-oh,' said Charlie. 'Surprise sectional.'

Eliot laughed. 'It's the switch from straight quavers to triplets. It's tricky.'

'Damn Brahms and his bloody twos-and-threes,' called Ann.

Marco looked over at the violas from his position in the first violins and grinned. 'Do you need a viola try first?'

A soft 'ooh' rippled round the strings. There's nothing like sectional rivalry to raise musicians' game.

'Alright, alright, calm down,' said Eliot. 'Look, violas, I know it's suddenly in treble clef and you have to divide a dotted minim into six, but—'

'It doesn't even add up,' grumbled Pete. 'We're in 4/4, then there's this misprint on our tremolo. We've got too many beats in the bar.'

'That's not tremolo, Pete,' said Eliot, not unkindly, 'it's triplets. You should have a little "six" under the dotted minim, and then a "three" under your dotted crotchets?'

Pete leaned right up to his music stand, raised his glasses, peered closely, put his glasses down on his nose again, and sniffed. 'Oh. I thought that was old pencil marks. These parts are terrible. Nobody rubs things out.'

The whole orchestra burst into laughter.

'Oh god, Pete, never change,' said Erin, wiping tears and shaking her head.

Eliot let the laughter die down before trying again. 'So, second violins, violas and cellos should all start playing triplets together, while firsts join in with the triplets on the last beat of the bar, and basses stick to straight slurs throughout. OK? Shall we try from letter D? Slowly? It's just those four bars.'

He brought them in at around half speed, and one by one the players who had been scrubbing out tremolo realised they should actually be playing (slower) triplets and fell into line with their section. After a while the raggedy mess coalesced into a rhythmic whole. The revelatory expressions around the whole string section were Eliot's answer.

'Brilliant!' he said. 'Now a bit faster? Don't fall off the triplets.'

He wound them up a notch, and then again, and after a few more tries he had managed to coax a string sound light years away from the scrubby mess of five minutes earlier. By the time he invited the wind and brass to join them again, it sounded like a different orchestra.

While they were working on this, Gregory lay down again and closed his eyes. Beatriz looked over at him and chewed the inside of her cheek until she had to play again.

Chapter 6

Later that week, Eliot arrived at the coffee shop ten minutes after he was supposed to. As he rounded the corner and reached the door, he could see David already sitting inside at a table with another man who had wispy, greying hair, rimless glasses and doughnut sugar all round his mouth. Eliot sketched a wave at them as he went past to order his coffee, miming 'ordering coffee' as he went. He hoped his miming skills conveyed apologies for his tardiness too, but wished, not for the first time that morning, that he didn't have to meet the TV producer hoping to ensnare Stockwell Park Orchestra into a televised music competition. Going viral over the summer with a Chris Hemsworth-esque poster boy horn soloist on tour had consequences, he was discovering.

Returning with his cup, Eliot leaned over to shake the rimless-glasses man's hand, which had been proffered from his position of slightly raised buttocks but not committing to standing up which would have involved moving his chair. Eliot digested this body language and accurately divined his perceived social standing with the man. It didn't make him feel any better.

'Eliot,' said David. 'This is Russell Donovan, the producer who emailed us. Russell, meet Eliot Yarrow, our conductor.'

'Hello, yes,' said Eliot. 'Sorry I'm late. Bloody Northern Line.'

'No worries,' said Russell. 'Been shooting the breeze with Dave here. Fascinating set up you have.' He took another large bite of his doughnut.

"Dave" shook his head infinitesimally at Eliot and sipped his coffee.

'Right,' said Eliot. 'What have I missed?'

Russell spoke enthusiastically round his doughnut. 'Well, as Dave knows, Quork Media – that's us – are sourcing acts for our new competition. Classical music groups. You know, a bit like the *Strictly* format but for musicians. A bit *The Voice* but groups. A bit *The Greatest Dancer* but—'

'Sitting down?' said Eliot.

David coughed behind his coffee cup.

'Well, yes,' agreed Russell. 'Or, no? I mean, I'm not against you standing up, if you prefer? Let's not go down the boring old stereotyped road.'

'Russell said our orchestra was flagged up to him because of our recent online fame,' said David, before Eliot could reply. 'He thought we could leverage that to bring some more viewers in. Possibly younger viewers?'

Russell nodded. A cloud of tiny sugar crystals drifted down from his chin and settled on his shirt. 'A symbiosis, obviously. Your profile would enjoy a huge boost from the broadcast. Maybe more than one, if you make it through to the final! We have it set up so the earlier rounds are pre-recorded and then the semis and final are live. Saturday early evening. Prime time.'

'BBC?' asked David.

'No, ITV. And we're getting some *preeety* sweet ad enquiries. This demographic rocks.'

'Best not go head-to-head with *Strictly*, I guess,' said Eliot. 'Some juggernauts of live telly competitions are best not interfered with.'

'From what I gather,' said David, 'there is a significant prize fund for the final – is that right, Russell?'

Russell nodded, busy with the end of his doughnut, but spread his hands wide and gestured with the distance between doughnut and coffee that the financial rewards were generous indeed.

'Meaning if we get through, we get to spend more on soloists next season?' said Eliot.

'Or boost the Stockwell Park Orchestra coffers generally,' said David. 'Which, as you know, can be precarious. The whim of supporters like Mrs Ford-Hughes…'

'…can blow in either direction, I get you.'

Russell was looking at them with a faintly uncomprehending expression. He finished chewing, swallowed and wiped his mouth. David and Eliot relaxed, not realising until then how tense the sugar beard had been making them.

'What other groups are signed up?' said Eliot. 'Are you allowed to say?'

Russell threw his screwed-up paper napkin on the table and spread his hands wide. 'Well, obviously I have to be a bit circumspect about all this.'

'Obviously.'

'But we're really excited about it. Our pipeline is huge! Massive. Think jazz bands, piano groups, horn quartets… I think we're even in talks with one of those Suzuki violin classes of tiny kids. Tiny! Playing sixteenth-size fiddles or some such! Incredible. Our working title is *Pass the Baton*. We're thinking, you know, classical conductor's baton, pass it on, get through to the next round kind of thing. It has kinetic energy. A connection.'

Eliot decided not to bring up the possible lavatory connection of an unfortunate constipated episode. He had spent too long as a conducting student and his mates' reflex scatological references were difficult to shake.

'So – what kind of commitment are you looking for?' said David. 'I mean, a whole concert, just one piece or what?'

'No, no – not a whole concert.' Russell laughed: a high, alarmed braying that conveyed his terror of over-promising in the age of tiny internet concentration spans. 'The nature of our show is more… episodic. Catch the zeitgeist. Viewers' attention. Our production team might want to come along to a rehearsal. You know, scope out potential. And then your piece for the heats would be around ten minutes, or less. Maybe less? It depends. Less, maybe.'

Eliot smiled. 'Well, David, I think we can probably crowbar ten minutes – maybe less? – into our rehearsal schedule this term without disrupting our concert preparations too much. Sounds fun. And we might even make some money. What do you think?'

'If you're happy to take this on, let's do it,' said David.

'Fabulous!' said Russell, clapping his hands softly in front of his sugar-encrusted chest. 'Now, I must run. Dave – I have all your details. I'll be in touch about when my guys want to come along to a rehearsal, yeah? Lovely to meet you, Eliot. Ciao!'

Eliot watched Russell's departing back with a broad grin. 'Well, *Dave…*'

David drank more coffee and flicked his eyes towards Eliot as the street door swung shut again. 'As you say, we could make some money. Rafael is all for it. And it's good publicity for the orchestra. I can put up with losing a syllable for a few weeks.'

'Hmm. He said he heard of us when we went viral with that Bruges thing last month.'

'Well, a lot of people did.'

'Do you think we would have been such a hit without our sexy star?'

David looked at Eliot and smiled. 'Perhaps not. What are you getting at?'

'I wonder who's in that horn quartet he mentioned.'

Chapter 7

At the following week's rehearsal, as everyone was chatting and getting their instruments out, David stood up. Gregory Knight was already there, standing close to where Beatriz was putting her bag down at the side of the hall. She walked over to the clarinet seats. He dug around in his satchel for a notebook and pencil.

David cleared his throat. 'Ah – hello everyone? Just a quick update. Hello? Um – Carl, do you mind?'

Carl left off his trombone warm-up exercises, which that evening consisted of the bass line of Stevie Wonder's *Superstition*, and gave David a thumbs-up.

'Thanks. Yes, well, you may have heard something about a television company being interested in us for their new competition programme.'

'Ooh – is it happening?' said Gwynneth from her place in the oboes. 'I'll tell Mam. She's only just got over our tour videos. We've been the talk of Merthyr.'

'Yes,' said David. 'Eliot and I met the producer last week. I'll leave Eliot to talk detailed programme stuff, but we'll be working up an extra ten minutes or so—'

'Or less,' said Eliot

'Or less,' agreed David, smiling. 'I don't know what Eliot wants to do. Someone from Quork Media will be popping into next week's rehearsal to see what we're up to, and then I think they record our thing a bit later on.'

'What? We don't get to go to a TV studio and do it live?' said Charlie.

'Thank God,' said Ann.

'If they like us,' said Eliot, 'and we get through to the next round, I think it's all up for grabs. Including prize money.'

A muffled '*wooo*!' rippled round the musicians, with a few exchanges of '*pub tab*' and '*get the beers in*' from somewhere in the brass section.

Gregory looked around the hall, directing a wave at Beatriz as she lined up the reed on her clarinet mouthpiece and turned the screws to keep it in place. Courtney, whose seat as first bassoon was next to Beatriz, leaned over. 'Think you might have caught Gregory's eye. Watch out.'

'Ugh,' said Beatriz, ducking behind her music. 'He wouldn't leave me alone in the break last week. Wanging on about... I dunno. Something to do with poetry. Like I had even asked. Draping his arm all over me. I think he wants me to collaborate on something. Said he's getting a band together called Ambient Sounds. Can you imagine?'

'Maybe you're his muse.'

Beatriz rolled her eyes. 'Can we get coffee together later? Don't let him corner me again.'

'Sure.'

'So,' continued Eliot, after the excitement of prospective life-changing windfalls had died down, 'we'll be working on the third movement of the Brahms today, but we'll save that 'til after the break and let the brass off early, since they're not

29

in it.' He acknowledged the cheers, led by Carl. 'Horns, I'm afraid we'll need you to stay, though. Meanwhile, let's get stuck into the first movement.'

'Are we doing the repeat?' asked Pearl.

'Yes, repeat is in. But we won't bother about it now.'

There was an audible relaxation from the string players on the inner half of the desks, whose job it was to turn pages – usually forward one at a time, but in the case of a repeat, back the correct number (which in a busy violin part full of semiquavers could be many pages) to the corresponding repeat mark. Nobody is *ever* ready for a repeat, no matter how much the non-page-turning desk partner raises their eyebrows or nods at the music stand. It's further complicated by some players taking the stern union position that Inner Player Turns Forward, Outer Player Turns Back. This sometimes results in a page-turning stand-off worthy of Clint Eastwood's poncho and cigar. Almost nobody outside the string section knows anything about these feuds. What with that and differences of opinion over bowing marks, sulking can fester for months.

'Yeah, it's only two sharps,' called Carl from behind Pearl. 'You won't need the second go to catch ones you missed the first time round.'

The entire string section drew in a shocked breath. Carl stuck out his tongue as only an unrepentant trombone player can.

'Settle down, kids,' said Eliot, laughing. 'The trombones have to play really quietly in a minute. We might get our own back. Can we have an A please, Gwynneth?'

He waited until everyone was tuned and ready, then brought in the cellos and basses for their bar alone to kick everything off – they were the nudge of the sledge at the top of a hill before gravity took over. It started in triple time: a dreamy, waltzing sort of feeling, where the horns were given the first phrase before taking turns with the wind, and then the first violins and violas crept in on a long, high, sustained note before making their way down the slope themselves, getting quieter and quieter, with the violas handing over their melody to the cellos as it got lower, everyone becoming more introspective until they disappeared altogether and left Max doing the quietest possible timpani roll completely on his own. Sneaking in after this were the three trombones and Leroy on tuba, accompanied by the cellos. Three... slow... chords – as smooth as warm chocolate. Technically speaking.

'Nope,' said Eliot, smiling at Carl and stopping his beat. 'Sorry. That's the bit I need you to shut up for, not blast away like a quartet of foghorns across the estuary.'

The strings felt understandably vindicated.

'Don't get cocky, you lot,' said Eliot, looking at the violins and violas. 'I don't want to hear a cigarette paper between your intonation on that exposed section. And then, when the violas hand it over to the cellos,' he turned to Erin, 'don't come thumping in. I shouldn't be able to hear the join. Shall we try it again? And I'm sure Brian and Gwynneth will float their little bits over the top when we get there, yeah?'

Eliot acknowledged their nods and gathered everyone up for another try. This time, Tracie tried so hard to be quiet, nothing came out of her trombone at all, and they collapsed in giggles.

'Go for it a bit more,' said Carl, kindly. 'If Leroy can keep a lid on it, we'll be perfect.'

'Oi!' said Leroy.

'He might have a point,' said Eliot, laughing. 'Again? Bar twenty?'

This time it went better, and they made it through to the first *forte* passage, bursting joyously through a door from their pastoral outdoor dance into the party happening inside, ushered in by the trumpets, who were finally allowed to join in. And here, Brahms employed one of his favourite tricks: switching effortlessly from laid-back, triple time bars into an energised, marching two-beat feeling – without bothering to change his time signature. Quite often he did that by bracketing two bars of whatever he was writing into one chunk, and dividing that by three, to make what is known as a hemiola or Getting An Orchestra To Vibe.

The players worked towards their coffee break, some exchanging fleeting half-smiles and glances as they polished the contours of the music. Irrespective of their sectional rivalries, they were all on the same side when it came to playing a better symphony, though Carl regularly despaired when he watched the back of the violas try to get into an off-beat groove. Pete was never going to be one of life's groovers.

Chapter 8

They piled eagerly through for Pearl's refreshments at the break. Gregory watched them all go from his seat at the side of the hall where he was writing in his Moleskine notebook. Courtney stuck close to Beatriz, and neither of them glanced at him as they walked to the foyer, so they didn't see his eyes follow Beatriz until she disappeared through the door. He flipped a page in his notebook and started scribbling.

Charlie and Erin were putting their cellos away for the break. Charlie nodded over toward Gregory, and whispered, 'Aye aye. Gregory has found his inspiration.'

Erin looked at Gregory, who was still writing intently, leaning the notebook on his satchel on top of his crossed legs. She pulled a face. 'He gives me the creeps.'

'Oh? Well maybe we should warn Courtney and Beatriz then. He was staring at them before he started haikuing or whatever.'

'Jeez, yes, definitely. Didn't you see him last week, when he'd cornered Beatriz in the break and had his arm round her? Ann was all for having it out with him, but then it was time to play and he had to leave her alone anyway. Maybe we should have said something then.'

'Oh? I was joking. Maybe I shouldn't be. Is this another one of those things I've missed because I'm a boy?'

'Probably.' Erin smiled.

'Sorry.'

'It's OK. You're a pretty quick learner.'

'Is he creepy enough that you reckon we should have a word with David?'

'What, you mean get him chucked out?'

'Maybe.' Charlie clipped his cello case shut. 'I don't think Gregory is bringing in a load of dosh like the telly guys, so it's not exactly a conflict of interest.'

'True. But Eliot will be so disappointed he hasn't found me my perfect man.'

'Perfect men don't appear out of nowhere. You need to do your homework.'

'Of course. You can be my benchmark,' said Erin. 'Come on, we need to check on Courtney and Beatriz. Gregory's just gone through.'

They walked out of the hall together, with Charlie mouthing *benchmark?* to himself and rolling his eyes. Tucking themselves in behind Ann in the coffee queue, they mentioned Gregory's stalking of Beatriz to her, wondering if he was an ideal person to loiter among the orchestra.

Ann glanced round and turned back to face the table. 'Fuck, no,' she said, and then immediately, 'oh god, sorry Pearl. That was *not* aimed at you. I'd love a coffee, thanks.'

Pearl, wide-eyed, nodded.

They looked over at Gregory. He had taken up position next to Beatriz, who was shifting closer to Courtney. Gregory followed, and the trio began drifting across the foyer as Gregory refused to give up his slow but relentless pursuit.

'I'm not having this,' said Ann, picking up her cup and striding away without waiting for Charlie and Erin. They apologised again to Pearl, took their own drinks and followed Ann.

Gregory was talking at Beatriz in the manner of one who confuses 'with' and 'at', but has given it no thought and also doesn't care, all the while inching into her personal space.

Courtney did her best to divert his attention and tried to interrupt. 'That's all fascinating, Gregory, but Beatriz and I need to discuss a section in the Brahms, don't we Beatriz? Sorry.'

'Yeah.' Beatriz nodded and turned back to Gregory. 'If you don't mind?'

'You don't need to ask permission to leave a conversation, Beatriz,' said Ann, appearing at Gregory's side and nodding at him cheerfully. 'If it *was* a conversation? Looks like you were doing all the talking, Gregory. That's a broadcast.'

'What?'

'Did you not hear me or are you too thick to understand?' Ann was still smiling, but nobody within earshot was under any illusion that this was anything other than a professional veneer over absolutely adamantine intent.

Erin and Charlie joined the group.

'What did we miss?' whispered Charlie to Courtney.

'Nothing much yet,' she whispered back. 'Ann's just got started.'

Gregory blinked and exhaled in disbelief. 'What the fuck? I was just discussing with this delightful young lady the possibility of a symbiosis between the spoken word and a responsive musical phrase, and whether—'

'Yeah, going to stop you there, my friend,' said Ann. 'Because I am not a "delightful young lady". And I have had it with your shit. Beatriz here *is* both delightful and young. I was like that several decades ago, and know more about "responsive musical phrases" than she's had cause to find out yet. But – let's not kid ourselves – there was no chance in hell of you approaching *me* to discuss any fucking symbiosis, was there?'

Gregory, wisely, kept silent.

'Go, Ann,' breathed Erin.

Several nearby conversations had paused. Beatriz and Courtney exchanged a look of combined awe and apprehension.

'We both know exactly what you were doing here,' Ann continued. 'It has nothing to do with musicianship, or art, or possibly even *listening* to what Beatriz thinks about either of those. It has nothing to do with whatever doggerel you've been scribbling in your grubby little notebook. It has everything to do with your ego and how you can manipulate a young woman. I have seen it all before, and I've had *enough* of your shit.'

A small round of spontaneous applause burst out among those musicians nearest to Ann. Gregory opened his mouth, looked at the people surrounding him, and shut it again.

'Oh, mate,' said Charlie. 'Have you been introduced to Ann? She's our orchestral mascot.'

'I didn't come here to get abused,' spluttered Gregory.

'Neither did Beatriz,' said Ann. 'And, if I were you, I'd be very careful using that word.'

Gregory flushed. 'When I approached your orchestral manager, it was to discuss, man to man, the possibilities of furthering my literary oeuvre—'

'I don't think your oeuvre's gonna be furthered much more here,' said Charlie, laughing.

'How dare you mock me?'

'Oh, don't worry, he mocks everyone,' said Erin.

'Yeah, you're nothing special,' said Charlie.

Erin giggled. 'Any minute now he's going to demand to speak to our manager.'

'Not if I speak to him first,' said Ann, looking round and waving at David across the foyer.

Chapter 9

In the pub, everyone was trying to tell Noel their own version of what happened next, with volume adjustments according to the amount of beer they had already drunk.

'So David got waved over,' said Erin, 'and Ann laid it all out for him, how Gregory was – what did you call him, Ann?'

Ann swallowed a gulp of beer. 'Predatory. Among other things.'

'But Greggy-boy wasn't taking it lying down,' said Charlie. 'He rolled out a rehashed version of his shite "work vision"' – he emphasised the air quotes, which was not easy as he was also holding a half-full pint – 'and tried to make Ann out to be this batty old lady.'

'Unwise,' said Noel quietly, smiling at Ann.

Eliot returned from the bar with Carl and Kayla and threw a pile of crisp packets on the table. There was a small flurry of hands diving in to search for their favourites. 'God, it's like feeding time at the zoo. Hello, Noel. Are you being updated on our latest rehearsal distraction? I can't seem to get a decent stretch to work on the Brahms without sex pests getting their comeuppance.'

'So I gather,' said Noel. 'But I've come to expect this kind of thing when I meet you guys here on a Monday night. Never a dull moment. Is that salt and vinegar going spare?'

'And so David took Beatriz off to one side to see what she thought about it,' said Erin. 'And Courtney told him too, and basically it was all the women's word against Gregory's.'

'Not just the women – some of the men as well,' said Charlie.

'Quite right too,' said Eliot.

'But then he kicked off,' said Ann. 'Which I probably should have anticipated.'

'Would it have stopped you?' asked Noel.

Ann snorted and shook her head. 'It's a glorious side-effect of being my age. Can't tell you the number of fucks I simply do not give.'

Kayla put her hand up to high-five Ann. 'You know you're my role model.' She turned to Noel and continued, 'But then he launched into a complete meltdown – a kind of "don't you know who I am?" thing.'

'Which of course we don't,' said Erin.

'And wouldn't want to,' said Carl.

'But that only made him more cross,' said Charlie, laughing.

'And the more we laughed,' said Eliot, 'the more angry he got. Oh god, it was brilliant.'

'Eventually he got so shouty I had to call on our friend Carl, here,' said Eliot. 'You know, to loom.'

'One of the best loomers I know,' agreed Noel.

'I didn't even have to take him beyond the door,' said Carl, almost sadly, as if he had been hoping for a more worthy opponent. 'He scuttled off to the tube station without turning round.'

'Hang on,' said Noel, putting his pint on the table in front of him. 'Did you say he was called Gregory?'

'Yep.'

'And he's a poet?'

'Yep.'

'His second name isn't Knight, by any chance, is it?'

There were open mouths all round.

Noel sighed and ran his hand through his hair. 'Ah.'

Everyone sat up straighter and leaned towards him.

'What do you mean, "Ah"?' said Eliot.

'You can't stop there,' said Ann.

'Well, technically, he can,' said Erin. 'He's good at doing that.'

Noel took another swallow of beer. The others knew he was not a man who could be hurried, so they munched crisps with as much chivvying energy as they could muster.

'Well, a lot of stuff is in the public domain anyway,' said Noel eventually. 'Goodness knows, Knight isn't the kind of man to keep anything secret when it can be spun into publicity.' He got his phone out and tapped some words into the search bar. 'Here we go, the details about the best incident are still up.' He fished into an inside pocket, flipped open his reading glasses with one hand, put them on and started to read. 'This is from a few years ago. "Poet Gregory Knight accused the committee of the Camberton Poetry Festival of 'performative wokeness' when he failed to win their Poetry Slam event last Saturday evening. The bard did not accept his runner-up status with anything approaching sportsmanlike gallantry, claiming the decision was 'silencing his right to speak' and 'clearly skewed to gain credit with the budget-holders'. Off the record, Camberton Poetry Festival staff suggested Knight may have put too many eggs in his enjambment basket and perhaps lost sight of the simple joy of metre and rhyme." Oh, hang on, this isn't the best report.' Noel tried another page.

'Is this about Gregory?' asked Erin. 'What's going on?'

'Did he go to the papers himself?' said Eliot. 'About losing a competition?'

Noel raised his eyebrows and chuckled. 'It appears he might have done. I think he thought it might be a celebrity incident. Look, here's the cracker. I'm no literary expert, but does this sound like impartial journalism to you? Have a listen. "Dr Knight, the multi-published—"'

'Dr?' said Ann. 'You're kidding.'

'It gets better,' said Noel. 'Listen. "Dr Knight, the multi-published poet who is ranked among the greatest living poets in the UK, has not taken his defeat lying down."'

Ann spluttered into laughter, which set everyone else off too.

'Who knew we had one of the UK's greatest living poets in our rehearsal?' said Eliot.

Noel smiled and carried on reading over his audience's guffaws. 'Shall I continue? "His response to the event – a collaboration with a didgeridoo player – is available to download. '*I internalised my anguish over the clearly rigged Slam, broke it down to its constituent base emotions, then built a piece from scratch to respond to the lack of reception to innovation in today's scene. I melded my noble poetic soul to one of the oldest human societies that exist. I became, if you will, a phoenix. And my fire will burn bright.*'" Did you notice much of his noble poetic soul this evening?'

By this time, most of the musicians round the table were helpless with laughter.

'We did not,' said Carl.

'He wrote that report himself, didn't he?' said Ann. 'What a wanker.'

Erin pulled a face. 'Do you think he wanted to meld his poetic soul with us? The orchestra, I mean?'

'Oh Christ,' mumbled Carl, putting his head in his hand.

'I think we dodged a bullet,' said Kayla.

Eliot put his head on one side and looked at Noel. 'But how come you'd heard of him? Did you mean professionally? That's hilarious and stupid, but not illegal, surely?'

Noel's face folded into a frown, and he chewed the inside of his cheek while he thought. 'You're right. I came across this little episode a few years back, when I had cause to – er, how shall I put it? – delve into Gregory's character. In the end we couldn't take things any further. The bar for evidence is high. Frustratingly so, in some cases. Anyway, from the things you were telling me earlier, sounds like he hasn't changed much and frankly you are well shot of him. How's the lass he was hassling?'

'Fine, I think,' said Erin. 'She knows we've got her back.'

'We all have,' said Carl.

'Good,' said Noel, nodding. 'But let me know if you get any more trouble from him.'

'Thanks, Noel,' said Eliot. 'Sometimes it feels as if we have a guardian angel.'

Noel laughed. 'You don't need one. You've got a Carl.'

Chapter 10

There was a definite something in the air at the following week's rehearsal. Erin walked over to where Charlie and Ann were putting rosin on their bows beside open cello cases at the side of the hall.

'Evening,' she said, easing her own case onto the floor from the strap on her shoulder and looking round at the musicians already there. 'What's going on? It smells like the start of a school disco in here, before anyone's Lynx has had a chance to soften up.'

'Did you forget?' said Charlie. 'This is basically our telly audition.'

'Oh god. I did.'

'They're not going to pan round the cello section,' said Ann. 'Look at us. Scruffs.'

'Unlike Pearl,' said Charlie.

Pearl wafted past them in a floor-length maxi dress with such a large floral print on it; she would have rivalled even Mrs Ford-Hughes on a trellis day. Huge green enamelled earrings completed the ensemble, swinging under her ears so low they nearly brushed her shoulders. Her eyeshadow glowed in matching green. The whole effect was one of a roving tropical rainforest in open-toed sandals.

'Are her earrings… parrots?' said Erin. 'Standing in enormous hoops?'

'I think so,' said Charlie. 'How is she going to play? They'll get caught in her chinrest.'

But Pearl was not the only one who had made an effort in case the cameras of Quork Media rested on them. Any casual Wimbledon tennis championship viewer knows that to stand out in a crowd, you have to have a gimmick. If you're not Cliff Richard or royalty, this usually involves revealing surprisingly large amounts of flesh or wearing extreme hats. Neither option being open to Stockwell Park Orchestra players, some of them had employed alarming levels of clothing one-upmanship, gravity-defying blow-dries, or theatre-grade slap.

Maureen, rosining her bow on the other side of the hall, watched Pearl walk past and sneered before making her way to her seat in the first violins. She sat down next to Marco, who coughed as the full force of Maureen's perfume hit him.

'You look nice,' he spluttered, wiping his eye.

Maureen had eschewed her familiar beige shirt-and-slacks combo for black satin leggings and a cerise silk blouse, plunging to a rare view of her bony décolletage. Her hair had been persuaded upwards into some sort of topknot, tethered by an accessory that flapped feathers in almost but not quite the same shade of cerise.

'This top? Just something I found in the back of the cupboard,' she said, without a flicker of a smile. 'Nothing special.'

'Right. Yes,' said Marco. He caught Charlie's eye and nearly lost his composure.

All around them, players who normally turned up to rehearsals in jeans and T-shirts, trainers or worn-out shirts, were resplendent in sequinned attire. Max, standing behind his timpani, wore a striped linen jacket that heavily implied he had put his matching boater down somewhere close by and he would be back in his punt momentarily.

Gwynneth, in her strappiest, shiniest top and with neon-lined eyes, looked like she was going clubbing. She glanced over at Carl, who had put on a black collared shirt instead of his usual floppy T-shirt and was playing *why do birds suddenly appear* as his warm-up riff in honour of Pearl. They were the only two players in the orchestra who knew British Sign Language. 'Nice shirt,' she signed to him.

He laughed and signed back. 'I need sunglasses to look at you.'

'Have you seen Pearl?'

'Everybody's seen Pearl.'

They both laughed, and Pearl, who was directly between them, had absolutely no idea why.

Eliot walked into the hall and stopped dead, grinning. His nod to possible television fame was a smarter shirt than his ordinary Monday-night level, but he could tell he was at the lower end of effort. He made his way to his stand and delved into his bag for his scores.

'Hello everyone,' he said, nodding in various directions. 'Blimey. Coming in here is like Dorothy suddenly arriving in Oz. You're all looking very… technicolour.'

Pearl raised herself into her meerkat lookout pose and directed a loud, enunciated stage whisper at him. 'It's the television people, Eliot. Remember?'

'I don't think they're here yet, Pearl,' said Eliot, glancing behind him to make sure. 'But yes. And, if I may say so, you look stunning.'

Pearl flushed and sat down, smiling. Her parrots swung backwards and forwards from her earlobes like avian trapeze artists.

David stood up from his place in the horns, looking towards the glass doors to the foyer. 'I think I see them arriving now.' He put his horn on his seat and went to meet them.

Eliot tried to dampen the flurry of excitement by asking Gwynneth to give an A for the strings to tune, but even he could see it had limited success. All eyes were on the doors.

'Do come in,' said David, holding one open for the two people hovering in the foyer, who were looking uncertainly around them as if doubting they had come to the right place. 'I'm David, Stockwell Park Orchestra's manager. Are you Gemma? Russell Donovan introduced us via email.'

'Aw, thanks Dave. Hi,' said a young woman, marching into the hall and hitching her bag higher up her shoulder. 'Come on, Arden. Stop dawdling.' She came to a halt and raised her gaze to take in the water-stained ceiling tiles, limp curtains and windows that had been painted shut for years. Sunbridge Academy's budget had been spent on other things.

An even younger person wearing yellow dungarees scurried in behind Gemma and almost bumped up against her stationary back.

'Good grief, it must be work experience week,' Charlie muttered to Erin, leaning over his bridge to adjust his strings to tune. 'That one looks about twelve.'

'I think we're getting old, that's all,' said Erin.

David ushered the pair towards Eliot, who – along with Richard, the orchestra leader – was trying to interest the woodwind in a communal A.

'Eliot, this is Gemma, from Quork Media,' he said. 'As you know, she's come along to watch some of our rehearsal and check out the lie of the land, as it were, for their future recording session.'

Eliot turned and let Richard and the wind get on with it themselves. 'Hello, Gemma. Lovely to meet you.' He shook her hand, then raised his eyebrows at her companion. 'Hello?'

'Hi,' said Gemma, shaking hair out of her eyes with a flick of her head. She flapped her hand toward the yellow dungarees. 'Yeah, this is Arden. Quork intern. Learning the ropes, that kind of thing, yeah?'

Arden turned big eyes up at Eliot, and said 'hello' in a small voice.

Eliot smiled. 'Welcome, Arden. Right, so… what's the plan? Do you just want us to rehearse as normal while you go around doing whatever you do?'

Richard chose this moment to invite Gwynneth to give her A for the brass, so Gemma's reply was drowned out by Carl, Leroy, and the other brass players tootling up and down arpeggios to check their tuning was roughly in the same area as everyone else. As always, the A given by Gwynneth's oboe was only the starting pistol for a minute or so of energetic twiddling. That's why the strings had to have their go first: if everyone in the orchestra tried tuning together, nobody would hear the oboe after five seconds, and the violins would find themselves trying to tune to a tuba segueing into 'Puff the Magic Dragon', or whatever had been on Leroy's mind. A tuning orchestra is like a game of word association, and you wouldn't want to let a psychologist loose in the heavy brass.

'Sorry?' said Eliot, after the rumpus had died down. 'Do go on.'

Gemma flicked her head again. 'OK. So we're just going to go round and get some shots, if that's OK? We'll take a few stills and some footage – just iPad stuff. Nothing major. We need some stock footage of you to slot into our boards. Plus, I'll take back my thoughts to Russell, of course.'

'Of course.'

'Let's hope they'll be good ones,' added David.

'Sure they will, Dave,' said Gemma. 'Sure they will. Do you know what you'll be working on for your piece? Gotta be around ten minutes. Maybe less.'

Eliot's lips twitched. 'Well, not knowing who else might be playing, we don't really know how to pitch it. But we're about to go through one of the pieces for our regular concert at the end of this term and you can tell us what you think: Rossini's *Barber of Seville Overture*. Do you know it?'

Arden's hand went up.

'Nah,' said Gemma. 'Dunno. You don't have to put your hand up, Arden. What? Do you know it?'

A nod.

'Brilliant,' said Eliot. 'And you might recognise it, Gemma. It's very catchy. And short. About ten minutes. Or maybe less.'

'I'll let you get to work, then,' said David, nodding Gemma in what was almost a little bow, and returning to the horns. He didn't, strictly speaking, need to sit in his seat for the Rossini, as it was scored for only two horns, but he thought he ought to be in place for any footage of the orchestra making its way back to Quork Media headquarters.

Eliot looked around his players. 'OK, folks. Who's played this before?' About half the hands went up. He turned to Gemma. 'Ah. We might have to stop and start a bit, in that case. Don't hold that against us – some of us are sight-reading, and it goes past at quite a lick.'

He grinned at Arie, who was standing next to Max in the percussion section, looking her usual level of mustard keen and ready to play. She had arrived in the orchestra with Tracie Scott, as they had both joined from Sunbridge Academy during the orchestra's recent invitations to a couple of local schools. Max had taken Arie under his musical wing and was in the process of forming a decent percussionist out of the tiny girl who hadn't even picked up a stick a few months earlier. Max had given her the bass drum to play, while he perched on a high stool behind his four timpani. Beyond Arie was a third percussionist standing ready with cymbals. Hitting things is a labour-intensive business.

'Right,' said Eliot. 'Strings, don't get carried away when you hear what I'm sure will be a spectacular intro. I know what you're like. We are *pianissimo* after that, OK? Pearl, are you alright?'

At the back of the violas, Pearl was holding her instrument at an odd angle, part-way down her arm instead of up on her shoulder.

'Yes, fine, thank you!' she said, brightly, nodding. Her parrots swung merrily to and fro, and the clunk of one of them repeatedly hitting her viola spread through the hall.

Eliot blinked, caught Ann's eye, and decided to press on.

'Let's go.'

He brought the whole orchestra in for its *fortissimo* fanfare and set the strings up for their quiet phrases by almost disappearing behind his stand and conducting in tiny movements. They crept up their scale sounding as if they were playing Grandmother's Footsteps, just as Eliot intended. After the strings had got into their groove, Gwynneth came in with a high, soft, sustained series of notes that were very hard for an oboist to put much expression into, so she did what all oboists do in such situations: flapped her elbows slowly up and down while leaning from one side to another. Even without circular breathing (which is another subject altogether), an oboe takes practically no air to play because of the unreasonably tiny gap in its double reed through which a player must force high pressure air to power the squawk. After a long phrase, an oboist often expels half the air left over in their lungs before taking another breath to play. It's not the blowing that makes them want to faint, it's that it takes so long to empty out one lungful. Their flute and clarinet neighbours, by contrast, are forever refilling their lungs to send more air down their greedy instruments. All of which is to say, don't ever challenge an oboist to a competition to see who can hold their breath the longest. No research has been published on the crossover between free divers and oboists, but that Venn diagram has to have one socking great intersection.

As the violins reached their first real melody, Eliot glanced round to see if Gemma and Arden were enjoying it. Arden was nodding along to the beat, smiling cheerfully, but Gemma seemed to be concentrating on the violas, who were plucking a pizzicato accompaniment to the tune. Because it was off the beat, several of them were jerking their heads *on* the beat to keep time, setting up a double rhythm in the section: heads going one way, hands plucking the other. Pearl had to contend with the pendulum effect of the parrot swinging from her left ear, which was adding a level of syncopation she hadn't anticipated, as well as trying to play the viola halfway down her arm, which wasn't, as it turned out, far enough. While her viola neighbours were going 'head, pluck, head, pluck', she was more along the lines of 'head, CLUNK, pluck, head, CLUNK, pluck', which pretty soon put Pete off too, and there was chaos on the back desk.

Ann got the giggles first – mainly because this was happening directly to her right and she could not ignore it – but she wasn't the only one. After a few bars, Eliot submitted to defeat and brought the orchestra to a halt.

'Um, Pearl?' he said, trying to stop laughing. 'Do you want to try it without your left parrot?'

'Of course, Eliot,' she said, unhooking her earring and putting it in her handbag. She settled her duster on her shoulder and nestled the viola back into its usual place under her chin. There was a muffled cheer from some of the players.

'Right, from the top?' suggested Eliot, and off they went again. The violins' tune went off without a hitch this time, and they really got settled into the ridiculously perky Rossini tune, first on Gwynneth's oboe (payback time for her earlier sustained section) and then repeated by Neema on the horn. As the piece began to wind itself up, and the engine of the string section set the whole thing thrumming, Eliot flung out his arms and pointed at the trombones. They needed no encouragement, and Carl led them in some razzing scales, trying to outplay the trumpets who were also letting rip. After a short recap of the soft tune, the whole thing revved

51

up again, and just as it sounded as if it might have reached its zenith, Rossini cranked it up to double time, forcing the double basses to join the rest of the string section in virtuosic scales – which they frankly were not used to and some players felt were way above their pay grade. Eliot grinned at Kayla, who coped with it better than the rest of the section.

It ended with a satisfying lot of percussion which Irie enjoyed enormously. Eliot brought them all off their final chord together and turned to Gemma, who was filming him on her iPad.

'Is that the kind of thing you had in mind?' he asked.

'Perfect, yeah. Nice one.'

Arden broke into a solo round of applause, and looked delighted. Eliot bowed.

'And it's only about eight minutes,' called David, who had been carefully timing it on his phone, using the lap function for the stops and starts. He had never been so grateful for the afternoons his son had insisted on being timed doing circuits of the obstacle course in their back garden: he'd never have learned how to do that otherwise. 'Which sounds nicely under our limit.'

'And bound to be a crowd-pleaser,' agreed Eliot. 'What do you think, everyone?' There were nods all round and general assent to the plan. 'Excellent.'

Chapter 11

Later that week, Ann invited Erin round for a progress check on the programme for her Royal Academy of Music audition. Erin, rather to her own surprise, had reawakened her love of the cello when she had to step in as a last-minute substitute playing the Elgar concerto on a Stradivari the previous year. Also to Erin's surprise, Ann had offered to coach her. Ann was mostly retired now but still retained her reputation for being a highly sought-after teacher. 'Chivvy' was the word Charlie used instead of 'coach' – approvingly – when he described Ann and Erin's musical relationship. Nobody who had heard Erin play the Elgar was in any doubt of her talent. Sometimes everyone needs a push.

'Come on through,' said Ann, walking back down her hallway and leaving her front door wide for Erin and her cello case to fit through. 'Just made a pot of coffee.'

'Fabulous. Gasping for one.'

Erin closed the front door, left her cello in the music room and walked through to the kitchen, where Ann was pouring coffee into two mugs. She waved her free hand towards a cupboard. 'Biscuit tin in there somewhere. Let's see what's left. I think I had some ginger nuts.'

Erin crouched in front of the open cupboard and fished out the tin from where it was leaning at an angle against an open packet of rice and a few tins of baked beans. 'You said you were going to clear out this cupboard months ago.' She leaned further in, and her voice became muffled. 'Ann, there's a tin of butter beans here that went out of date in the last century.'

'Nobody believes in best before dates,' said Ann. 'Anyway, if I never cook them, I'll be safe. They can be an heirloom.'

Erin laughed. 'All those statements are wrong, and you know it. Look, I found a new pack of ginger nuts, just as you said. You've got your priorities right.'

Ann put the mugs on the table, sat down and crossed her legs up on another chair. 'Come on. Coffee before work. How's it been going?'

Erin sat opposite her and opened the biscuit packet. 'OK. I think. Got back into a rhythm after the break for our tour – except now, apparently, we've also got this telly thing going on. It's all happening at once.'

'But your audition's not until – what? – first week in December?'

'Yeah.'

'Well then. It's only September. Plenty of time for everything.'

'And a bit of temp work too. I told the agency I'd do the odd week, but nothing long-term.' Erin took a gulp of coffee and dunked her ginger nut absentmindedly. 'Oh! And there's this – did you get a text from Mrs Ford-Hughes as well?' She dug in her bag for her phone.

'Dunno – what? I haven't checked recently.'

'It only came in when I was on my way here… yep, look. She wants to "convene a cello ensemble" and asked if I can go round to her house this Saturday at two-thirty. I can't imagine she's going to "convene a cello ensemble" without you too.'

Ann had found her phone under a stack of post on the worktop. 'So she does… yeah, I've got it too. What's she up to now?'

Erin's phone pinged, and she read the incoming text. 'Ah. Charlie's asking about it as well. I think she must have texted the entire Stockwell Park Orchestra cello section.'

Ann stared at Erin, suddenly still. 'Oh god.'

'What?'

'I bet I can guess what she's up to.'

Erin spread her hands wide, waiting for Ann's insight. 'Well?'

'I don't think the orchestra could get itself onto television without Mr and Mrs Ford-Hughes knowing about it, do you?'

'Probably not.'

'And I don't think it's possible that Mrs Ford-Hughes would let an opportunity to grab a bit of that limelight for herself slide through her fingers.'

Erin started to smile. 'You're right, of course. So?'

Ann shoved the last of a ginger nut into her mouth and talked uninhibitedly round it. 'So, what's the piece any soprano wants to sing if they can call on a few tame cellists?'

'Oh… yeah.' Erin flicked her fingers a few times to try and retrieve the name. 'Whasshisname? The Spanish one?'

'Not quite, my friend. Heitor Villa-Lobos. Brazilian.'

Erin looked shamefaced. 'Oops. Yes. But it's the one with no words, isn't it? Which would suit Mrs Ford-Hughes down to the ground.'

'Well, again, not quite. *Bachianas Brasileiras No.5*. Not an umlaut in sight for the first bit,' agreed Ann. 'But… then it goes into Portuguese. She won't be daunted though – bet you anything that's what she's planning. I think you and I might have not just one but two telly auditions in the offing. Could look good for your Academy CV.'

'You mean, you think we should do it? Voluntarily make music with Mrs Ford-Hughes?'

'I think we should certainly go along on Saturday and find out if I'm right. And arrange for some sort of prize if I am. You never know, she might be paying us.'

Erin laughed. 'Shall I tell Charlie to say yes too, then?'

'Why not?

* * *

Erin, Charlie and Ann agreed to meet up on their way to Mr and Mrs Ford-Hughes's house. Erin, the only one who had been there before, had told them enough about it that nobody wanted to run the risk of being the first one there and have to deal with the full force of the Ford-Hughes hospitality on their own – Erin had found her previous visit daunting. Although, this visit was at the request of Mrs Ford-Hughes herself instead of turning up to ask a favour, as they had before. And they had shared quite a few musical triumphs together since then, so Erin guessed the welcome might well be warmer.

Three cellos on a London bus is three more than the ideal number. By the time it got to their stop in Battersea, they had apologised more times than the number of dirty looks other passengers had given them, but apparently it was still not enough. They clambered down and swung their cello cases onto their shoulders as the bus pulled away. The passenger who had to get out to let them off before re-boarding the bus looked back at them and shook his head slowly.

'Tell me again why I couldn't bring the car?' grumbled Ann.

'There's nowhere to park anywhere near their house,' said Erin. 'And all the restrictions will be up. And it's greener.'

'I knew there was a reason I never go out during the daytime. You can park anywhere if you sneak around London at night.'

'Said by the woman with the burgeoning collection of parking fines,' said Charlie, grinning. 'Come on. Is it this way?'

They skirted Battersea Park and walked along Prince of Wales Drive towards the tall mansion with immaculate gravel and highly polished door furniture that Erin remembered well.

'In here,' she said, taking the first scrunching step onto the drive and, as before, feeling nervous about disturbing the millimetre-perfect raked gravel arrangement.

'Oh yes!' said Charlie. 'You've been here before, haven't you? Didn't you come with Joshua to beg them not to sue after our doomed stand-in conductor squashed Mrs Ford-Hughes while he was rudely dying?'

Erin grimaced. 'Yeah. The less I remember about that episode the better, thanks.'

'It worked, though,' said Ann. 'Top grovelling.'

'Top gravelling,' said Charlie, glancing at the driveway. 'Who's going to knock? Ann, go for it. You're the oldest. You can pull rank.'

'Fuck off.'

The heavy door swung open before they reached it, and – in complete contrast to Erin's last visit – the vision of Mrs

Ford-Hughes greeted them with a wide, welcoming smile and literal open arms. Ann hoped she hadn't heard her last remark.

'Erin, honey – you made it!' she cried. 'And Ann! And Charlie! Hi. Come on in. Great to see y'all.'

She stood to the side to let them all into the hall. The table Erin remembered was still there, with its enormous vase of flowers positioned in its centre as before.

'Go on through to the drawing room,' said Mrs Ford-Hughes, gesturing across the hall towards double doors. 'The others are here and setting up.' She shut the door to the street and immediately the ever-present background noise of London was silenced by four inches of really, really expensive security.

Erin and Charlie exchanged looks, and followed Ann. Erin couldn't resist running her finger along the polished table as she passed and, just as before, it came away completely dust-free.

Spread out across the vast expanse of the Ford-Hughes's drawing room carpet were six cello cases. Five of them belonged to other members of the Stockwell Park Orchestra cello section, who looked over to Erin, Ann and Charlie, and smiled. The sixth person had her back to the door, next to the baby grand piano in the corner of the room, and was leaning down to unclip her bow from the case. Her long hair fell in a shining curtain, until she straightened and used the impetus of that to carry on the movement of her hair away from her face with a practised flick of one hand. She turned to the door and smiled.

'Hello, Fenella,' said Erin. 'How lovely to see you.'

Chapter 12

'Erin! You're looking great,' cried Fenella, and sashayed across the room towards her, holding her arms out, one hand still holding her bow. She air-kissed the general area around Erin's head. 'How marvellous. And Ann, and Charlie!' They got the treatment too, during which all three stood very still in case of error, like Bathsheba when Sergeant Troy whizzed about her head with a sword. Nobody can successfully predict how many air kisses there will be, especially if they didn't initiate the encounter. Bumped noses are just the start of potential crippling embarrassment. Full lip contact, even if just a glancing blow, can stay with a person for life, inhibiting all future social interactions. In any case, nobody wanted a mouthful of Fenella's hair by mistake.

'Maryanne told me [*mwah!*] you'd be coming [*mwah!*] along too,' Fenella continued.

There was a moment of confusion until Erin remembered that Mrs Ford-Hughes's first name was Maryanne, and then she took another moment to register Fenella had clearly risen in social status to receive permission to use it.

'Funny,' said Charlie. 'She didn't mention you at all.'

Mrs Ford-Hughes swept in behind them and clapped her hands with delight. 'And here we all are! I'm so thrilled y'all could make it. Before we get going, I'll have Paola bring in some refreshments. Can't make a start if we're thirsty!' She stepped over to the hall door and called. 'Paola? We're ready now, please.'

Erin was still standing with her cello case hitched over her shoulder and could see Fenella looking at it carefully. She took it over to a wall and set it down gently on the carpet. 'It's not the Strad, Fenella,' she said, 'if you were wondering. I don't take it around for most things. In case you were worried.'

Fenella nodded. 'I know, I know. I was half hoping to see it but didn't really think you would.'

Ann put her own case down on another side of the room and leaned on it casually with her elbow over the top, as if she were at a bar. Charlie walked quietly up to her and did the same.

'Awkward,' he whispered. 'What's going on?'

'Fuck knows,' she said. 'It's always been complicated with those two.'

'I know Erin's got the Strad on loan, to apply to music college, but I thought that was only because of Fenella's broken wrist?'

'Last time I saw her she couldn't play,' Ann agreed. 'So what's she doing here?'

'Do you think she's taken up singing?'

Ann snorted with a laugh that was a lot louder than she had anticipated, and smiled her apologies when everyone turned to look. 'Sorry. Charlie's being stupid. Again. As you were.'

They nodded with understanding.

'Count the cello cases,' said Ann. 'She's playing.'

Just then, Paola came into the drawing room wheeling a trolley loaded with teapots, coffee jugs, and small towers of clinking mugs. She set them down on the low table, then reached onto the lower shelf of the trolley for platters piled with cakes.

'Thank you, Paola,' said Mrs Ford-Hughes, bustling over to that end of the room. 'Come on, everyone. Help yourselves to tea or coffee, and a little something to eat, and come and sit down. Plenty of space. Paola sure bakes the best carrot cake I've tasted outside Arkansas.'

When everyone was holding a beverage of their choice and a piece of cake wrapped in a napkin, Mrs Ford-Hughes cleared her throat and beamed at them.

'I thought I should say a few words about why I've asked y'all to come round here today – and I'm so grateful that you made time.'

Erin and Charlie exchanged glances. It was not like Mrs Ford-Hughes to sound so indebted to anyone. Charlie leaned close to Erin and tried to whisper through his mouthful of carrot cake, which wasn't easy, especially with sibilants. 'Thee wanths thomething.'

Erin brushed some cake crumbth out of her hair and nodded.

Mrs Ford-Hughes continued, oblivious. 'When I heard that Quork Media had reached out to Stockwell Park Orchestra for their new TV competition, I was so thrilled. It was all because of Erin's wonderful work on the social medias in Europe last month, of course!' She tried to lead a small round of applause, but because everyone had either one or

61

two hands already taken up with a drink or cake, it quickly evolved into a rippling chorus of '*hear hear*'s instead. Erin blushed, still wondering what was about to come next.

'Who would have thought that our little orchestra could first take Europe by storm, then the internet, and now television! It has been such a wonderful few weeks. Anyhow, as I said, when David mentioned this television opportunity, Mr Ford-Hughes and I immediately hit on another peachy idea! What if we could showcase *another* aspect of our orchestra at the same time? Show our range? Wouldn't that be wonderful?'

'So, you want the cellos to do something on their own?' asked Ann. She half turned to Erin and winked.

'What's going on?' whispered Charlie to Erin.

'We've got a bet going. Wait and see. I think we're about to find out if Ann was right,' said Erin.

Mrs Ford-Hughes carried on, nodding as if she completely agreed with Ann. 'Yes, indeed. All the wonderful, wonderful cellists in this room. Imagine you all playing together! What a sound that would make. And of course, I immediately called Fenella to see if her wrist was better because I couldn't possibly convene the section without asking if our former esteemed section leader could play, of course.' Fenella smiled benevolently. 'And we were musing to ourselves, Mr Ford-Hughes and I, one evening, and we hit upon the perfect repertoire! Have any of you heard of Villa-Lobos?'

Ann reached one hand behind her back for Erin to high-five.

'The Spanish composer?' said Fenella.

'Brazilian, actually,' said Charlie. 'He spoke Portuguese. But I guess they sound similar. An easy mistake to make.'

'Yeah, everyone knows that,' said Erin. 'Duh.'

Fenella looked crestfallen.

'Oh, no, Fenella, I'm sorry!' said Erin hurriedly. 'It's just that I made that exact same mistake – I mean assumption – I mean, I got it wrong just a few days ago, and I… oh dear.'

'She did,' confirmed Ann. 'She knows nothing and should never speak again.'

'So you two were talking about Villa-Lobos a few days ago?' said Charlie. 'Interesting.'

'Shut up, Poirot,' said Ann. 'Sorry, Mrs Ford-Hughes. Feel free to ignore Charlie. We all do. You were saying?'

'Yes, thank you. I was about to suggest that we read through the *Aria* of Villa-Lobos's *Bachianas Brasileiras No.5*, here, today – well, now – and Mr Ford-Hughes has insisted I sing the *Aria* myself.'

Chapter 13

'I think that's a lovely idea,' said Fenella, flicking her hair over one shoulder away from where it had been dangling over her cake. 'I'm so pleased you invited us all to do it.'

Mrs Ford-Hughes beamed and looked around at everyone else. 'Well? What do you think?'

'It's a wonderful piece,' said Ann. 'Some quite tricky ensemble sections. Did you have a conductor in mind?'

'Oh, no,' said Mrs Ford-Hughes, draining her cup and standing up with determination. 'I'm sure we can feel our way through it together. There aren't many of us – it's a chamber piece really. We're all musicians.' She walked to the other end of the room and started leafing through a pile of sheet music that had been placed artistically askew on the baby grand piano in the corner.

Bachianas Brasileiras No.5 by Heitor Villa-Lobos is an extraordinary piece for solo soprano and 'an orchestra of cellos'. The minimum number in this 'orchestra' is between eight and nine, depending how much double stopping you want to be bothered with. There are four separate cello parts, each of which split into two, though the piece is often performed with more than one player to a part. The first section, *Aria*, is one of Villa-Lobos's most famous compositions, using traditional Brazilian folk melodies but also managing to combine them with harmonies and contrapuntal techniques used by Bach. Villa-Lobos – street musician, traveller, composer, cellist, conductor, guitarist – was a master of fusion.

Like most chamber pieces, there are individual lines with tunes at the top and lines that lay down the bass notes, and then there is the hazy middle ground of inner harmonies. This middle ground is a broiling turmoil of egos and frustrated dreams, as any choral alto or tenor can tell you. Just as in a choir there are people who sing soprano who should really be singing alto but don't because they like the tune, there is a type of instrumentalist who will never be happy relegated to the plinky-plonky accompaniment if there is a soaring tune to be had. In *Bachianas Brasileiras No. 5*, Villa-Lobos takes the idea of plinky-plonky to its logical extremes, and instructs many of the inner cello parts to pluck their rhythmic harmonies while their colleagues to right and left sustain tunes and bass lines alike. It is a thankless task, but one that requires fierce concentration. Without this inner engine of rhythm, there would be no piece as a whole. There are those, however, who deem it beneath them. The fact that it is much harder to play a tricky inner part correctly is apparently not enough of a draw. Every cellist in that room who had played this piece knew intimately that, however politely it would be played out, a fight for dominance in the pecking order was about to happen.

They drank up, stuffed the last pieces of carrot cake into their mouths and wiped as much of it off their hands as they could before their fingerboards got sticky. Mrs Ford-Hughes indicated a heap of folded music stands at her feet and dining chairs lined up along a wall, and slowly a circle of stands and chairs formed itself around her, as if she had been summoned into this realm by an incantation for raising wobbly sopranos from the netherworld. She laid out the parts on the stands in order: two copies each of *Cello I, II, III* and *IV*, around the circle.

'So who's taking the *Cello I* solo part?' she called, then, without waiting for an answer, 'Fenella darling? Are you gonna sit here?'

Seven cellists turned to look at Erin, who had taken over as leader of the section after Fenella's broken wrist enforced her retirement from the orchestra. Fenella, on the other hand, took her cello straight over to the seat Mrs Ford-Hughes was indicating and sat down, smiling up at her. 'I'd love to, thanks Maryanne.'

'Okaaaaay...' said Charlie. 'Do we, um, want to talk about this?'

'Oh boy,' muttered one of the other cellists from the orchestra, who remembered what the section was like with Fenella at its helm. He became suddenly preoccupied with tightening his bow.

Fenella's mouth smiled at Charlie but her eyes remained completely unmoved. 'What did you want to talk about, Charlie?'

Charlie looked at Erin and Ann, who shrugged.

'Well,' said Charlie to Fenella, 'how is your wrist? I didn't know you were back playing, that's all.'

Fenella waggled her left hand at him. 'It's basically fine. I can't play for very long at a time, but it's improving. We'll see how it goes.'

'And we're all so pleased and relieved it has healed so well,' said Mrs Ford-Hughes, patting Fenella on the shoulder. 'How about you all take a seat? Pick a part and we'll give this thing a test drive.'

Ann walked over to a *Cello III* stand and thought quickly. 'Look, why don't I take the upper part of *Cello III* – that's mostly the bass line and I can pretend I'm sitting at the back of the orchestra section again, and Erin can take the lower line in *Cello I*, and Charlie can do the upper line of *Cello II*? Would that work for everyone?'

'Suits me,' said Erin, and sat where she was told.

Charlie sighed, and nodded. 'OK.'

What Ann had instantly arranged (and Charlie and Erin trusted her to make calculations for them all) was for herself to lead the bowed bass line, so she could keep a handle on the pulse of the whole piece, for Erin to take on the possibly thankless task of duetting with Fenella at the top end to try and keep her under control, and Charlie to take the lead plinky-plonk part – which was possibly the hardest because of its rhythm and also because it spent a lot of its time up in the treble clef. Charlie had a good head for heights.

'Where do you think it's best for me to stand?' asked Mrs Ford-Hughes, still stuck in the middle of the circle of chairs and stands and, now, cellos. 'I feel like one of those chorus girls in a dance routine from the movies that they're about to shoot from above!' She dissolved into girlish giggles and gave an excited twirl, looking up at her crystal-festooned chandelier while the rest of them imagined what a dance number led by Mrs Ford-Hughes would look like.

Ann leaned forward to Fenella. 'If you shuffle sideways and open up a gap next to you, she can fit in there. You two have a lot of lines together. As you know.'

After a few more minutes of arranging the chairs, finding another stand for Mrs Ford-Hughes and settling her on a tenth seat in the circle, they were ready to start.

'So,' said Fenella, opening her music and flattening the crease in the middle so it stayed flat. 'Ah. It's in 5/4. Yes.'

Erin braved a glance at Ann, as memories of Fenella's idiosyncratic approach to timing flooded back. Ann was already pressing her lips into a flat line to stop herself laughing but pulled herself together for the sake of the group.

'Well, that's OK,' said Ann, 'because you and Erin and Mrs Ford-Hughes don't come in for two bars. I can kick off with the beat – and I think the other *Cello III* is with me, yes? – and everyone else has got semiquavers, so you three can just slot in at the start of the third bar... how does that sound? It's only *adagio*. We'll be fine.'

Mrs Ford-Hughes raised her eyebrows and nodded. Fenella waved assent at Ann.

Ann counted them in, and dug into her bass line. After one semiquaver rest, the others picked up their pizzicato rhythms straight away, Charlie using his body language to communicate to the other semiquaverists how fast to go and how much energy to put into them. Between Ann and Charlie, they managed to arrange to slow down at the end of the second bar, as marked, in preparation for Mrs Ford-Hughes to come in.

The accompaniment hovered, waiting for the voice and *Cello I* to arrive in unison: the wordless voice as written by Villa-Lobos seeming to embody a cello in human form.

What actually happened was that Fenella flopped into her entry slightly late, coming in after Erin but, because Fenella was closer to Mrs Ford-Hughes and Mrs Ford-Hughes had been expecting to hear Fenella play the note she had to sing, she ended up singing a third lower in pitch than she should have been because she had been lulled by Ann's repetition of an A. Fenella gamely played C a bit louder, too late, into Mrs

Ford-Hughes's left ear, while from the other side of the circle Ann's meandering up her A arpeggio only seemed to confirm to Mrs Ford-Hughes that A was indeed the note she needed.

The *Cello I* part and Mrs Ford-Hughes see-sawed up and down their melody in parallel thirds for a bit, until Ann decided maybe a second take would be worth it after all. Looking at it in a benevolent light, the wordless voice part, as sung by Mrs Ford-Hughes, did have the advantage of such a wide vibrato that any number of notes could be said to inhabit it, but containing multitudes was not quite the effect Villa-Lobos had been aiming for.

'Shall we try again?' said Ann, rather too brightly. She knew she did not have the temperament to lead rehearsals like this one and swore silently for manoeuvring herself into leading this one.

This time, with firm intonation from Fenella, Mrs Ford-Hughes landed right, and off they went together, soaring hand in hand over the 5/4 plinky-plonk meadows. With no words to distract her, Mrs Ford-Hughes made good progress for at least two bars, at which point the 5/4 turned into 3/4 for a single bar and then switched into 3/2. They were flying blind – without a conductor – into some rocky territory indeed and took any number of metaphors to help them on with their journey. Luckily, Mrs Ford-Hughes had to reach a top B flat at that point, which distracted everybody in the room from anything else that might be going awry.

Erin helped where she could, when her part mirrored Fenella's, and together they shepherded her back down again. The trouble was, to create the effortless feel of floating, Villa-Lobos had taken what can only be described as a carefree attitude to time signatures, and the changes piled in thick and fast – 6/4, 5/4, 4/4 – during which time Charlie's part had gone right up into the treble clef and no matter how forcefully he plinked his plonk, there is only so much resonance he could extract from his cello when he was leaning halfway up the fingerboard.

Mrs Ford-Hughes made it through to the end of her first wordless section, and settled back in her seat to listen to the cellos reprise the gorgeous tune. Erin and Fenella started off playing it together, and Ann and Charlie were not the only ones to notice Erin's obvious lack when her part dropped out and left Fenella to continue as soloist. Erin joined the accompaniment with a rueful smile at Charlie.

With concentration and a lot of goodwill, the nine cellists held it together through some more timey-wimey shenanigans without a conductor, by looking at each other and reading body language accurately. They slowed down, sped up, and slowed down again just before Mrs Ford-Hughes's next entry.

This time, in a triple Ford-Hughes whammy, she was singing in Portuguese, it was marked *più mosso* (more movement), and she had to come in on an upbeat. To confuse her further, Fenella and Erin were now sent up into the treble clef to add some chromatic atmosphere, while it was left to Charlie to hammer out the line Mrs Ford-Hughes was supposed to be singing. After looking nervously at Fenella for a moment, her eyes locked onto Charlie's as she realised which part was her friend at that point. Looking on the positive side, it wasn't so much a tune they had but more of a series of repeated notes falling slowly down a flight of stairs one tone at a time. All Charlie had to do was line her up on her next note and try to keep up as she flailed through the Portuguese and elastic timing until the next step. Mrs Ford-Hughes made up for what she lacked in accurate pronunciation with absolute conviction, so if the audience had never heard a word of Portuguese it would probably be OK. She delivered her lines as if channelling Brünnhilde.

Mercifully for everyone's eardrums, at the end of that section she was instructed to sing *bocca chiusa* (mouth closed, i.e. humming), and the cello arrangement reverted to Fenella doubling her part while Charlie was banished back to the pizzicatos. He made the mistake of catching Ann's eye, and they both fought giggles for the rest of the piece.

Humming is not as easy as singing 'ah' – especially when going high – so, when Mrs Ford-Hughes was sent up to her top B flat again, her timbre transformed from a distant chainsaw into an angry mosquito that had got into your bedroom and was flying very close to your ear prior to taking supper. A mosquito that had learned how to do vibrato.

Ann, who had mostly been successful at quashing her laughter, managed to ride the first mosquito moment, but she knew the piece well and doubted she could hold it together for the last bar. It called for the soprano to float out of nowhere onto a top A, marked *pianissimo*, and hold her note with a pause while the rest of them find a chord afterwards, and also pause. It is very difficult to retain composure when nobody knows who is in charge of bringing the note to a close and there is an increasingly red-faced mosquito rapidly falling off her top note. In the end, Ann seemed to be the one everyone was looking at by default since Fenella had closed her eyes to lean into the beauty of the moment and was no help to anyone. Ann gestured to end the note as well as she could, leaving Fenella drifting away by herself until she realised, and stopped too.

Mrs Ford-Hughes took a few deep breaths and returned to her normal colour. They were all startled by a sudden volley of clapping from the hallway, and turned to see Mr Ford-Hughes beaming with such pride at his wife he had tears in his eyes.

Beside him, looking at her employers with what can only be described as horror, was Paola. She was, after all, Brazilian and had heard everything Mrs Ford-Hughes had just attempted to sing. The previous fortnight of Mrs Ford-Hughes pestering her to read aloud a particular poem in Portuguese to her now made sense, though it didn't make it any easier to hear the result. Mr Ford-Hughes glanced at Paola and jerked his head toward the musicians, making his views plain. Paola unwillingly joined in the applause duet.

'Oh, honey!' trilled Mrs Ford-Hughes, 'I didn't know you were back home so soon! We were just giving this Villa-Lobos a first run-through. We're not up to performance standard yet, are we, folks?' She laughed with easy artistic camaraderie with her fellow musicians, who let her have it this once, mainly (in the case of Ann, Erin and Charlie) because they were embracing the freedom to laugh out loud.

'Enchanting, my darling! Enchanting!' cried Mr Ford-Hughes. 'Shall I open a little something to celebrate?'

'Oh, we've just gotten started, silly,' said his wife. 'We are *rehearsing*. Ain't that right, folks?'

'Well…' said Ann.

'It might need a bit of polishing,' said Erin, diplomatically.

'Top and tail, kind of thing?' added Charlie.

Mrs Ford-Hughes beamed at her husband. 'Give us another half an hour, honey. Then bring enough glasses through for everyone.'

With the promise of that reward, the cellists turned the pages of their music back to the beginning and started work.

Chapter 14

If Eliot had been amused by the level of dressing up the orchestra indulged in when they were merely being scouted out by Quork Media, he was not prepared for the bling-fest greeting him the next week when there were lights and cameras and microphones and adrenaline.

When he arrived, earlier than normal for the rehearsal time, the hall at Sunbridge Academy was already buzzing with people. David was talking to Gemma in the middle of the floor. They were both gesticulating in turn, as if they were carrying on a complicated semaphore conversation at a distance of a metre. A lot of the musicians were already there, bunched around the edges of the hall pretending to get their instruments out while also insouciantly lifting their chins to iron out jowl droop and smiling over-brightly at whatever their conversation happened to provoke, with half an eye on where any roving camera might be. Nobody wanted to be in the stock footage of Stockwell Park Orchestra looking grumpy.

Pearl was in another maxi dress: this time sporting bold vertical stripes of yellow and white. She had not brought her parrot earrings again, having learned her lesson, but kept it subtle with pearl (of course) studs. Her enthusiasm to make an effort had been diverted into her hair, which had been curled into rolls of bouffant undulations that continued their own momentum after every turn of her head. She knew the eye of the camera could point in her direction at any time, and it never lied, even though it made her put on weight. She tried not to let her resultant confusion show though. She put her faith in the slimming properties of vertical stripes and went about her usual orchestral business with a fixed smile.

Charlie and Erin waved at Eliot when they saw him come in, and he sauntered over to where they were rosining their bows.

'Look at you: couple of scruffs,' said Eliot. 'You could have made an effort.'

Erin looked down at her jeans, and over at Charlie's, and shrugged. 'Shall I go home and change?'

'God, no. We need all the good players we've got. As it is, half of them aren't going to be making a noise as they'll all be employing Performing Mime.'

'Oh shit, he knows about Performing Mime,' said Charlie to Erin, in a theatrical whisper.

'Of course. Did you think you can get away with frowning, leaning close to your stand and fluffing the semiquavers in rehearsal, only to sit with a beatific smile on your face in a concert and appear to be doing it all effortlessly?'

'I don't do that!' said Erin.

'*You* don't, no,' said Charlie, nodding. 'But there are some – I'm not naming names – who might.'

Eliot laughed. 'Anyway, I doubt we're going to be getting much real rehearsal done tonight. We have to "lay down our track" – I believe that's the technical term.'

Charlie laughed. 'Get you, with your industry knowledge.'

They looked round the hall at the mingling clumps of musicians setting up stands and fetching chairs, trying to look as if they were unaware of a couple of roving cameras scouting out the place. The cameras were being sent to check out various angles by Gemma, who stood holding her iPad, scrolling up and down the list she had on it in between her semaphore exchanges with David. Arden was close by, attentive and alert for requests.

Ann walked into the hall, took a moment to clock what was going on then came over to the others, rolling her eyes and shaking her head slightly. 'Should've stayed outside for a fag. This lot will take forever to settle down.'

'We don't all have your vast international professional experience,' said Erin.

'We don't all have Pearl's wardrobe,' said Charlie. 'Oh, that's a point. Do you think Mrs Ford-Hughes will have us in matching uniforms for her thing?'

'You what, now?' said Eliot. The mention of Mrs Ford-Hughes had given him an involuntary jump. He had not factored her into any rehearsal plan.

Ann snorted with laughter. 'Oh yeah. We haven't told you yet – she's half-inched the cello section to launch her own bid for stardom. Go on. Guess what she's got us doing.' Her eyes drilled into Eliot's with a twinkle.

Eliot looked at Erin and Charlie, then back to Ann. 'Christ, you're not joking. Tell me she's not doing the Villa-Lobos?' They all grinned. 'Oh lordy. Really? *In Portuguese?*'

'Yep,' said Erin. 'We went round to her house at the weekend. And that's not all... she's got Fenella on board too.'

'What?'

'It was quite the reunion,' said Charlie.

'She's playing again?' said Eliot. 'I thought she couldn't anymore.'

'Not much, apparently,' said Erin. 'But I think she's made an exception for Mrs Ford-Hughes.'

'And television stardom,' added Charlie.

'She didn't want her cello back, did she?' Eliot asked Erin. 'Nope.'

Eliot ran his fingers through his hair and continued to look poleaxed, but was distracted by David calling him over to where he and Gemma were sorting the timetable. 'I need to hear all about this later,' he called over his shoulder as he went.

The orchestra were arranging themselves into the right seats to play the Rossini, which left David with a dilemma about whether he and Simon – together, the third and fourth horns – should sit in their places or not.

'What do you think, Gemma?' he asked. 'I mean, we *are* part of the orchestra, but it might look a bit weird if we were just sat there twiddling our thumbs…?'

Gemma looked at him vaguely, her finger still hovering over her iPad. 'What?'

'Eliot, what's your opinion?' David said. 'Should Simon and I sit this one out completely, or stay there with our horns on our laps and look like we're part of it?'

Simon was loitering on the edge of this conversation to find out where he should be. 'I'm OK with either,' he said, waving a paperback cheerily. 'Got my book.'

Eliot looked at them both: Simon happy to get back to his book, and David looking as though he would be sad to miss the excitement of a TV appearance since he had done a lot of the work to make it come about in the first place. He dredged up a diplomatic answer.

'Um… how about, if Simon would prefer to read while we record this, he can sit off to the side so we don't look as if we're a travelling library, and David, if you want you can sit in the horn section looking as if you're about to play. With the camera panning around and cutting and so on, I bet nobody will notice you're not actually playing. How does that sound?'

David smiled. 'Perfect. Thanks.' He went over to join Neema and Ryan in the horn section.

The two camera operators returned to Gemma like boomerangs and awaited their next instructions. She turned to Eliot.

'Are we all set then, do you think? Shall we try a take?'

'How many attempts do we get?' asked Eliot. 'Is it a one-take thing, or can we cobble different ones together in case of howlers? Not that I'm expecting howlers, of course.' He smiled. 'But, you know, nerves might get the better of… some of them.'

He glanced round the hall. Max was flattening down his hair and smoothing the lapels of his glorious jacket, which had been taken out for a spin for the second week running. Pearl had settled herself at the back of the violas in her yellow and white stripy maxi dress with the vibe of a whole bank of Wordsworth's dancing daffodils. Maureen had expanded on the hair feather idea, and now it looked as if a group of young peacocks were having an energetic stag do on her head. She sat in the second desk of the first violins, just behind Richard, the leader. Eliot doubted if he was going to be able to make eye contact with any violin player further back. Samira, the extra flautist the orchestra invited in to play if they needed a piccolo part, was on the end of the flute section line next to Amber and Brian, her piccolo in her lap. Together, the three of them represented the entire gamut of the Stockwell Park Orchestra's tellytastic outfitting: Brian had made no change whatsoever to his accustomed crumpled shirt and slacks; Amber had upgraded to a more colourful top and some make-up; while Samira shimmered in full sequinned, false-eyelashed glory. It was like having a small disco glitterball slotted into the woodwind ranks.

Gemma smiled. 'Let's aim for one straight through, but if you need another go I'm sure we can accommodate it. Let's go, shall we? Come on, Arden. Get all those lights on.'

Multiple sets of bulbs on tall stands flooded the orchestra with white light, and the players over fifty relaxed muscles in their eyes they weren't aware they had been tensing every rehearsal before then and made mental notes to buy one of those clippy LED-bulb lights on an adjustable stalk to fix on their music stands. The lighting in a public sector school hall was not really up to the job of reading music, and there was nothing like experiencing an alternative to help them literally see the light.

Eliot gazed out over the orchestra. Every newly-lit sequin glittered back at him. Feathers quivered, and ironed shirts boasted crisp arm creases. 'You all look, and smell, wonderful,' he said. 'Let's see what this new posh orchestra sounds like, shall we? Everyone good to go? Are we all tuned? Gemma here says we might get another go if it all goes pear-shaped, but don't bank on it. Let's regard this as a concert performance. Wind up whatever attention you've got and keep your eyes on me.'

He turned to Gemma, got a thumbs-up, and set the Overture going.

Chapter 15

Noel Osmar was halfway down his second pint before any of his friends from the orchestra joined him in the pub later that evening. There were other players he recognised, but not the people he was waiting for. As always, he had a book with him, propped himself in a corner and successfully kept his table free of anyone else wanting to share it by saying he was expecting friends momentarily. The sight of several of those space-seekers throwing glances his way from their places at the bar or on the edge of another occupied table didn't worry him in the slightest.

Noel was a nondescript man when he chose to be, which was a boon in his line of work (as several criminals who underestimated him had discovered to their cost), but he had a core of utterly apodictic resolve he occasionally decided not to hide. It wasn't obvious how it happened, which was perhaps part of its power: not dependent on the line of his shoulders, or his expression, or movement. He could open a vent at will to let heat beam out of an inner furnace, and people either backed off or got burned.

Luckily, he was content with his own company, a book, and a pint. The vents remained closed most of the time.

An hour later than usual, another gaggle of orchestra members piled into the pub and headed for the bar, led by Carl. There was valuable drinking time to be made up, so he got a double round in for himself, Kayla and Ann. Carl spotted Noel and ascertained he didn't want another pint (thank you) via the medium of hand signals over the heads of other punters. Noel didn't have Gwynneth's vocab in British Sign Language, but Carl got the gist.

Erin, Charlie and Eliot weren't far behind, and pretty soon they were all settling themselves round Noel's table. Eliot, as usual, threw a pile of crisp packets into the centre and watched the feeding frenzy.

Noel put his bookmark in place and closed his book. 'Evening. Was beginning to think you weren't coming. I saw the others,' he nodded over to where some other orchestra members were drinking, 'and was on the verge of checking up. And you know how I like my evenings off.'

'It wasn't our fault,' said Charlie. 'We had to be future telly stars.'

Noel raised his eyebrows over his pint glass, and looked at Eliot for an explanation.

Eliot nodded. 'It's all go, Noel. No sooner had we seen the back of Gregory Knight than we were co-opted into some televised competition. Just recorded our ten minutes of music. Called *Pass the Baton*, if you can believe that.'

There was a general snigger around the table.

'I will never not laugh at that title,' said Charlie.

Erin shook her head. 'It's your lavatorial mind.'

'It's not just me.'

'No, you're right,' said Ann. 'Never mind. It took all bloody evening, Noel.'

'Some of that was Maureen's feathers, to be honest,' said Erin.

'They looked hilarious from our side of the hall,' said Kayla.

Carl laughed. 'Yeah. Like a David Attenborough wildlife programme – some weird bird popping up over the savannah type thing.'

Eliot turned to Noel. 'I would have been willing to carry on conducting—'

'Ha!' Charlie broke in. 'Now *there's* our film title.'

Erin shushed him, and Eliot carried on. 'Even if I couldn't see to the back of the violins, but then one of them started sneezing.'

'Feather allergy,' said Kayla, nodding.

'So we had to stop the whole thing and start again.'

'And then, after the break, they decided to record soundbites with us all,' said Ann, sighing. 'To cut in to the broadcast, you know. For *context* or some bollocks. Give me strength.'

'David and I got more than just soundbite attention,' said Eliot, sounding ever so slightly boastful. 'We had to do a whole talking heads thing.'

Ann wasn't impressed. 'Yeah, we noticed. And we weren't allowed to heckle, which wasn't fair.'

Noel smiled. 'Something's telling me you're not a fan of all this, Ann?'

She grimaced and drank a lot of her pint in one go.

'But the upside is we might make some money,' said Erin. 'I mean, that's why we're doing it.'

'Speak for yourself – I'm in it for the glory,' said Kayla.

'She means prize money,' said Charlie, leaning in towards Noel. He had sunk his pint very quickly. 'All above board.'

'Well, of course. I'd expect nothing less,' said Noel. 'When should I tune in for this orchestral extravaganza?'

'I think they said these recorded segments will be broadcast next month – they were going to let David know which episode we'll be on,' said Eliot. 'And then, if we get through to the semi-final, that's when the fun will really start with live shows. God knows when we're going to fit in our regular rehearsals. We're supposed to be doing our own concert in December.'

'Nobody is going to care about that, Eliot,' said Kayla. 'We have stars in our eyes now. I won't be able to control the kids from our school if we go through.'

'And Erin's got her music college audition in December too,' said Ann. 'She's got to work towards that.'

Noel smiled at Erin. He had not forgotten hearing her play the Elgar concerto the previous year. 'I'm sure that's a foregone conclusion. They'd be mad not to take you.'

Erin pulled a face and ate a crisp. 'I dunno.'

'He's right,' said Charlie. 'Who knows, by then, you might be a telly superstar and get in on celeb credentials alone.'

'Who does the selections for the semi-finals?' asked Noel. 'Public vote?'

'Ah. I didn't think to ask that,' said Eliot. 'David would know. But he's not here. His tic started up after the feather incident so he went home for an early night.'

Chapter 16

The autumn deepened and settled in on itself. Days that had felt more like summer during September started to chill, even in south London, as leaves dried and curled on the trees. The chestnuts, as always, began to drop first. Shops hurried to shift their Halloween stock before pivoting big time into Christmas and turning window dressing colours from pumpkin orange into festive red and white.

Toward the end of October, the pre-recorded heats for *Pass the Baton* started to be shown on Saturday evening TV. Out of the dozen or so hopeful acts each week, only two would be voted through to compete in the semi-finals. Quork Media hoped to create a juggernaut of hype the show could ride until Christmas.

They had invited in a studio audience who watched the pre-recorded films live on the show, seated in their specially equipped studio chairs fitted with voting panels. The audience members were not screened for their opinions or knowledge of any kind of music, let alone classical, and were thus as illogical, prejudiced and partisan as the wider British public. But they knew what they liked. Quork Media knew this, and hoped for – if not actual fights – decisions that might spark debate. Actually, a lot of Quork Media's senior management *did* hope for actual fights. That was viewing figures gold dust. They all walked the thin line between entertainment and outright exploitation, and had watched the demise of *The Jeremy Kyle Show* with a 'there but for the grace of God' kind of feeling. Never uttered out loud, of course.

The fighting end of the competition would come later, during the semi-finals and final, when all votes would come from the audience. Before then, the bulk of voting clout was in the hands of three judges: Maria Romano, an operatic mezzo-soprano in demand on stage and in recording studios; Anthony Popkin, a conductor chasing celebrity status; and Olive Yessel, a retired violinist with a long international career behind her. Each judge had their own reason for being involved in *Pass the Baton*, some of which they had said out loud in publicity interviews, some not. The boyish enthusiasm for the show embodied by Russell Donovan, in all his sugar-bearded glory in that coffee shop weeks earlier, was not necessarily shared equally by the judging panel.

Stockwell Park Orchestra's turn was in the middle of October; the third of four weeks of heats. Scattered across south London and beyond, orchestra members gathered together or watched alone – but they all watched. David settled on his sofa with his wife and son, leaning his elbow on the arm of the sofa and resting his cheek in his hand, in case the judges' decision kicked his tic back into action.

Pearl was cosy under her blanket-with-sleeves, custard creams to hand. She had a cup of tea on a nearby table in her insulated, lidded mug that held over a pint. Her cat kneaded a part of the fleece blanket that was tucked round Pearl's leg until it was suitably cat-shaped, and curled into a perfect circle, revving up into a deep purr of contentment. Pearl's phone was on the arm of her squashy chair, ready to speed-dial David in case of victory – when he might need an instant chat with a fellow orchestra committee member. She wasn't going to phone Rafael, the financial director of the orchestra. She would leave that to David. If it were required.

Gwynneth was back home at her family's house in Merthyr Tydfil for the weekend. Her mam was beside herself with excitement and had invited too many cousins and aunties and uncles to fit on her three-piece suite. Several uncles had been relegated to a back row of folding garden chairs retrieved out of the shed from where they eyed the thick cushions of the seats in front of them with some envy, shifting their buttocks every now and then. But Gwynneth's moment of glory would be worth it, they were sure. The front room had the spirit of the 1953 coronation.

Amber, Beatriz and Courtney were round at Amber's flat, all squashed onto her sofa, drinking rum and cokes, ignoring the thunka-thunka-thunka of the bloke downstairs playing his music too loud again. Amber had tried inviting him up when she had friends round, just to stop the noise, but after he had given drugs to her mates and then thrown up on her carpet, she wasn't trying that one again. She kept the volume on her telly high and was trying to find another flat.

Noel Osmar was on duty that weekend but leaned his phone up against the pot of pens on his desk and watched the live broadcast out of the corner of his eye on mute, ready to turn the volume up when he saw the orchestra. He wasn't going to miss this.

Ann, who had a bigger house than many of her fellow players, offered to host a party that Saturday night so they could watch it together and either celebrate or commiserate as the mood took them. Depending on people's hopes, both those reactions could be to an identical result. So that Saturday afternoon, Erin, Charlie, Carl, Kayla, and Eliot turned up at Ann's Victorian semi-detached villa near the Oval. They brought alcohol and many, many snacks. Nobody was going to have to go through that evening sober or alone if they didn't want to.

The kitchen table had turned into an impromptu bar, littered with bottles and pizza delivery leaflets.

'We'll order a load of pizzas later,' said Ann, waving a hand vaguely at the leaflets, 'in one of their zillions of ad breaks. Go on through, it's nearly starting.'

'Aw, man,' came a shout from the living room. 'Eliot's already nicked the best spot.'

'You're not in charge here, mate,' called Ann, walking into the room. 'And there is no best spot anyway. Except for that chair by the fireplace – you'll get a crick in your neck if you try and watch the telly from there for too long. That's definitely the worst spot.'

'Carl could move it, if you like?' said Kayla, taking Carl's drink from him. 'He's useful like that.'

'Go for it,' said Ann, so Carl picked up the large armchair as if it were thistledown and set it facing the television at a better angle. He promptly sat in it and pulled Kayla over to sit on his knee. Remarkably, she managed to keep both glasses she was holding level and didn't spill a drop.

'Idiot,' she said, but looked happy.

'I do have enough chairs,' said Ann. 'You don't have to canoodle all evening.'

'We like it, Ann,' said Carl, canoodling into Kayla's neck.

'Try not to take any notice, people,' said Ann, flopping into another armchair on the other side of the room.

'Look, look – here it comes!' said Charlie, turning up the volume. 'God. This is an awful theme. What were they thinking?'

Some string arrangement of a perky tune accompanied the graphics starting the programme, recorded in the driest of dry acoustics beloved of quiz shows like *University Challenge* or *Only Connect*.

'They're going for an intellectual BBC-esque edge, I reckon,' said Eliot. 'They've got the cerebral filter on that recording.'

'Way to go to open up classical music to the masses,' said Kayla.

'Not exactly breaking boundaries, I agree,' said Carl, nodding.

'Haven't you seen the other heats?' said Eliot. 'I've been watching out for your Villa-Lobos thing, but nothing yet. Would have thought you'd be keen to see how you got on?'

Erin wrinkled her nose. 'God, no. We're on next week's episode, I think. Mrs Ford-Hughes has us all on a WhatsApp group and keeps us informed. Dunno how she's getting her info – she must be haranguing the producers.'

'We agreed never to speak of that Villa-Lobos again,' said Ann, with her nose deep in her wine glass.

'Well,' Eliot continued, 'they *have* been trying to open up the stiff-shirt world of classical music, I think. There has been a whole lot of stuff featured already that canters merrily to the crossover fence, and, not content with munching a few mouthfuls of grass from the other side, crashes straight through and frolics in the daisies in the far field, kicking up its heels.'

The others had turned to him with frank admiration for his sustained imagery.

Charlie turned to Erin. 'See? That's why he's a conductor. Not only does he do the homework for us by watching the other episodes, he can paint us a picture like that!'

Eliot threw a salted cashew at him from the other end of the sofa, which Charlie caught deftly in his mouth.

The first studio shots of *Pass the Baton* showed the host, Barney North, and the three judges walking on stage in front of the backdrop of a huge screen, to whoops from the crowd. Maria Romano and Anthony Popkin looked completely at ease, raising their arms to acknowledge the applause and smiling and nodding to all. Trailing slightly behind them, Olive Yessel stepped, precise and bird-like, across the stage directly to her chair, leaning on a silver-topped walking cane. Her white hair was in a neat bun. Her slight, upright frame and turned-out feet suggested a childhood of ballet lessons, as well as the violin study for which she was more famous.

'Who's this now? The compère guy?' asked Kayla. There were several answers, none of which seemed to be definitive.

'Didn't he win that Island thing?'

'No, he started off in stand-up but then did that radio show.'

'I thought he married the guy from the awards thing?'

'You're all wrong,' said Eliot. 'Or right, sort of. Yes, he was a stand-up. Yes, he married the guy who scooped all those awards. And yes, we all think Awards Guy got him this gig, no he didn't win the Island thing he just looks like him and gets a lot of stick for it.' There was a respectful silence for Eliot's bravura display of unexpected knowledge. He looked defensive. 'As I said, I've been watching it from the start. You kind of pick it up.'

'You do,' said Charlie. 'And we are definitely not having opinions on how you choose to spend your Saturday evenings.'

The judges and Barney North settled themselves into their matching plush armchairs. Olive still hadn't cracked a smile.

'Oh, I love Olive,' said Eliot. 'She takes no prisoners. Nobody knows why she's doing this show, but we're glad she is.'

'The other two seem to be enjoying it more,' said Erin.

'They're younger than Olive,' Ann pointed out. 'I reckon she's seen it all before, but those two still think they can have a career-defining moment.'

'Cynic.'

'Realist. Old realist.'

'What's Olive going to make of us, then?' said Charlie. 'We've got Maureen's feathers, remember. And Pearl's stripes.'

The others laughed. The programme went into a preview of the groups being judged that evening, and they cheered as Stockwell Park Orchestra footage went past in the montage. Their opposition comprised a clarinet quintet, a close harmony singing group, two sets of identical twins playing two pianos, someone who yodelled while standing on a ball, a flamenco guitar ensemble and three xylophone players dressed in luminous skeleton suits.

'Yeah,' said Eliot. 'David and I were talking after we recorded that – maybe we need to be in concert dress if we get through to the next round. I know Russell said he wanted realism and down-to-earth, relaxed behaviour, but compared to – say – those xylophone skeletons, we all look like scruffs. Except for Maureen, of course. Who was a startled pheasant. And Samira the glitterball.'

Each act got ten minutes (or less) to play a piece of their choice, just like the orchestra had. After each segment of recorded music, the three judges on stage discussed what they had just seen and heard, guided through their comments by Barney. Their scores were tallied up on a grid at the side of the stage.

'Oh god, here we come,' said Ann, as the orchestra's turn came up. Barney's intro mentioned their recent viral success from Bruges, but lamented the lack of their 'star horn soloist who was so integral to that success story'.

'Why are they mentioning Alexander?' said Erin.

'Why not?' grumbled Charlie. 'He does tend to take over. Even if he's not bloody here.'

'Charlie,' said Ann, frowning at him.

'Well, when David and I met Russell at the start of all this, he did mention a horn quartet,' said Eliot, with an apologetic glance at Charlie. 'Who knows? It hasn't turned up yet, but there are a couple more weeks of heats to go.'

'Great,' said Charlie.

'Shh,' said Kayla. 'We're on.'

They watched the segment of themselves, which not only included their Rossini performance but also a series of cut-together sections of them talking, either to the camera or, in the case of Eliot and David, to each other.

'God, do I really sound like that?' groaned Eliot.

'Yes,' they all chorused.

'It's OK, we like it,' said Erin, patting his knee since she was sitting next to him on the sofa.

The end of the Overture was rousing enough to provoke enthusiastic applause in the studio as the camera cut to the judges.

Barney beamed straight down the lens, his improbably luminous teeth drawing everyone's eye. They were impossible to resist. 'Stockwell Park Orchestra there,' he said through his smile, sounding as if he were running down the radio Top 40 chart, 'with Rossini's Overture to *The Barber of Seville.* Let's turn to you first, Maria. What did you think?'

'We didn't have any singers, so she's not going to like it,' said Eliot.

'Well, Barney, although they didn't have any singers, it was still a valiant effort!' said Maria, leaning into Barney from her place at the end of the judges' line, and laying her hand coquettishly on his arm. The audience loved her. 'But seriously, I think the standard of this amateur orchestra is to be commended. Tuning good, ensemble tight: altogether a very pleasing rendition.'

'Anthony?' said Barney, after the applause had died down.

Anthony Popkin cleared his throat. 'I hesitate to bring a harder edge to my judgement merely because there happens to be a conductor in this group.' The audience started to boo quietly. 'But, but – hear me out – there were some excellent dynamics and, as Maria noted,' he bowed his head gallantly to Maria, 'the ensemble was indeed crisp. No small achievement from an amateur group!'

Eliot snorted. 'What they don't know is that Anthony Popkin can't conduct his way out of a paper bag these days. He does his best work with old pros who can play the whole thing blindfolded without him, and all he has to do is sink a few glasses of red before the show and wave vaguely in their direction all evening.'

'Unlike you: a teetotaller of renown,' said Ann, laughing gently.

Eliot lifted his glass. 'Ah, but I'm off duty tonight. I don't wave my stick drunk. Cheers.'

Barney was turning to the final judge for her opinion. 'And Olive – what was your opinion of Stockwell Park Orchestra?'

'Christ, here we go,' said Eliot. 'Shh.'

Olive raised her chin, showing her angular cheekbones and the hollows under them in the bright studio lighting. 'Some of the tuning in the woodwind left something to be desired, especially the flutes.'

'Oh, Brian,' said everyone in Ann's sitting room.

'And I did see some discrepancy in timing between the violins and violas at one point.'

'I think Pete was put off by Pearl's dress,' said Charlie.

'But overall, the dynamics were acutely observed, and the tempi crisp. I particularly enjoyed that young conductor. I can see he had full control and the trust of his orchestra, which is a rare quality indeed.'

She finished speaking without even glancing at Anthony, whose face was filling the screen at the behest of a quick-thinking director. He was looking at Olive with a mixture of annoyance and grudging acceptance that she might be right.

'Woo, go Eliot!' shouted Kayla.

'Olive likes you,' added Carl. 'Although she didn't mention the trombones, which I can never forgive her for.'

The orchestra ended up with a score of twenty-six out of thirty on the board: somewhere near the top, below the identical piano-playing twins but above the yodelling ball-walker and skeleton xylophone players.

The programme ended, as always, with Barney asking the audience to vote via their chair panels. As their votes were tallied up by some off-stage computer, the dry string theme tune swirled around in another arrangement and the screen showed Barney having earnest-looking silent conversations with the three judges, who were all still on stage. After a few seconds, the new column on the scoreboard lit up with the audience ratings, then they were juggled into the correct weightings and combined to give the overall results for the evening.

'The numbers are jumping about all over the place,' complained Ann. 'What the fuck is going on?'

Eliot laughed. 'It jiggles like this for a bit while they sort out… stuff. I dunno. It'll settle in a second. Top two go through.'

'I'm strangely nervous,' said Erin. 'Do we want this?'

'We want the money,' said Charlie.

The board flashed, and stopped moving, to a fanfare. Stockwell Park Orchestra was on the second line down, under the piano twins. The audience erupted into another wild cheer, no doubt egged on by an enthusiastic studio manager off to the side out of shot.

'Bloody hell,' said Eliot.

'Olive came through for you, mate,' said Carl.

'Shit,' said Ann, and drained her glass.

'Now we've got to think of another piece to do in the semi-final,' said Eliot. 'At this rate, we'll never get our concert programme up to scratch.'

'That's *your* problem,' laughed Carl.

As the theme tune proper started up, Barney spoke to the camera over the applause. 'So, there we have it! The Honkytonk Twins win this heat, and Stockwell Park Orchestra come second, so they both go through to our live semi-final in a few weeks' time. Join us next week for the next heat of *Pass the Baton*! Good night!'

Chapter 17

The following Saturday, Mrs Ford-Hughes invited all the cello group to her house to watch *Pass the Baton*, along with a large number of her friends. It was quite the soirée. Paola had been joined in the kitchen by a catering company who produced an endless supply of canapés artfully arranged on slates – measured into bite-sized pieces designed to be chewed and swallowed in the time it took for your casual party acquaintance to update you on the skiing at Verbier at that time of year, or whether anyone could afford to have children these days with school fees being what they were.

Even before Charlie's socialist conscience knew it was going to be rubbed up the wrong way, he, Ann and Erin were not keen to go: memories of the recording session they had endured were seared on their retinas, and none of them thought they had a chance in hell of going through with Mrs Ford-Hughes.

The same camera crew who had recorded the orchestra had made an appointment to capture Mrs Ford-Hughes in action, on a weekday evening quite soon after they had done Stockwell Park. That first run-through had ended with everyone drinking an awful lot of champagne – which sent them home with an altogether more rosy view of the proceedings than they perhaps warranted. They had only managed one more rehearsal since then, and now they had to record it. In short: they were not ready. In longer: Mrs Ford-Hughes would never have been ready, and her happy enabler, Fenella, wasn't going to help.

After three takes had disintegrated, either because of pitching issues from Mrs Ford-Hughes or timing issues from Fenella, Ann emerged as the default ensemble leader. They should have had a conductor. The piece usually does. However, after desperate looks from both Erin and Charlie, Ann decided she was too old to bugger about any longer and took charge. Rather to her surprise, both Fenella and Mrs Ford-Hughes buckled under meekly, and the fourth attempt was a (relative) success. They all finished together, put it that way. Mrs Ford-Hughes's final top A teetered around its correct frequency, and Ann – by dint of watching how red Mrs Ford-Hughes's face was getting, and how engine-damaged her mosquito flight sounded – managed to bring everyone off at the same time.

The camera operator had breathed a silent 'thank you' to Ann before Mrs Ford-Hughes or Fenella had opened their eyes. She had winked back, and the Villa-Lobos recording was in the bag.

That Saturday, as soon as the Ford-Hughes front door was opened to them by a neatly uniformed member of staff, they knew the kind of evening they had ahead of them.

'Behave,' Erin whispered to Charlie as they went inside.

After only a small tussle during which the staff member persuaded him to give up his donkey jacket, Charlie looked at the calibre of coats it was joining in a walk-in cloakroom off the hall. 'There's enough fur in there to keep Shackleton in business for years. I thought it was supposed to have gone out of fashion?'

'It's never been about fashion,' said Ann. 'Come on. Let's go in. The sooner we start drinking, the sooner it might end.'

They accepted a glass of champagne each from a proffered tray and walked into the crowded drawing room which had so recently been the scene of various crimes against Villa-Lobos. Fenella was already there, standing by the baby grand and swishing her hair at the small group of people gathering attentively around her. The sheet music parts of *Bachianas Brasileiras No.5* were displayed in a precise yet careless fan arrangement on the top of the piano. Fenella had one hand on top of them, her fingers laid out carefully like a starfish, as if drawing strength from that physical connection.

'Darlings! You've arrived!' Mrs Ford-Hughes caught sight of them in the doorway, broke away from a knot of guests and hurried across the carpet, her arms reaching to gather them all in for a group hug. Erin found her cheek pressed against Charlie's, and they eyed each other blurrily at a distance of about an inch until Mrs Ford-Hughes released them.

'Hello,' said Ann, who had recovered her breath before the other two, having been in a solo position on the other side of the hug. 'What a splendid evening you've arranged here.'

Mrs Ford-Hughes fluttered her lashes and chuckled. 'Oh… I just love entertaining. A few friends, that's all. It's not every day you get to sing on national television!'

'And I'm sure all eyes and ears will be on you and you alone,' said Charlie. 'As indeed they should be.'

Erin let out a quiet squeak as she sipped her champagne, to try and rein Charlie in before he got going.

Ann was on it, diverting swiftly. 'Have you heard about any of the other acts who'll be on tonight? Do we know who our competition will be?'

'Do you know, honey, those naughty producers wouldn't tell me. I will admit to trying to sneak that information out of them, but they clammed up.' Mrs Ford-Hughes shook her head in mock outrage. 'Anyway, come along in and meet everybody. I want all my friends to know my wonderful musicians.'

She twirled round and led the way into the centre of the room, silk sleeves billowing behind her. Logs in the fireplace gave out the quiet, steady heat of a fire that had been settling in all day. On the opposite wall was an enormous television screen showing muted pictures of the programme scheduled before *Pass the Baton*.

'Was that there earlier?' asked Charlie, jerking his head at the screen. 'I don't remember it. You don't think she's put it up specially for tonight, do you?'

'Wouldn't put it past her,' said Ann.

'Maybe it gets disguised?' said Erin. 'I mean, there are a load of pictures around. Could it have had a curtain over it before?' She looked at the other furnishings in the room, which did tend towards the fringed pelmet and skirted furniture end of interior design taste.

The three of them watched Mrs Ford-Hughes work the room, ably helped by her husband, who looked just as proud of her as he had done after the first run-through. Black-uniformed waiting staff mingled, bearing the slates of canapés, or more champagne to top up their glasses. The friends split up and chatted to other guests, explaining over and over again that yes, they were part of the cello ensemble they were going to hear play tonight, and agreeing (with varying degrees of believable sincerity) that yes, Mrs Ford-Hughes was a wonderful singer who deserved this limelight.

After a while, they found themselves eddying back together again.

Charlie was delighted with the snacks. 'Look at these! Can you believe it? It's a tiny roast dinner on a stick: beef, Yorkshire pudding, red cabbage and horseradish!' The waiter kindly loitered for him to take five at once before gently sliding away. Charlie munched happily. 'And I've had mini quiches – of *all* flavours. I mean *all*. Even bloody goat's cheese. Which is not like me, as you know.'

'Yes,' said Erin. 'We've been right here, and had to watch.'

'Oh my GOD. Tiny garlic mushrooms!' His arm darted out to intercept another passing tray.

Ann shook her head. 'Do you think he ever eats at home?'

'Free food,' said Erin. 'It's his weakness. Undercuts all his political principles.'

Just then, Mr Ford-Hughes turned the volume up on the television and all eyes swivelled towards it. 'It's starting!' he said, walking backwards with the remote in his hand. 'Darling, would you like to sit here?' He indicated the sofa with the best view of the screen to his wife, who simpered and settled herself on the cushions.

'I'm as nervous as a little girl,' she confided to the whole room. 'Fenella, honey, come and sit by me.' She patted the place next to her, and Fenella went to take up her guest of honour position.

'I see Fenella hasn't lost the art of power networking,' said Ann.

Charlie smiled. 'She was always better at that than playing, in any case.'

Mrs Ford-Hughes's friends joined her on the sofa and nearby armchairs, and other guests found places to sit around the room, on scattered chairs and stools.

Erin, Ann and Charlie managed to secure a window seat to themselves towards the piano end of the room.

'Do you think we can leave before it's shown?' asked Erin quietly. 'I don't know if I can bear to watch.'

'Not a chance,' said Ann. She held her glass out to a passing waiter, who filled it to the brim with ice-cold fizz. 'Cheers. In for the long haul.'

Conversations in the room rose and fell during the programme as, one by one, other acts were shown, judged and marked on the leader board on screen. Olive Yessel was predictably hard to please, while Anthony and Maria gamely offered encouragement and criticism in equal measure when prompted by Barney North. A group of around thirty tiny children playing an arrangement of Britney Spears' "Toxic" on miniscule violins got huge applause, with particular praise from the judges for their choreography. A colliery brass band marched while they played, with the ease of long practice.

'We should have moved more,' said Charlie. 'Strapped our cellos on and just – you know. Gone for it. Dancing. The works. Strictly Los Villa-Lobos.'

Ann snorted. 'You think Fenella could have played with her eyes closed *and* strutted around?'

'Fair point,' said Erin, drinking more champagne. 'These all look very good. I mean, I knew we didn't stand a chance, but we *really* don't. Now I'm just hoping we didn't embarrass ourselves appallingly.'

'Oh god, look,' said Charlie, for once not automatically putting his next canapé into his mouth. He was staring at the screen.

'Is it us?' said Erin, turning to watch. 'Oh. Oh god.'

'Holy shit,' said Ann.

Chapter 18

Filling the screen was not the ample bosom of Mrs Ford-Hughes and nine cellists. They were at least prepared for that eventuality. No, the camera panned over a figure standing at a microphone, surrounded by men with piano, double bass, violin, alto flute and triangle. The triangle player dangled his instrument from an outstretched arm in front of him. Ambient Sounds had become a reality.

The bass and piano started up a riff, and then the violin joined with a rhythmic side-beat. The alto flute's low notes boomed in occasionally, not giving any clues as to whether this music would lean toward ultra-modern, atonal classical or ultra-free, atonal jazz. (Like political parties, they tend to meet round the back of the continuum of musical style, which eventually bends onto itself in a circle. Nobody admits this.)

The triangle player stood motionless: the sword hanging over Damocles.

Eyes closed, head nodding to a vibe only he could feel, Gregory Knight grabbed hold of his mic and started to recite in an urgent monotone that only deviated from its pitch at the ends of lines, either by going up or down by an equal amount. There was no correlation between the meaning of the line and whether his voice went up or down. A poet's voice is as inscrutable as custard.

'*A shower gel girl*
Dried out in the wet
Philosophy of all that thinks
And hits with the violence
Malevolence
Of the thing.'

Nobody listening was in any doubt about the initial capitals at the beginning of his lines.

The instruments held their chord. The triangle player raised his hand that held the beater in a slow circle and gave the triangle a mournful *ting* on its way past before settling back in a position of repose as before. He had been much influenced as a teen by Pete Townshend's windmilling and had resolved to incorporate it into his musical persona as far as he could. No matter what the tempo.

The rhythm started up again, this time with more energy. It wasn't as if there was a tune, as such, developing; more that the flute decided to meet its 1970s new age/jazz destiny head-on and break out in a cadenza. The flautist, a man of around sixty sporting an unkempt beard and sunglasses, started walking round in small circles, which did nothing for the sound pickup from the static microphone. The whole effect was of a terribly slow Hammond organ rotation.

'Oh shit. There's a second verse coming,' said Ann.

Everyone in Mrs Ford-Hughes's drawing room was transfixed. Some had looks of horror on their faces. Mrs Ford-Hughes's hand reached out to hold Fenella's, and they sat side by side on the sofa, gripping each other in disbelief.

'You know it's bad when even Fenella and Mrs Ford-Hughes are horrified,' said Charlie, nodding over to the sofa.

'Here it comes,' said Erin.

Gregory Knight approached his microphone for the second time.

'All the while the water
Runs plugward
Hellward
Heavenward
Oh my word
And the shard of my heart
I blurt to her bare
In the shower for an hour.
The curtain falls.
The violin calls.
We are all… new once more.'

The instruments seemed to settle on whatever note they had just arrived on. After a couple more triangle *ting*s with what felt like an ice age between them, Gregory stepped away from the microphone and relaxed into a huge grin, nodding his vibing thanks to his fellow musicians.

Erin had covered her face with her hand. 'Has he finished?'

'Yeah, safe to come out,' said Charlie, and started eating again.

In complete contrast to the stunned quiet in the room, a swell of applause slugged out of the screen. Mrs Ford-Hughes and Fenella looked at each other in confusion. A murmur of disbelief started to ripple through the guests, as the realisation that Ambient Sound's performance had been met with rapturous approval in the TV studio. Barney was nodding and smiling, waiting for the clapping to die away.

'They liked it?' said Ann.

'What the fuck's that about?' said Charlie, through an improvised double-decker mini quiche.

Anthony Popkin had started to speak. 'This searing comment on modern lives – I mean, what can one say? And the bravery to cut his instrumentation to the bone. Flawless.'

Barney turned to Maria, who was also nodding. 'Obviously I cannot speak to the use of amplified voices – it's not how we go about opera, for instance – but I can see the attraction for this kind of fusion. A pared-back Strauss. One to watch, certainly.'

Olive Yessel was shaking her head as Barney turned to her.

'I cannot believe what I'm hearing from my fellow judges. I may be a little old lady, but has none of you heard of *The Emperor's New Clothes*?'

Charlie, Ann and Erin cheered from their window seat, making everyone else turn to look.

'Go, Olive!' shouted Charlie.

Olive hadn't finished. 'I think we would do well to take a good look at ourselves as gatekeepers before holding this ragged confection up to the British public as something to venerate.'

Barney twinkled a smile at the audience. 'Well, Olive, don't hold back – tell us what you really think!'

A huge laugh from the audience answered him. Olive merely shrugged.

As the judges' scores were entered on the leader board, Barney was already into his next announcement. 'And now, our second-to-last competitor. With not four, not five, not six, but *nine* cellos, here is Maryanne Ford-Hughes and her cello orchestra with the *Aria* from Villa-Lobos's *Bachianas Brasileiras No. 5*!'

'Oh my!' squealed Mrs Ford-Hughes. 'Here we go!'

Everyone in the room straightened up to watch with their full attention, apart from Erin, Ann and Charlie, who leaned further back into their window seat and tried not to look at the screen.

'Eliot's texted,' said Erin. 'He saw Gregory too. I can't read this. It's basically all swears. Oh, now he's gone all fingers-crossed-emoji-for-luck.'

'I think we're beyond luck,' said Ann. 'As Eliot well knows. But it's nice of him to try.'

The opening bars of the Villa-Lobos drifted from the television.

'You sound nice, Ann,' said Charlie.

'As do you, my friend,' she said. 'Aaaaaand, here's bar three.'

As the unmistakable voice of Mrs Ford-Hughes swooped up to her note, Ann and Erin each put a hand over their eyes and drained their glasses. Charlie waved at a passing waiter with a full bottle and managed to get them all refills.

Given what could have happened, the piece was delivered relatively unscathed. Charlie had managed to keep Mrs Ford-Hughes vaguely on the right road during the Portuguese section, even if Paola cringed in the hallway as Mrs Ford-Hughes's mangling of the language filled the room in surround sound. The same waiter who had just refilled Charlie's glass walked past her to the kitchen, only to reappear instantly with a clean champagne flute. He handed it to her and filled it up, putting a finger to his lips with a smile. Through the doorway, Paola caught Charlie's eye as she lifted the glass to her mouth. He grinned and toasted her, and they drank together.

It ended, as all things will. The studio audience's applause was full and genuine, but it was drowned out by whoops and cheers from her friends beside her in the drawing room. Mrs Ford-Hughes blushed and smiled. Fenella leaned over and kissed her cheek. Mr Ford-Hughes stepped forward from his place by the wall, and raised her hand to his lips.

'Brava, my darling,' he murmured. 'Brava.'

Mrs Ford-Hughes gazed at him with utter love.

'Aw,' said Erin. 'They are rather sweet together, aren't they?'

'Quite the team,' agreed Ann.

The attention in the studio turned to the judges, and Mrs Ford-Hughes shushed everyone to hear what they had to say.

Barney turned to Maria Romano first. 'Maria, as our resident opera singer, let's find out what you have to say about this ensemble first. Give us your expert opinion!'

'Well, Barney, this singer clearly has a trained voice and can handle the repertoire,' she started. 'I wondered about the lie of the register, and whether she is more of a mezzo than a soprano. Some of the top notes were a little strained.'

'Oh!' squeaked Mrs Ford-Hughes, both hands over her mouth and her eyes wide. Fenella patted her knee.

Maria continued. 'But overall, I'd say a competent stab at what is a tricky ensemble piece to pull off, especially without a conductor.'

'Thank you,' said Barney. 'And speaking of conductors, what's your view on that, Anthony? Should they have attempted this without one?'

'Absolutely not,' said Anthony sternly, before breaking out into a huge grin. 'Otherwise, we'd all be out of work!' He rode the laughter like a pro. 'No, seriously, I was impressed with the cello ensemble too. There are some fine players there.'

Olive, as usual, was given her turn to speak last. She looked as if she was used to it. 'Despite all the lack of technical skills so evident in this performance, I applaud the love of the music she so obviously brings. And I concur with Anthony, the cellos are to be commended. It is not an easy piece.'

'There you have it, folks,' said Barney. 'Judges' scores going up now, and on to our final group of the evening: a quintet of trombones and tubas!'

'Where are we on the board?' asked Ann, squinting. 'Haven't got my glasses on.'

'Kind of middling,' said Erin.

'Please god don't let us go through.'

'Amen,' said Charlie. 'For one thing, we can't play anything else, and we have to do a new piece if we get into the semis.'

'Christ, that's true,' said Ann. 'I'm not doing any more rehearsing with those two.' She looked over to the sofa where Fenella and Mrs Ford-Hughes were laughing together.

The room talked loudly over the trombone/tuba quintet segment, only turning their attention back to the television when all the judges' scores were up and Barney was about to tell the audience to vote.

Erin's phone buzzed again. She looked and snorted with laughter. 'Eliot,' she whispered. 'He says, "*THOUGHT YOU WERE WONDERFUL BUT HOPE YOU'RE CRAP ENOUGH TO LOSE. GOOD LUCK.*" He knows.'

'Good man,' whispered Charlie.

Barney gave the audience the go-ahead, and the scoreboard did its now familiar swirling and jiggling so nobody could tell who was going where. It settled in a cascade of lights to show the little marching violin troupe in the top spot, with Gregory's Ambient Sounds just underneath. Mrs Ford-Hughes was third, by a tiny margin of votes.

There was a heartfelt sympathetic 'aw' in the room for Mrs Ford-Hughes, which she acknowledged with a bow of her head and a hand over what was probably meant to be her heart but ended up slipping down over her left bosom.

'It was so close!' said her husband. 'Bad luck indeed. It should have been you and not that awful poet man.'

Ann was still looking at the screen. 'Seems Olive agrees,' she said, as the camera panned over the judges' faces. Olive was rolling her eyes and shaking her head. 'Still, hoo-bloody-ray, eh? Let's try to look sad until we get out.'

'Roger that,' said Charlie.

The dry yet jaunty theme tune played out, and Mr Ford-Hughes snapped the television off with his remote control. As if summoned, a flock of waiting staff filed into the room with fresh canapés and cold bottles, and people hummed into conversation again.

Mrs Ford-Hughes got to her feet and raised her glass. 'I just wanted to say a few words before we go any further. I've had a helluva time with y'all putting this little ensemble together, and I want to thank each and every one of you for the time you spent with me.'

The room applauded the nine cellists, noticing with surprise that three of them had been lurking in a window seat all evening. The three grinned cheerily and raised their glasses in thanks.

'I wanna thank my husband: my strength, as always,' she continued. 'And all of you, my dear, dear friends, for supporting me in this little bit of fun. It's a shame it had to stop but sometimes things are just how they are. I had a blast. Now, let's party!'

'She's a trouper, I'll give her that,' said Erin.

'Not a bad old bird,' agreed Ann.

'Try the haggis,' said Charlie. 'They look disgusting but taste amazing!'

And so they partied into the night.

Chapter 19

Before the orchestra played a note at the next rehearsal, Eliot put down his baton and led a round of applause for the cello section, who sat there looking embarrassed. Everyone had watched them on telly, it turned out, and therefore knew exactly what reserves of musicality and perseverance it had taken to shepherd Mrs Ford-Hughes safely to the double barline at the end of the piece.

The applause went on for so long Erin had to wave at them to stop. 'Thank you,' she said, laughing. 'On behalf of the best cello section I could hope to play in.'

The cellists behind her cheered and shuffled their feet on the floor as a secondary round of musicians' applause, and that was that.

'Well deserved,' said Eliot. 'Now, before we get going, you'll have seen we have a new piece of music on our stands. David, Pearl and I have had to do a bit of jiggling with our programme this term. Because you were all so bloody good, we appear to have got ourselves involved in a live broadcast situation in two weeks' time.' He paused for more cheers. 'Which requires us to play a new, very short piece we haven't played them before, which seems unfair, since we played the last one so nicely. Anyway, after the minimum of communal research –' he broke off to grin at Pearl, '– well, OK then, over last week's coffee break, we decided to give the Glinka *Ruslan and Ludmila* Overture a whirl.'

'Nice,' said Charlie.

'Nice and short,' called Ann, from the back of the cellos.

'Have you seen our part?' said Marco, leafing through the one on his stand.

'I admit,' said Eliot, 'that the first violins will be sawing up and down scales like billy-o, but in my defence, it is in D major, and I reckon after rehearsing Brahms 2 for a few weeks, you should be a dab hand at those. There was some method in this madness.'

The violins laughed grudgingly, accepting the logic.

'This change of programming also means we need a contrabassoon,' said Eliot, 'and I'm delighted that Dev agreed to help us out at short notice.' He waved at Dev, who was sitting next to Rafael at the end of the bassoon section, holding his contra balanced on its spike on the floor, similar to a cello. The contra, or double-bassoon, sounded an octave deeper than an ordinary bassoon, and its polished wooden 18-foot-long tube was folded up on itself four times so, to the uninitiated, Dev looked as if he were grappling with a large python. Dev waved cheerily at everyone saying hello.

'Huge thanks also to Pearl,' said Eliot. 'I don't know how many favours she had to call in, or what magic she wove, but she has managed to hire a full score and all our Glinka parts within a week. Truly, she is a marvel.' He blew her a kiss through more applause. Pearl looked shyly delighted.

'And we'd better win some prize money to offset the hire costs,' called Rafael. Nobody knew if he was joking or not.

'Right,' said Eliot. 'Let's have a go at this. It's only short but chock-full of notes, and we haven't got long to learn it. Concentrate. And I apologise now to the entire string section, who have to wear their fingers to the bone before we even get to the tune.'

He grinned at the string desks near to him in solidarity and set off at the hectic *presto* speed indicated. The entire brass and wind joined in with brisk chords, before dropping out to leave the violins, violas, cellos and even the double basses (who usually were let off Fast Work) negotiating furiously rapid scales in unison before the wind and brass dropped in again briefly. It should have sounded as if the strings were being carelessly tossed in the air by the wind and brass, flying up and back, only to be caught and thrown again.

What actually happened was that the wind and brass nailed their chords to Eliot's beat, while the string sound grew increasingly ragged as their scale progressed. Some of them hadn't made it back home before the next triumphant orchestral chord arrived, and then of course they were late starting off on the next run, like a schoolchild puffing at the back of a cross-country race. The first couple of scale sections were only two bars long, so there was time for a quick reset if needed, and some players could skip what they knew they were not going to get around to in time and plop themselves into the next bar on time.

The third go, however, was an eight-bar sequence that sent the strings up and down the same basic scale but with added meanderings, culminating in a bar and a half of extra sharps and flats just to throw them off the scent. It was all too much for some of the back desks and, by about the sixth bar of the final scale passage, the time lag between Richard, Charlie and Erin on the front rows of their sections, and some of the players further back had got so wide, and the giggles of those helplessly mired had got so infectious, the whole ensemble collapsed and Eliot stopped beating to laugh.

'Right,' he said, waiting for the laughter to stop. 'Maybe the tempo was too ambitious. That wasn't really fair, but I wanted to see what we could do. Let's take it again, at a slightly more sensible pace. But I reserve the right to send you away to have sectionals.' A sarcastic 'woooh' drifted over the orchestra from the trombone section, which Eliot tried not to laugh at. 'Shall we try just the strings slowly from bar eleven?'

After a few practice runs at increasing speeds, the strings felt ready to rejoin the orchestra and have another go. This time, they made it to the first big tune everybody recognised. Several faces expressed a revelation that they knew the tune but hadn't clocked it was from this Glinka Overture. Having been used as the theme tune to John Finnemore's BBC Radio 4 comedy *Cabin Pressure*, the first few bars at least were familiar to a lot of players, some of whom involuntarily overlayed it in their mind with Benedict Cumberbatch reading out the credits in an increasingly silly voice. It was a jaunty tune. It could cope.

The horns had a dovetailed rhythm of crotchets that allowed them to build an irrepressible momentum: Neema and Simon (first and third horn) played off the beat, while Ryan and David (second and fourth) played on the beat. The overall output was a horn note on every beat, but because each player only had to play half the time, the effect was more energised. It had an added advantage of allowing them to breathe without interrupting the rhythm.

That kind of orchestral writing could be tricky to pull off (as Brian and Amber had discovered while playing the Strauss horn concerto flute parts on tour that summer), but the Stockwell Park Orchestra horn section was an effective unit. Keeping their peripheral vision on each other and their concentration on Eliot, the quartet pumped out a tightly controlled rhythm for the rest of the orchestra to use as a base. Eliot nodded at them during their first few bars of that arrangement, to make sure they knew he knew how well they were playing. Neema raised her eyebrows in recognition on behalf of her section without taking her lips away from her mouthpiece. Gestures like these are the glue that holds an orchestra together.

The violins and violas shared their first tune with both flutes and, if in that first run-through it had the air of a couple of Pied Piper experts leading a trail of variably able followers, there was no going back. Several viola players, unused as they were to *quite* so many notes going past per bar, were not capable of playing them all. Some missed out the ends of bars to give themselves time to launch into the next one on time. Some tried playing the longer notes and whichever individual ones in the quaver runs took their fancy on the way through. Pete, at the back, tried his best: sitting on the very front edge of his chair, his tongue poking out of the side of his mouth. It didn't take long before he was attempting the scales by moving the neck of his viola from side to side and keeping his bow still. It never worked as a tactic, but he never failed to give it another chance.

Eliot encouraged everyone to spot the *sforzandos* every now and then, which are supposed to leap out of the furious texture like rocks in the road making a car jump. A lot of the time, when faced with sight-reading pages of fast quavers, players tend to overlook the tiny printed marking of *sf* under one of them. The sound of unremitting 'terrified loud quavers' becomes dull after a while. Eliot tried to encourage it more along the lines of 'terrified (for now, but will improve) and yet still capable of surprises'. He did this by doing actual star jumps, knowing that the energy gearing system in place between conductor and orchestra required a ridiculous input on his part to gain any traction with them. Also, he enjoyed it.

After what seemed like several years to the string players, the tune shifted over to the wind, who threw it around between themselves deftly as if they were playing catch with it. All the strings had to do was count some rests and then see if their next note was bowed or plucked, which was another whole level of difficulty for some of them.

Just before the next big tune, Eliot brought them to a halt.

'I know we're just reading through for the first time, but can anyone tell me your dynamic in bar seventy-five?'

A few people shouted '*fortissimo!*' with the happy conviction of sixteen-year-olds at the back of a coach on a school trip.

'Correct. Now – and I can see some people know what I'm about to ask next – what's the dynamic in bar seventy-seven?'

A shame-faced mumble.

'Sorry? Couldn't hear you. And I realise how hilariously ironic that is.'

'*Piano*,' murmured a few people.

'Correct!' Eliot smiled. 'Within three bars, I need you to go from the loudest you can possibly play to the softest you can possibly play. Which is really difficult, I grant you. But it's written right there for you on the page. So? Again from bar seventy, and shut the flip up when it says so. I mean that in the nicest possible way.'

After being reminded, the orchestra did indeed shut up, and the glorious tune swelled out on the cellos, violas and bassoon. They let everyone else join in after a while, and – with only one more yell from Eliot of 'minor!' when it switched from major to minor and some people didn't notice the accidentals – it went swimmingly.

The Overture wound itself up over the next few minutes. Near the end, when the strings' quavers were almost entirely drowned out by the brass and wind with sustained chords and random accents, plus Max rolling away on the timpani, the orchestra was thrown another curveball in the shape of a *più mosso*. More movement. More than the scurrying around that they had already been required to perform. Even faster, in other words. Pete shuffled further to the front of his chair and leaned forward. Eliot's beat grew wilder. It was the home straight: the violins went into triplets, Max bashed as if his life depended on it, the entire brass section were smashing out chords together in a wall of decibels that laid down most orchestral musicians' future tinnitus problems. The wind and strings had to fall onto their final note via four demisemiquavers, which Eliot allowed them to fudge with a mental note to work on later.

He brought them off with a triumphant clenched fist, and nodded, breathing hard. 'Not bad. Not bad at all. That should blow their socks off in a fortnight. Now, let's get to work on it.'

Chapter 20

In the last week of October, Eliot texted Alexander Leakey on the off-chance his hunch had been correct. He was willing to bet Alexander – their Thor-hunk horn soloist who had joined the Stockwell Park Orchestra's recent European tour – would have been first on the contact list for Russell Donovan at Quork Media. A man like Russell would not be oblivious to rock star charisma and a huge ready-made following of internet fans.

They met at two o'clock on a cold, bright Tuesday in Jubilee Park on the South Bank, and shook hands with warm enthusiasm.

'Good to see you!' said Alexander, his soft Scottish accent slipping through his smile.

'Glad you could make it,' said Eliot. 'Didn't know if you were still going to be in London. I guess you're busy?'

Alexander chuckled. 'Yes, funnily enough I am. Diary's filled up considerably after our little jaunt. Can't imagine why. I did enjoy myself on that trip – how is everyone?'

They strolled along the South Bank, under the looming curves of the London Eye and onto the path by the river. The vast dark waters of the Thames rolled past. Across the water,

London's skyline chucked as many famous landmarks as it could into one horizon: Parliament, Big Ben and Whitehall.

'They're all very well,' said Eliot. 'And we're busy too. More than usual. I wondered if we might be busy with the same thing? Have you been watching much telly recently?'

Alexander laughed, properly this time. 'I wondered if you wanted to compare notes on that. Yes, I have, and you sounded brilliant. Congratulations on going through.'

'Compare notes? So you *are* involved?'

'Yeah. I've got a quartet together. Our recorded thing goes out this weekend – I think it's the last heat before it goes into the semi-final.'

Eliot clapped him on the shoulder. 'I knew it! When the producer met David and me for coffee, he mentioned a load of other acts he was interested in, and said something about a horn quartet! I should have rung you then.'

'Yeah, he found me via my site and got in touch. I knew he'd contacted you lot because he was going on about our tour and how it had "caught the zeitgeist" or some such bollocks.'

It was Eliot's turn to laugh. 'He does talk bollocks a bit, doesn't he? But then imagine having his job.'

'Our jobs are pretty silly too.'

'Maybe.'

They wandered on companionably.

'So if your episode doesn't go out until this week,' said Eliot, 'that doesn't sound fair for prep time if you go through. Which you obviously will. I mean, we knew three weeks ago and have already had a fortnight to work on our next piece. Mind you, maybe they did that deliberately. We need the time – you've met Pete. Your lot probably don't.'

'You're very kind. And that had crossed my mind – though even thinking about it maybe puts the kibosh on things. We've worked on another piece just in case, since we recorded the first one, I mean. If we need it, I guess next week will be rehearsal-tastic.'

Eliot nodded. 'God knows what we'll do if we get through to the final. That's probably only a week after the semi. And we're sailing pretty close to the edge with our Glinka.'

'Oh-ho! The *Ruslan and Ludmila* Overture? Good luck with that!'

'I probably shouldn't be telling you. You might be our opposition.'

Alexander put his hands deep into his pockets out of the wind and gazed over the water. 'I don't think a bit of healthy competition will come between us.' He looked at Eliot. 'It would be brilliant if we each got through, wouldn't it? Though we're both maybe a bit traditional for them – have you *seen* what else has been winning? Christ alive. That poet.'

It was Eliot's turn to laugh. 'Yeah – my cello section were simultaneously appalled at him – for many reasons – and yet relieved not to have to progress with Mrs Ford-Hughes.'

'Ah, yes. I did watch that one. The cellos sounded good – on the whole.'

'Fenella used to lead our orchestra cello section. It's a whole other story.'

Alexander nodded. 'What's with the poet?'

Eliot grimaced. 'He's local, apparently – somewhere in south London, anyway. Couple of months ago he approached us asking about a "residency" or something. Can't remember how he phrased it. Anyway, turns out he's a weapons grade arsehole who was creepy to one of our clarinettists – Beatriz, d'you remember her? Super creepy. Ann flipped out, which was educational to watch, let me tell you, and he was basically escorted from the premises by Carl.'

Alexander stopped walking and stared at Eliot. 'You're kidding?'

'I wish. Though the Ann and Carl double act was a sight to behold.'

'Bet it was. They kind of complement each other, don't they?'

'You don't mess with either of them, put it that way.' Eliot paused and frowned. 'The thing is, and this is the bit that pisses me off, he must have heard about *Pass the Baton* while he was hanging round with us for those couple of weeks. David mentioned the production company. It would have been easy to google them. And – get this – we were in the pub with Noel Osmar and he showed us a whole load more of hilarious stuff on Gregory. That's the poet. Stuff Noel only knew about because of something *else* he'd had to look into, which I don't even want to think about. But I can't get away from feeling guilty that it's only because of us that Gregory heard about the whole TV thing. And now he's in the bloody semi-final. Spouting that utter shite.'

'You didn't vote him through,' said Alexander gently. 'That bit's not your fault.'

Eliot shrugged and nodded, and they started walking again.

'That triangle player though.' Eliot started to giggle.

Alexander shook his head in incomprehension. 'Look on the bright side. He'll have had to come up with something new too. The triangle player could be a thing of the past.'

'Will that improve it, overall? We might yearn nostalgically for something to distract us from Gregory. Oh god.'

They walked on, past the Oxo Tower and Blackfriars Bridge, towards the Globe. Eliot noticed Alexander getting a fair few glances and double-takes, either from people thinking it was perhaps Thor himself walking along the Thames, or simply admiring his ridiculously off-the-scale good looks. It was a glimpse of a life he knew he would never experience, no matter how boyishly attractive he might be on a good day. And that was OK by him.

As they approached the Swan pub next to the Globe, Alexander looked at his watch. 'Fancy a pint?'

Eliot grinned. 'Why not? We can plot our coordinated takeover of early evening telly.'

'God, I love not having a proper job,' said Alexander, and pushed open the door.

Chapter 21

Alexander's horn quartet did go through to the semi-final, as Eliot predicted, along with a group of opera singers. In the end, after four heats, Quork Media had eight groups of musicians lined up for the next stage of *Pass the Baton*. Four would compete in each semi-final, with one group going home and three going through to the final. To keep a competitive edge, each pair who had made it through from the recorded heats had been split up for the semi-finals, so they would not be competing against the same people again before they got to the final.

The first semi-final week comprised Stockwell Park Orchestra, the group of tiny violinists, a harp ensemble, and the opera singers. The second week had Alexander's horn quartet, the Honkytonk Twins (the piano act who had been in the orchestra's heat), a jazz band, and Gregory Knight.

And so, one by one, on a rainy Saturday lunchtime in November, members of the orchestra arrived at the TV studio in central London. They were checked in by security staff and given red lanyards to wear saying *PERFORMER*, then directed into the centre of the building to wait in an airy atrium until called. The space had an industrial vibe, with whitewashed, textured concrete walls and huge pipes suspended from the ceiling. A brightly-lit bar selling drinks and sandwiches took up most of one side of the space, and tables and chairs were scattered about in groups. The atrium slowly filled with people, most of whom also wore *PERFORMER* lanyards. Some were yellow, green or blue.

'The opposition,' said Charlie to Erin, flipping his red oblong of plastic toward a gaggle of kids wearing yellow ones. 'They're tiny. We can take them out.'

'I don't think that's how this works.'

'You never know. It's semi-final territory now. Maybe we have to do hand-to-hand combat too. For the ratings.'

Erin laughed and waved at Eliot, who was being lanyarded up by a security guard. He walked over.

'Hello! Nice and early, jolly good. I think most of today will be waiting around until we do our thing, but I thought I'd get here in time for a good loiter first.'

'I'm starving,' said Charlie, eyeing the sandwiches at the bar. 'Watch my cello, would you? Can I get anyone anything?'

Erin shook her head. 'Some of us had lunch before we came, Charlie. Don't you ever plan ahead?'

Charlie stuck his tongue out at her and walked off.

'No alcohol!' called Eliot after him. A few of the tiny violinists' adult chaperones turned to stare. He smiled, only slightly awkwardly, and turned back to Erin. 'Now they're judging us. I can't believe they've got the moral high ground already.'

'Relax,' said Erin, laughing. 'It's a music competition. They're the odd ones out.'

'Well, they are children, I suppose.'

She snorted. 'What are you talking about? Didn't you ever play in a youth orchestra? Legendary drinking habits.'

'Fair point. Although some of them are *very* tiny.'

More and more people arrived and naturally congregated in their colour-coordinated groups. The blue lanyards stood together by the windows. Every one of them wore a scarf wrapped around their throat and carried a water bottle, and the aroma of Vocalzones swirled around them before being sucked into the exposed grilles of the ventilation system piping.

Charlie returned with what looked like an entire baguette stuffed full of cheese and salad, by which time most of the orchestra had arrived and was milling around Eliot. The people who played large instruments had put their cases on the floor to rest their shoulders, while a lot of the violinists and viola players still wore theirs as backpacks. Players of tiny instruments like flutes and oboes were free to dart about at will, unhindered by their art, having tucked their microscopic instrument cases into normal bags. They were the breed of musician who could use public transport without quips (or "quips") from fellow passengers or sore backs and shoulders from lugging things about.

Eliot was concentrating on something David was telling him about timings for the afternoon when his attention was diverted by the latest group arriving at security and being issued with their (green) lanyards.

'Oh my god,' he said.

David stopped talking and turned to look.

'Shit,' said Charlie.

'I thought you'd seen all the heats,' said Erin to Eliot. 'You could have said. Didn't you know?'

'I missed one. She must have been on that week.'

Leading her ensemble through the security gates as if she were hauling another dimension behind her like a cloak was a tall, elegant woman with black hair pulled up on top of her head in a sleek bun. Her pallor contrasted with her dark red lipstick, which was painted on in a stern flat line. She wheeled a harp on a silent, rubber-tyred trolley until she arrived at an area of floor space free of anyone else, then stopped. Her fellow harpists gathered around her, and also tipped their harp trolleys flat to rest. They stood motionless, surrounded by shrouded harps taller than themselves, like witches at midnight in a stone circle.

'Should I... go and say hello, do you think?' said Eliot, suddenly aware his voice had gone croaky.

At that moment, the lead harpist turned her head directly towards him, and inclined it slightly, still unsmiling.

'Think you'd better now,' said Charlie. 'She's practically jumped up and down in excitement to see you.'

Eliot cleared his throat and walked over to the harps. 'Hello, Bożenka,' he said, holding out his hand and – too late – wishing he hadn't.

'Eliot,' said Bożenka, in her low, heavy accent. She clasped his hand tightly. 'Good afternoon.'

Eliot felt his hand shrink in Bożenka's icy grip and extricated it as soon as he could, which seemed to take an age because his arm failed to register it needed to move. 'Lovely to see you again. I – er – didn't know you were playing in this.'

'We pass the time as we must,' she said, gesturing to her fellow harpists. 'The winter dark approaches.'

He laughed an abnormally high laugh, as if trying to inject some warm-blooded human life into the air again.

'Yes, yes. It is, I suppose. November. Right then, better get back. Good luck!'

Bożenka inclined her head once more, and released Eliot back to his orchestra. He returned to them massaging his hand, trying to work some kind of feeling back into his fingers. Charlie and Erin were laughing at him.

'You plonker,' said Charlie. 'We need your right hand to hold the baton. Have you learned nothing?'

'Apparently not,' said Eliot. 'She doesn't get any more cheerful, does she? Do you think they're all like that?'

'If they weren't before, they probably are now,' said Erin. 'Nobody can rehearse with her for long and remain immune.'

'Wonder what they'll be playing,' said Carl, who had watched Eliot's attempt at cordiality.

'The main thing is not to look at her for too long before we do our bit,' said Eliot. 'We don't want all our energy sucked out.'

Just then, Gemma and Arden appeared from a doorway on the far side of the atrium. They each wore a microphone headset and carried clipboards.

'Hello everyone,' called Gemma. The conversation hum in the room died away. 'Welcome to the first semi-final of *Pass the Baton*! If you'd all like to come this way, Arden will show you through to the studio and we'll go through the timetable for the rest of the day.'

Everyone slowly eddied toward Arden, who marched in front of them through the door like a tiny dungaree-wearing warrior leading an army into battle.

Chapter 22

They were led into a studio even bigger than the atrium. The roof was criss-crossed with lighting rigs and cables snaking in all directions. The lights dazzled, making it impossible to see how high the ceiling actually was above the rigging. The floor space was sectioned off: a large part was given to ranked seats for an audience. There was a stage area at the far end with its now-familiar enormous screen on the wall behind it, and down one side of the stage there were four groups of chairs and small tables. Each group was clustered round a small pennant on a miniature flagpole – one each of red, yellow, green and blue. The number of chairs around the pennants varied hugely, with the most by far in the red zone, around thirty yellows, and fewer than ten each for green and blue.

Arden gestured at the chairs round the pennants. 'We've colour-coded your seating areas. Please find a seat in your colour zone.'

The orchestra's red zone was furthest from the door they had just come in by, so they straggled past the other groups peeling off to settle themselves around their flags.

Gemma appeared from yet another door, and behind her emerged Russell Donovan, clapping his hands with delight at the sight of all his competitors readying themselves.

'Greetings!' he cried. 'On behalf of Quork Media, may I congratulate you all on reaching the semi-finals of *Pass the Baton*. In a very real sense, you are all winners already!'

'Give me strength,' said Carl quietly, before being shushed by Kayla.

Undaunted by a heckle he had completely failed to notice, Russell continued. 'It's wonderful to welcome you all – I want to say "back", even though you haven't actually been to the studio before in person. I feel you have in spirit. Dave! Hi!' He gave David a thumbs-up and a grin. David lifted his chin in acknowledgement. 'Great to have Stockwell Park Orchestra on board. And Fiddle Me This!' He waved at the tiny violinists, who squealed and waved back, bouncing on their seats until their grown-ups calmed them down. 'Congratulations. You are definitely the youngest act in our semi-finals.' He turned to the opera singers and bowed. 'And of course, Arioso – welcome. I hope you have all come in fine voice?' The singers immediately sang 'yes!' back to him, building up into a perfectly tuned chord, and then flustered around taking sips of water and popping throat sweets.

Finally, Russell faced Bożenka and her harpists. He swallowed, and tried to keep his grin plastered on his face even as it threatened to melt away and whimper on the other side of his head. 'And last but – and I cannot stress this enough – *by no means* least, we have this truly outstanding ensemble: The Dark Harps.'

'You called,' said Bożenka. 'We came. Let it begin.'

Charlie leaned in towards Erin's ear. 'Are you not entertained?'

'I just hope we don't have to go on after Bożenka's lot,' she whispered back. 'Imagine having to get the audience jolly again after that.'

'So,' continued Russell, 'Gemma here will take you through the nuts and bolts of this afternoon and evening. I'll be up there –' he pointed to a glass-walled room at the back of the studio, up a flight of steps, '– doing my thing. Let's make a great show!'

He bustled away, leaving Gemma and Arden.

Gemma smiled. 'Your current seats will be your base – your Green Room, as it were, and you'll go from here to the stage when it's your turn to perform. We're keeping you in the studio so our cameras can show the viewers shots of you when you're not performing, that kind of thing. We'll show you to your dressing rooms to change before the broadcast this evening, and hair and make-up, and then you'll come back here in good time. There'll be soundchecks and things like that. But most of all, have fun!'

One of the tiny violinists put his hand up. 'I need the toilet.'

Gemma turned to Arden. 'Over to you.'

* * *

After everyone who wanted to had visited the toilet, each group was given a short while for a soundcheck, during which the technical team decided which shots they wanted and how to choreograph it. Stockwell Park Orchestra were up first.

'Leave your instrument cases here,' said David. 'They've set up for us on stage, so we just need you, your instrument and your music. Max, I think they've already spoken to you about your timps, haven't they? Let's go.'

Eliot led the way onto the vibratingly bright stage area and was delighted to find that the stagehands had efficiently laid out the right number of chairs and stands in the correct arrangement. Max's timpani and stool were arranged at the back. He waved a heartfelt thank you to the guys milling all around the studio, who could accurately follow a plan without fussing. Their uniform was coordinating black trousers, black T-shirts and black belts festooned with all manner of spare tape, tools and coils of wire. Eliot wouldn't have been surprised to see any one of them shimmy up a cable into the ceiling rigging if required. He reflected he was used to Pearl's level of administration which, although far and away the best in terms of beverages, custard creams and maxi dresses, lacked a little in terms of the effortless efficiency of these wall-to-wall black-outfit ninjas.

Several of the players were blinking under the bright lights.

'We've only got about twenty minutes, so let's crack on,' said Eliot. 'Gwynneth, could we have an A, please? What's the matter, Pete?'

Pete was walking round in small circles, looking at the floor. 'I dropped my music.'

Ann bent down and picked something up. 'Here you go. It was right behind you.'

She caught Eliot's eye and sighed. Pete was always going to 'Pete', even if he was about to be on telly.

They started the Glinka Overture, ran it for a short while until Eliot stopped them, nodding. 'Yeah, that's going to be fine. Superb string sound, well done.' There was a shuffling of congratulatory feet. 'Let's try the final section.'

They topped and tailed a bit more until Eliot was satisfied it wouldn't fall apart later on, then he waved them offstage to let the others have their turn. The army of furniture movers swarmed onto the set and whisked the orchestra chairs, stands and timpani away, leaving a bare space for Fiddle Me This to perform their very own brand of choreographed marching violins.

'Right, we can put our feet up for a while now,' said Carl, stretching his long legs onto a spare chair in front of him. 'Hey – look at this! Magic.'

He waved Kayla and Charlie away from the small table nearest to him, as he had seen some catering staff approach bearing huge oval trays piled high with sandwiches covered in clingfilm. They kept coming, in their own version of choreographed marching catering staff, putting the trays down at regular intervals until most tables had a selection of sandwiches. A second wave of caterers followed, setting out water bottles.

Carl peeled off the clingfilm on his nearest tray and started munching. 'Come on, Tracie,' he said, jerking his head to beckon his young trombonist protégé towards the food. 'Fill yer boots. It's free.'

She didn't need telling twice, and soon they were sitting side by side eating double decker sandwiches and laughing.

Kayla folded her arms and smiled. 'It's so sweet how he's teaching her to be a proper brass player.'

Charlie pushed past her and took a sandwich for himself. 'Not just brass players, mate. Always room for another sandwich, even if you've had lunch already.'

'Keep telling you,' said Ann to Erin. 'Worms.'

On stage, the small violins were playing an arrangement of "Bohemian Raphsody", somehow managing to play it all off by heart and know where to walk to make intricate patterns on the stage as well. Because some of the children were really very tiny, and they were playing extremely small violins, frequencies were pushed right up to their squeaky limit. When they got excited, their repertoire was in danger of sounding like a 33 rpm record being played at 45.

Placed at strategic points around the stage, their grown-up handlers waved what looked like table-tennis bats to remind them which way they should be walking. The adults weren't on camera, but for those in the studio who could see what was going on, it looked like aircraft ground staff had been recruited to divert a determined column of musical ants.

'Fenella would be rubbish at that,' said Charlie, nodding over what was occurring on the stage. 'I mean, leaving aside the walking-with-a-cello thing, she would forget she needed to see and close her eyes whenever it got to a soulful bit. Pile up. Carnage.'

Ann laughed. 'We'll never know how close we were to having to do something like that. I'm so glad we didn't get through with Mrs Ford-Hughes.'

'God, yes,' said Erin. 'Can you imagine Fenella and Mrs Ford-Hughes here?'

'Yes,' said everyone within earshot.

The operatic ensemble, Arioso, were starting to warm up in their blue corner. Strictly speaking, they had never allowed themselves to warm down, and had been sirening quietly to themselves since breakfast. Now, however, they began to produce the strange noises a human voice apparently requires to dislodge even the tiniest obstruction on the vocal folds. There was facial massaging going on, as well as several of them enunciating 'Popocatépetl' to themselves quietly up and down scales, with exaggerated mouth movements. Some were blowing raspberries, which upset a few children on stage who thought it was directed at their performance.

After a fourth child had burst into tears, Arden had to go over to Arioso and ask them to refrain from such exercises that might be open to misinterpretation.

'You want us to stop warming up?' asked the largest soprano, clutching her scarf ever closer around her neck.

'No, no,' said Arden hurriedly. 'Just, maybe, a bit, um, quieter? And with less raspberry-blowing? You're upsetting Fiddle Me This.'

'Might we be allowed to use a dressing room for our warm-up? If the harps are doing their soundcheck before us?'

Arden couldn't see any reason why not, and led the singers through a door. The sounds of 'Popocatépetl' and raspberries receded.

Ann sat down next to Carl and helped herself to a sandwich. 'What the fuck have we let ourselves in for?'

Fiddle Me This finished their rehearsal of "Bohemian Rhapsody", which ended with them all lying on their backs, still playing. Several of them looked exhausted and closed their eyes but were chivvied off stage by extra-vigorous gestures from the wielders of the table-tennis bats.

Gemma finished a conversation into her headset and approached Bożenka's group, who had unzipped their harp covers, but the instruments remained on their trolleys. 'You're up next. We're setting up your chairs now. So, do you want to move your harps?'

Bożenka stared at Gemma without smiling or moving. The other harpists stared at Bożenka. Time seemed to etiolate. Civilizations were born and crumbled.

'Oh god,' Eliot whispered, watching in sympathetic horror. 'Gemma's getting Bożenka'd.'

Nobody moved.

'They'll have to crack soon,' said Ann. 'Those singers will be back before long.'

Bożenka blinked: a slow, deliberate sweep of her long lashes. 'Good. We shall arrange ourselves.'

Gemma walked past Eliot and the others, widening her eyes and shaking her head slightly – not enough to be perceived by the harpists behind her. Or so she thought. Eliot smiled at her in sympathy.

When the last sleepy little violinists had been swept up and five chairs for the harpists were arranged in a semicircle, Bożenka led the procession of silent-wheeled trolleys to the stage area. They eased their harps to the floor, removed the covers completely, rolled them up into bulky piles, re-strapped the pile to the trolley, and wheeled them back to their green zone seats. Returning onstage, Bożenka and the others reached into bags and produced their tuning keys – a bit like oversized radiator keys that could fit over the pegs at the top of each of their strings to adjust their pitch.

And so the tuning began. A four-string violin or cello can take some time before the player is satisfied each string is perfectly adjusted to the micro-pitch accuracy required to play. Guitars have six. An orchestral pedal harp has forty-seven which, unless you are having a game of one-upmanship with a piano, seems excessive. The harpists checked each of their seven pedals was in its neutral position and set to with their tuning keys, checking each frequency against a little black electronic box they held close to the string and adjusting accordingly.

Arden returned alone from showing Arioso their dressing room, and stood with Gemma at the side of the stage area, just in front of the orchestra seats.

Gemma was finishing a conversation with someone in her headset. 'Yeah, yeah, I know. Do you want to tell them to crack on with it? Jesus.' She flicked a switch by her ear and sighed.

'I said I'd fetch the singers when the harps have finished,' said Arden, looking at Bożenka. 'I didn't say how long that might be.'

'Yeah,' said Gemma, chewing her thumbnail, 'Russell's getting antsy about it already. He was like this the last time they were here. He's an idiot. I told him to fix for that fabulous boy trumpet group to go through instead – they were up for playing with open shirts and leather trousers in the final. They're well fit. Russell said the viewing projections weren't reliable enough to swing it. Think he might be regretting that now.'

Erin, who was on a chair in their group nearest to the stage, turned to the others with her eyes wide, and mouthed silently '*Did you hear that?*'

Eliot and Charlie nodded. Ann, a little further away, shook her head, grabbed one of her own ear lobes and mouthed '*old ears*'.

Charlie shifted round next to Ann and quietly filled her in.

Gemma was still talking to Arden. 'I need to make him see sense. He's not on the floor having to deal with it.'

'Well,' said Arden, in a reasonable voice, 'we could switch the order round for tonight, at least? Have the harps go on first. That way, they could tune up before the show starts, and be ready to play on time.'

'Yeah. That's actually a great idea. Let me talk to Russell.' Gemma moved the switch by her ear. 'Russell? Yeah, Russell, let's change the running order for tonight. *Tonight*. Russell? Can you hear me?' She fiddled with the switch on the headset. 'Christ, these things are fucking useless. Russell? Nope.' She tore the headset off and threw it on the floor, starting to half-walk, half-run to the stairs leading up to Russell's glass room, shouting back to Arden. 'Find me another headset, will you? *Now!*'

Arden jumped, and hurried away.

Gemma's headset lay on the floor not far from Erin's seat.

'Chuck that over here, Erin,' said Charlie.

Erin scanned quickly around the studio, but nobody seemed to be looking their way. She scooped up the headset and threw it to Charlie in one movement, before sitting down again and trying to look innocent. 'Gemma said it was broken, though? What do you want it for?'

'These things are never as broken as you might think,' said Charlie, having a close look at the connections between the headset and microphone. A few delicate probes later, he looked at once shifty and triumphant. 'Bingo. Russell hasn't turned his headset off.'

He turned a volume control. The tinny voices of Gemma and Russell rose into the air. Erin, Eliot, Ann, Carl, Kayla and Tracie all leaned in to listen.

'They're a fucking nightmare, Russell. She's practically certifiable. You can't let them go through to the final.'

'But they score very well on our viewer responses. Especially with those low-cut concert dresses they wear to perform.'

'Stuff the viewer responses. What about my *response?'*

'Not to be funny about this, Gemma, but your responses don't pay my salary.'

'It's all about the money, isn't it?'

'Well – yes. You know the deal. Maria and Anthony are on board. Wait 'til our vox pops kick in between the semis and the final, and watch this baby go up. Trust me.'

'You're going ahead with that?'

'Playing the game, darling. Just playing the game. Now get back on the floor and put a rocket up those harp arses.'

The sound of a door opening and closing broke the spell of the crowd around Charlie's handiwork, and he flicked a switch on the headset and stuffed it into his bag.

'What are you doing?' said Erin.

'Think this might come in very useful, don't you?'

'But – you can't nick it.'

'Aw, come on. Can't we be a daring orchestral crime-fighting unit?'

Erin and the others laughed, a little too loudly for Bożenka's liking. She looked up from her tuning and treated them to a glacial stare.

Gemma was intercepted at the bottom of the stairs by Arden, who had found her a replacement headset. Arden then walked back to the orchestra's area and scanned the floor. Everyone did their best to look especially innocent and in other directions.

Arden addressed anyone within earshot. 'Has anyone seen a headset around here? We dropped one…'

'One of those roadie guys in black picked it up a while ago,' said Charlie without blinking. 'Took it off over there somewhere.' He waved his arm vaguely in several directions.

'Oh. Thanks,' said Arden, and lost interest.

Erin shook her head silently at Charlie, in disbelief at his capacity for an instant lie but was impressed nonetheless. Eliot patted him on the shoulder, and Tracie gave him a thumbs-up. Charlie shrugged, unrepentant.

Gemma strode back to the stage and interrupted the harp tuning. 'Gotta roll, girls. You have ten minutes left. Use it for tuning or a soundcheck, I don't care.'

She turned as she walked away, making eye contact with Bożenka who, after a slow blink, carried on tuning her harp.

Chapter 23

Somehow all the soundchecks were done, and then Arden showed the four groups to their dressing rooms. Once changed into performance clothes, they were filed through hair and make-up at industrial speeds, and dealt with efficiently by professionals well used to this pace of work.

The tiny violinists needed the merest hint of colour to avoid pallor under the lights. The opera singers, old hands at stage make-up themselves, encouraged the television staff to ladle it on, but were not indulged too much. After all, as one of the make-up artists assured the singers, the camera wasn't going to be squinting through opera glasses from a cheap seat at the back of the balcony and if she was them, love, if they wanted a bit of advice for free, less is most definitely more on the telly, as she had been saying to Ant or Dec only yesterday. Since everybody in Arioso was wearing an eighteenth-century-style wig, all the hairdresser had to do was make sure it was secured. Some of the wigs, while not originals, were more aged than others, and their aromas were not in the full flush of youth, so they got a spritz of perfume pretending to be hairspray.

The orchestra were given help where help was required. Eliot tried to fight off a small triangular sponge with foundation on it, but was overcome. Pearl wanted green eyeshadow, but was denied. Maureen had brought her own feather hairpiece and asked for help to affix it, but the hairdresser had been given advance warning from Eliot, and heeded his plea by persuading Maureen to abandon it. Max's pate was liberally powdered. Pete's forehead got similar treatment. Ann sat in the chair and laughed, daring them to do what they could. She emerged slightly more bouffant but not unrecognisable. One by one, the Stockwell Park Orchestra took their seats on the studio floor, looking like touched-up and colourised versions of their everyday selves.

The five harpists swept into the hair and make-up room together, wearing matching full-length, rich purple gowns with fitted bejewelled bodices and somewhat thrusting décolletages. Each had put their long hair up in a sleek bun to match Bożenka. Their make-up was flawless and striking. They emerged again almost immediately – it having been wordlessly agreed that they needed no assistance whatsoever with their appearance.

The audience started to take their seats, having been let through security and given a wristband each. Eliot stood up and reminded his wind and brass players (after apologising for teaching their grandmothers to suck eggs) that they might like to keep their instruments warming up quietly while everyone else performed, as they weren't going to get a chance to do anything more than a quick tune when it was their turn.

Once all the performers were in their zoned areas, Russell walked briskly in front of the stage and addressed them directly, while the audience to his side chattered and milled about finding their seats.

'So, we're live tonight, as you know. We've switched up the running order, so Boż darling, you and your gorgeous girls can move your harps onto the stage area right after my little speech here, OK? That way you can do all the tuning you need to do, and then you'll perform first, yeah?'

Nobody dared turn round to see how Bożenka was taking her name being shortened with such familiarity. They surmised it was not well by the amount of jiggling up and down of Russell's Adam's apple and the number of throat clears he had to do before continuing with his speech.

'So… yes. Then next up will be you guys in Fiddle Me This.' He gave an exaggerated thumbs-up to the kids, in the way people who don't personally know any children will do. 'And I know you will be spectacular! Then third, we have Arioso, and finally you guys in Stockwell Park Orchestra. It's easier logistically if we leave you until last, with all the stage management issues.'

'Fine by me,' said Eliot.

'And, so, right, we'll be live, as I said, and we'll be going to our ad breaks after each of your performances. That'll give us time to reset the stage and take a moment. If we need one.' He laughed nervously. 'Then the fifth segment of the show is a recap of what we've heard, recap of the judges' scores – yada yada – then the audience vote live, and we know which three of you are going through to our final! Sound good to everyone?'

The violinists cheered, the orchestra and opera singers nodded, and the harpists stared at Russell with unblinking eyes.

'Great. So, I'll go back to my room up there – the nerve centre of the whole thing – and get this show on the road! Gemma is in charge here on the floor, but you'll see a whole load of other people doing their jobs too. Ask if you need help, but otherwise, perform when you're told to, and good luck! Oh, I'm not supposed to say that, am I? Break a leg! But that sounds so much more violent. I don't know – have fun, anyway!'

And with that, he ran up the stairs two at a time and disappeared behind his glass wall.

'What a twat,' said Ann, making those around her collapse in giggles.

'Let's focus on the prize money,' said Eliot. 'It'll be worth it if we win.'

'Do you think they have us in mind to win?' said Charlie. 'No luck involved in a fixed race.'

'Shh,' said Erin. 'Keep your voice down. Let's get through tonight before we take that any further.'

'Agreed,' said Carl, calm but looking like thunder, hissing through his teeth as if trying to duck under a lipreader's radar. He didn't trust any of the cameras. 'But then we need a shitting debrief at the pub on Monday evening.'

'Aw, that's not fair,' said Tracie.

'You can come,' said Kayla. 'I'll buy you a lime and soda specially.'

Tracie grinned.

Shortly before transmission time, the three judges appeared on their side of the stage, accompanied by Gemma, who was pointing at each performer section in turn and talking rapidly. The judges nodded, concentrating, looking at the groups sitting in colour-coded seats, and at The Dark Harps who were already on stage, tuning up.

'Olive is miniscule!' said Charlie. 'She's not much bigger than those little fiddlers.'

'Still wouldn't want to cross her though,' said Kayla.

Eliot frowned. 'I wonder what she knows. You know, about this programme. She almost cracked when Gregory Knight got through, don't you remember? She's certainly not in the pay of Big Game Show, even if the other two are.'

'Yeah, she really let rip about him, didn't she?' said Erin. 'What was it she said – something about *The Emperor's New Clothes*?'

'Why is she doing this at all?' asked Tracie.

Ann sniffed. 'She's older than me. She's not playing anymore or teaching much, I think. Maybe she needs the money. And that's not a dirty reason to work.'

Gemma had finished her explanations, and the judges retreated into the wings in order to make their entry at the start of the show. Barney North came out to chat to Gemma briefly, before following the judges backstage.

Gemma walked towards the audience and raised her arm. 'Nearly there, folks. Thank you for being so patient. Are you excited?' They whooped in answer. 'Good! So, you'll hear the theme tune on playback, then keep your eyes on my colleagues here at the front. They'll tell you what you need to do and when. You've all had a practice with your voting panel, yeah? Great. Let's have a great night!'

She walked over to Bożenka and the other harpists, who had finally stopped tuning and were sitting behind their harps, resting their hands on their knees. 'You all look beautiful. Barney will introduce you when it's time, and you can take it from there.'

'Of course,' said Bożenka. 'We wait in readiness.'

Gemma turned and walked to the centre of the studio, where the paths between audience, stage and performers met, wide enough for cameras to roll along. She nodded to the nearest camera operator and spoke into her headset.

Charlie leaned towards Erin. 'What is Bożenka going to play? They never did get around to it while I was in here earlier.'

'Dunno,' Erin whispered back.

'Tenner says it's Chopin's funeral march.'

'No bet.'

The lights dimmed, the audience squirmed with excitement, and the now-familiar theme of *Pass the Baton* boomed out of speakers all around the studio rigging. The far end of the stage was suddenly illuminated, and Barney North bounded into view, his teeth shining a welcome for everyone in their beam, like a walking lighthouse.

He pattered through his script, reading the prompter but throwing his gaze around the audience too. As the judges came on stage, Gemma's colleagues in front of the audience orchestrated a huge burst of applause and encouraged them to cheer as well, before directing them in a diminuendo and then cutting them off at the right time.

'Jeez, it's just like conducting,' said Eliot. 'They're naturals.'

Anthony Popkin and Maria Romano waved to the audience, looking completely at ease. Maria even went as far as blowing them kisses. Olive Yessel leaned on her stick and looked around the studio with a keen gaze. They all took their seats as the noise levels fell, and Barney went straight into explaining the format of the evening's show, and who was going to be competing. As he said a little bit about each group, a spotlight flooded their area and a couple of cameras pointed their way. This threw the violinists completely, and they immediately jumped onto their seats and started shouting and waving in excitement, before being talked down by their handlers.

'Shit, I wasn't expecting they'd film us sitting here,' said Erin.

'Getting their pound of flesh,' said Ann. 'Just don't jump on your chair and embarrass us.'

'Roger that.'

When their turn came, Eliot felt it was incumbent on him to acknowledge the attention somehow, so he raised a hand and smiled in the vague direction of the judges.

'Nicely done,' said Charlie. 'Very classy.'

Eliot poked his tongue out at him.

'Always assume you're on camera,' said Ann. 'We know their game now.'

'Oops,' said Eliot. 'Too late now.'

When Barney introduced The Dark Harps, the stage lights above them were turned up to full wattage. Their bodices sparkled, and the rich colour of their dresses showed off the gold embellishments on their harps.

Barney introduced a video montage on the screen behind him, showing highlights of the harpists' performance in their heat, cut with footage of them wheeling their harps around and unpacking them from their cases. He wound up his speech and nodded at Bożenka, who raised her hands to her strings and checked her fellow harpists were also ready. They were playing without sheet music, so could look at each other all the time.

With a flick of her head and elbows, Bożenka brought them in expertly for the first scurrying bars of their arrangement of Mozart's *Rondo Alla Turca*.

'Bloody hell,' whispered Charlie. 'I wasn't expecting that.'

Chapter 24

The Dark Harps' performance was outstanding, exhibiting skill and musicality. Whatever power Bożenka exerted over her musical colleagues socially, when they played, they came to sparkling life. As the final cadence of *Rondo Alla Turca* died away, Bożenka lifted her chin and placed her hands on her lap with a look of satisfaction just as intense as Mrs Hurst's when she played the same piece at the 1995 incarnation of the Netherfield Ball.

After a moment's awed silence, the studio erupted into hearty cheers and applause, joined by all the performers with just as much enthusiasm. Several of the tiny violinists had already decided to give up the violin and learn the harp. What they hadn't realised was that because a full-size harp is about six feet tall, it would take about four of them stacked in a trenchcoat to attempt it.

Barney echoed the audience's praise. He turned to the judges, who were uniformly complimentary. Even Olive Yessel looked genuinely impressed, handing out high marks and warm words. Barney winked at the camera, reminded viewers that Fiddle Me This would be performing right after the break, then relaxed as live transmission stopped for the ads.

A dozen black-clad men swarmed to the stage, waiting for Bożenka and the harps to vacate the area before whisking their chairs away and making sure the correct space had been cleared for the marching violins. The table-tennis bat grown-ups marshalled their small musicians into lines on the stage ready to perform, running from child to child to sort last-minute hitches of bows not being tightened or strings slipping out of tune. One of the smallest children put his hand up.

'There's no time now, Zachary,' snapped the nearest adult. 'You'll have to hold it for five minutes.'

Zachary nodded but looked worried, standing with his hand pressed over the front of his shorts in the international language of needing a wee.

'That doesn't look good,' said Kayla. 'When my son was that age, by the time he looked like that we had about thirty seconds to get to a toilet.'

'Tenner says he leaks,' said Charlie.

'Will you stop betting on things?' said Erin, laughing.

'I'm bored.'

'It would liven the competition up,' agreed Carl.

After a couple of minutes, the cameras were back on and Barney was introducing the video montage of Fiddle Me This, showing clips from their rehearsals and a lot of footage of them filing on and off their coach in car parks, in height order. The lights changed to the start of their "Bohemian Rhapsody" setting, illuminating the children on stage, and they started to play.

At first, they remained standing in place but, when the tempo of the song picked up, their choreography started: rows and columns peeling away from the original block and walking in all directions. They continued to play, somehow filing past each other with centimetres to spare, almost interlocking bowing elbows as they turned corners. When the high energy middle section kicked in, they incorporated some dance moves as well as walking, swinging hips and flicking feet in time to the beat.

Zachary did his best, but the mind control of a six-year-old was no match for the pressure on his bladder. Cornering at the back of the stage and preparing to traverse the diagonal, the floodgates opened. To his credit, he didn't stop playing. He tried to stem the flow by exaggerating the swing of his hips, but that only succeeded in spraying over a wider area. His gaze was clamped on the face of the table-tennis bat adult directly in front of him, who was oblivious to what was happening until the children following Zachary started to skid. They might have got away with it if it hadn't happened at the energetic height of their dance. As it was, children who had a turn of ninety degrees or more had a good chance of going down. The table-tennis bats grew more frenzied. Any child who found themselves suddenly sitting in some of Zachary's pee promptly jumped up and carried on. Some fell over multiple times. By the time they reached their final choreography, which involved most of them lying on the floor playing dreamily and staring at the ceiling, a lot of them were not keen to make close contact with the floor tiles again, especially with their hair. The piece ended with children arranged in their planned shape, but all trying to suspend their limbs and heads off the floor, so it looked like a scene of catastrophically upturned beetles waving their legs in the air but failing to right themselves. Kafka would have been proud.

By this point, most of the orchestra were stuffing hands over their mouths to stop hysterical laughter bubbling up. Carl was openly wiping tears of mirth. Erin and Charlie were doubled over. The opera singers looked aghast. The Dark Harps merely observed the frailty of humankind.

The audience kicked off with enormous applause and loud cheers, absolutely undaunted by what had just happened. They responded to the kids' spirit of carrying on in the face of disaster with a warmth nobody could have expected. Slowly, the children climbed to their feet, took a bow, and filed back to their seats – in Zachary's case, squelching slightly.

Fighting to keep his composure, Barney turned to the judges and asked for their thoughts on what they had just seen. Olive and Maria had kind words to say, glossing over what everybody was thinking and commenting on the musicality of the children, the imagination of their choreography, and their dogged determination that the show must go on, which Maria said was one of the fundamental lessons to learn in a performing career. Anthony Popkin positively revelled in the difficulties Fiddle Me This had found themselves in, not even trying to hide his amusement or save the blushes of poor Zachary. From behind the glass in the control room, Russell was making damn sure every shameful tear dropping down Zachary's cheeks was caught on live television and beamed to living rooms all around the country. He could feel his ratings soaring by the minute.

The second the judges' scores were recorded and live transmission stopped, a cascade of ninja stagehands appeared with multiple mops and buckets, and soon the smell of hot disinfectant was wafting through the studio – claiming to be fresh pine but actually just reminding people of cheap taxi journeys. Another wave of ninjas went in behind the buckets, drying and buffing and polishing until the stage floor was liquid-free and pristine again. The damper members of Fiddle Me This were taken en masse to the toilets to change out of their costumes into dry clothes, returning to their seats as jaunty as if nothing had happened. Even Zachary had cheered up and was basking in all the attention.

Arioso needed no chairs or stands setting up, so they managed to get themselves into position in plenty of time before the commercial break finished. They were going to perform the last minutes of the finale of Act II of Mozart's *The Marriage of Figaro*. The full finale takes around twenty minutes to (famously) build up from a duet to a trio, then a quartet, then quintet, then sextet, until finally a septet of individual soloists are singing their own inner thoughts about the latest discoveries and frustrations of the plot. Because Russell had been so insistent on only having ten minutes (or less) of music, they had decided to cut into the scene at the quartet stage, when the Count, the Countess, Susanna and Figaro were trying to cover up the fact that Cherubino had just escaped through a window dressed up as a woman after hiding in a cupboard in the Countess's bedroom… It's complicated.

Instead of a tame orchestra, they had a backing track lined up, which was being cued in by one of the Quork Media sound managers to replay through speakers by the stage. Arioso had decided on full authentic costume even though they weren't performing on a stage with props, and so each of the eight singers wore heavy eighteenth-century clothes: long skirts and petticoats for the women and ornate brocade coats, knee breeches and silk stockings for the men. The wigs were curled and powdered. The Countess's, in particular, was so tall she had to take care to keep it balanced on her head, but they all felt weighed down by their unfamiliar headgear and tried to avoid turning their heads too quickly from one side to another in case the inertia of the wig kept it stationary, and they might suddenly find themselves forced to sing into the inside of their hairpiece.

After the cameras started rolling again, before introducing Arioso's video, Barney chatted a bit to Maria Romano. He asked her about the demands of an international operatic career and how she might have approached singing the role of the Countess in *Figaro*.

'Well,' said Maria rather grandly, 'I probably wouldn't have gone in for this faux dressing up on an empty stage. It's a sure sign of the insecurity of a young singer, I'd say, if you have to hide behind a silly costume. And those wigs!' She tittered behind her hand, fluttering her eyelashes. 'But, I'm sure Arioso will rise to the occasion.'

The Countess was unnerved, an expression perfectly caught in a cutaway shot with a side camera, as if the operator had been primed to focus that way. She put a hand up to her wig to check it was stable.

'I'm sure they will!' agreed Barney, and led into their video, which featured a lot of warm-up exercises and intercut contrasting vowels. The audience started laughing. The Countess looked as if she was about to cry.

Charlie and Erin exchanged frowns, wondering how obvious Quork Media's manipulation was appearing to anyone who hadn't listened in to Russell and Gemma's earlier conversation. Erin looked back to the stage where the singer playing the Count was trying to explain in thirty seconds who was who, and the basic plot of one of the most complicated opera farces. He did his best, as well as pointing out that it ended up in the famous septet, but that if the audience had counted the singers carefully there were clearly eight and this was because Antonio came in and went out again, followed by three others who joined the four people already in the Countess's bedroom, not including the person who had jumped out of the window and run off to Seville. He laughed, suddenly aware he was on live television and nobody will have understood what the hell was going on, plus they were about to sing in Italian. Opera plots and soundbites do not mix.

The singers in the roles of Antonio the gardener, Marcellina, Bartolo, and Basilio stood in a huddle on one side of the stage, trying to convey the impression of being on the other side of an invisible door rather than a wrestling tag team waiting outside the ropes. Antonio held a pot of geraniums which was trailing compost through its drainage holes all over the newly washed floor.

A Mozart orchestral accompaniment suddenly jumped out of the speakers, galvanising those on stage into life. They wound themselves through the cleverly written scene, acting their socks off in an empty space where the only two actual props were the bowl of geraniums and a scroll of paper the Count could unroll theatrically to read and then roll up again. What with the falling compost and the loud crinkling of the paper, it was probably for the best they had only those two at their disposal.

The Countess threw herself into the role despite earlier knocks to her confidence. As the scene grew more intense, she became more urgent as she looked over the Count's shoulder, passed information about what was written on the paper to Susanna, who passed it onto Figaro at the end of the line, who was pretending to have hurt his leg (I said it was complicated). This back-and-forth whispering became so committed, the women's wigs began to obey the laws of physics. The Countess felt hers detach and start to sway, and flung her hand up to steady it. Susanna's did the same, although because it was less grand, the risk of total separation was also lower.

By the time the septet reached its climax, the Countess was singing with her head on one side, desperately trying to keep underneath her wig which had slid far past the point of no return. After their final notes, the sound of laughter was roughly the same as the applause coming from the audience. Arioso bowed and curtseyed as best they could, given the wig situation and gravity, and made their way back to their seats, where Figaro did remedial wig realignment repairs for the Countess. Antonio shoved the geraniums under his seat and tried to kick most of the earth out of sight.

With the exception of Olive Yessel, the judges took no prisoners. They were egged on by Barney and proceeded to trash what they had just witnessed. Olive did her best to praise what had been fine singing and pointed out the unfortunate circumstances had not been the fault of any musical decision, which was what they were there to judge. By the time the next commercial break arrived, the singers were whispering anxiously among themselves and several members of the audience were openly laughing again, caught perfectly by a panning camera.

Chapter 25

However sympathetic the orchestra felt to the opera singers, they had their own performance to concentrate on. During the break, they got their instruments ready while their chairs and stands were carried into place by a disciplined army of stagehands. Max supervised the placing of his timpani. Eliot walked to his stand and opened his Glinka score, waving his players onto the stage to hurry them up.

'Don't worry about the compost,' he said. 'We're last so, brass, you can tip your water anywhere and make as much mud as you want – nobody's going to care. Gwynneth – quick as you like please.'

Gwynneth played her A for the strings and, after them, the wind and brass. Max put his ear down close to his timpani, tapping gently with his stick, and adjusted their tension by turning the taps round the circumference.

'Great!' said Eliot, when they had all quietened down again. 'OK, whatever happens, I want you to enjoy this. Does anybody need the loo?' After their laughter had died down, he carried on. 'We've got this. Nobody's wearing a wig.'

'That we know about,' called Carl.

'True. Now, when Barney plays our montage, don't look. Concentrate on me – whatever they throw at us. Strings, eyes on me like hawks from the start of the Overture, OK? Remember our dynamics. We'll be fab.'

The lights blazed, and the eyes of the world were on them yet again. Barney cued up the orchestra montage. Eliot didn't even turn round to watch the screen, and swept his eyes round the orchestra to make sure everyone was looking at him, pointing the index and middle finger of one hand at his own eyes to remind them not to waver. He'd never felt more like a hypnotist. Needs must.

As the video montage played, he heard a few bars of them playing that had obviously been recorded in their rehearsal and, when the audience laughed in a sudden eruption of mirth, he guessed some of them had been caught at unflattering angles or maybe swearing within camera range. Blanking it out, he held the gaze of his players.

Sounding almost regretful not to get a reaction from the performers, Barney handed over to Eliot and introduced the orchestra, saying they would be playing Glinka's Overture to *Ruslan and Ludmila*.

Eliot nodded, smiled, checked everyone was ready and set off. Richard, the leader of the first violins and consequently the whole orchestra, leaned into his quavers with such gusto he pulled the whole section with him, injecting an infectious energy that passed through all the string players like electricity. Eliot grinned and held them steady: the last thing he wanted was to let them loose to scamper around at will and then be unable to gather them later on when they might need gathering. An overexcited violin section suddenly realising they have run off the edge of the cliff is a scary place to be, and it is a wise conductor who can persuade them back onto solid ground before they realise, cartoon-like, they are about to plummet.

Neema and her horn section set up their alternating rhythm bang on target, and from then on, the Overture positively fizzed along. It was their best performance of it yet. Not quite at world-record setting tempo, their brisk pace nevertheless got them comfortably under their ten-minute limit. Eliot brought their final chord off and nodded his thanks to them for doing everything he had asked and more.

The audience – wowed by the decibels and sheer force of a full orchestra enjoying themselves – leapt to their feet, whooping and yelling so much Eliot had to turn to them and, with a huge grin, take a bow. He gave an extra bow to the violinists of Fiddle Me This, who were up on their chairs again in support – this time allowed by their grown-ups. He turned to clap his musicians, who looked pumped they had made it through so many notes so successfully. As had been requested, they remained in their seats and waited for the judges to give their verdicts.

Maria was effusive. 'Such a dynamic range, and tight ensemble! It is hard to remember that these are amateur players! Bravo indeed!'

Olive was similarly impressed, although she delivered her opinion with considerably fewer exclamation marks. 'This is an orchestra of real flair and substance. I don't mind admitting that I was wary of their so-called "viral internet" qualifications, but am most happy to be proved wrong. Excellent playing of, what I know is, a piece full of hidden dangers.'

Barney turned to Anthony Popkin last, with a mischievous grin. 'And Anthony? As a fellow – and one might say "senior" – conductor, how would you rate Eliot's handling of this piece?'

Eliot turned to the orchestra and pulled a face. Erin blew him a kiss.

'Well, with all young conductors, there is an element of bravado,' Anthony said. 'A showing-off, if you will. One grows out of that and perhaps learns that the true art of conducting can be found in the less obviously rococo, filigree pieces – in those with real depth of soul.'

Charlie leaned down behind his cello and whispered to Erin. 'What's he talking about? Has he been on the sherry?'

Erin smiled and did her best ventriloquist act. 'You can't plumb the depths of a soul in less than ten minutes.'

Anthony hadn't finished. 'I must say, however, that despite some significant conducting lacunae, Stockwell Park Orchestra managed to get through the Glinka with only a few mishaps. They are to be commended.'

The judges' scores for the orchestra were added to the board, and even factoring in Anthony's rather harsh contribution, they lay in second place.

'See you after the break for our live audience vote!' said Barney to camera. The audience was exhorted to cheer once more, and the cameras stopped.

Charlie looked round the studio. Gemma was talking urgently into her headset, holding the mic closer to her mouth with one hand, and he could make out the figure of Russell standing close to the glass, facing down to the studio with his hands on his hips. The hum of audience chat, anticipating their own vote, rose to excited decibels. Charlie leaned his cello forward, reached into his jacket pocket and pulled out the headset. Erin widened her eyes and quickly checked to see if any Quork Media staff were nearby or if any cameras were facing their way. Satisfied, she leaned towards Charlie as he flicked a switch, holding the earpiece close to both of them as they bent down behind their cellos. They could just make out the tinny conversation.

'– *thought we were gonna cull the orchestra, but cutting across this audience will be a nightmare now. Did you hear them? They went insane. There'll be a riot.'*

'Agreed,' Russell's voice sounded resigned. *'Anthony did his best, but hey. So, do we back the kids or the singers? Harps through, obviously – not going to stop those cleavage weirdos. The singing wigs were gold – our social media's gone crazy over them. But kids are always popular.'*

'*You didn't have to clear up after them.'*

'*Neither did you, darling. Don't sulk. Yeah – let's go with the kids. Those singers might be a one-trick thing.'*

'*OK. I'll get on it.'*

Gemma put her hand to her ear briefly and strode to where a confluence of cables ran through what looked like a junction box behind a screen. She lifted the lid and punched something into a keypad, then quickly closed the lid and walked back round to the centre of the studio. She looked up at Russell who was still standing by the glass, and nodded to him. He raised his arm and turned away.

Charlie surreptitiously slipped the headset back into his pocket and straightened up in his chair. Eliot had seen what they had been doing, and looked over enquiringly.

'This whole thing is fucked to buggery, Eliot,' said Charlie quietly.

Eliot nearly laughed.

'Not for us,' added Erin. 'But – god. We need to talk.'

Before any of them had time to say any more, the cameras were rolling again and Barney was sweeping everybody into a voting frenzy. The scoreboard on the screen did its usual jiggling about.

'Tenner says the singers go out,' said Charlie.

Erin just shook her head, looking grim.

When the numbers had settled, there was what sounded like elation from the audience. The children from Fiddle Me This screamed with the realisation that they would be on national television again in a couple of weeks' time. Bożenka turned to her fellow harpists and infinitesimally inclined her head. They returned the gesture.

The singers in Arioso tried to put a brave face on defeat, and turned to their competitors, clapping gallantly. Eliot stepped off the stage and walked over to them, shaking hands and kissing their cheeks in solidarity. He spent the next minute or so getting strands of the Countess's wig out of his mouth, but tried to be subtle about it. The orchestra also got to their feet to applaud Arioso, who accepted their support with graceful thanks.

As the programme drew to a close and the applause died down, the post-mortem had only just begun.

Chapter 26

The following day, a WhatsApp conversation that started between Erin and Charlie expanded until it included Ann, Eliot, Carl and Kayla too. All through that Sunday, it wound on as Charlie and Erin related what they had eavesdropped on the previous evening, and what – if anything – they could do about it.

By the next evening, at their usual Monday evening orchestra rehearsal, they all knew what had happened but weren't much further forward with what to do next. What they *had* agreed was to meet Noel Osmar in the pub later. Things always seemed clearer when Noel was part of their conversation, as if he lent them all his detectorly acumen.

First things first, however. Before they had even tuned, Eliot put his baton on his stand, grinned at them all and gave them a solo round of applause. 'Top bloody work, my friends,' he said. 'You do it every time, even though you insist on claiming you can't right up to the final rehearsal. Even the violas. *Especially* the violas.' He blew Pearl a kiss. 'I'll start trusting you one day. Superb performance on Saturday. Thank you.'

An awkwardly British half-cheer rippled round the orchestra, and that was that, but everyone looked pleased.

'However,' Eliot continued, 'because of your brilliance, in two weeks' time we have to perform yet another piece they haven't heard. As well as practise for our own concert – remember that? Where are we going to find all this extra time to rehearse without adding extra rehearsals in – which I know you will flatly refuse to do?' The players laughed, knowing Eliot was right. 'Don't worry: I have come up with a plan. Fact one: they need a piece lasting ten minutes.'

'Or less!' several people shouted. They were a good team like that.

It was Eliot's turn to laugh. 'Absolutely. Fact two: we need to rehearse for our own concert. So… I thought, why not play them the last movement of our Brahms symphony? It's the perfect length, snappy, practically the most uplifting music you can hope to hear and, if you promise not to get too bored by it, we'll end up being very slick and may romp home with the prize money.'

'Steady on,' said Ann. 'Let's not get ahead of ourselves. But I like the plan.'

'Does it sound OK to everyone else?' said Eliot, looking round.

There were various nods and thumbs-ups.

'Great. So, let's put a bit more time into it now. I want to work backwards if I may, towards what is of course the finest trombone chord in the history of any symphony ever – am I right?'

'Damn right,' called Carl.

'For any of you who don't know this symphony well – and Tracie, this will be essential for you, at the youthful start of your playing career,' Eliot winked at her. 'On the very last page – after we've all been fanfaring our arses off, and the trumpets and horns have been flashing about giving us all tinnitus – there's this brilliant moment five bars from the end when the rest of us shut up entirely and we're left with the three trombones, holding a tied chord over the barline, showing us what can be achieved if you simply puff a raspberry into a bit of metal with enough oomph. Honestly: that bar should knock us sideways. The trick, of course, is for your trombone section to have enough lip left at the end of the whole symphony to razz that out with absolutely no mercy. Right, Carl?'

'Oh yes.'

'However, given that we'll only have played this movement and not the whole symphony on the telly, you'll have absolutely no excuse not to break whatever microphones they have pointed at you. Do we have a deal?'

'I guess?' said Tracie, looking bemused. She turned to Carl. 'Is he serious?'

Carl nodded, finding the place in her part and pointing. 'It's a cracking bit, look. You'll understand when we get to it. We've got four bars to fill our lungs, then it's flamethrower time.'

Tracie looked keener at that description, and nodded, looking determined.

'So,' said Eliot, turning to the end of his score and flicking the pages backwards, 'let's go from the fifth bar of letter P.'

'Do you want us to all play at the same pitch, or are you not bothered now you're a telly superstar?' called Gwynneth.

Eliot, theatrically crestfallen, invited her to play an A, and everybody tuned.

'OK,' he said when they had all agreed, more or less, what the correct pitch was. 'Fifth of P.'

He brought them in, and immediately the upper strings sawed at their quavers, the flutes joined them three ledger lines above the stave, and the rest of the orchestra started getting themselves all stirred up. Eliot stopped them before they had gone half a dozen bars.

'Yes, yes, that's all very well, but trombones – I love you, but it's not your moment yet. I know you have accents, but look ahead. You have nine bars of crescendo before you even hit *forte*. You can't blast a *fortissimo* at the very start. You won't have anywhere else to go. Start around *mezzo forte*. Again!'

The trombones pencilled in an *mf* dynamic to remind them, and they set off again.

Eliot stopped them once more. 'I'm sorry guys. I know you want to go for it. But this ending simply isn't going to work unless we have the light and shade beforehand. We're not Deep Purple. We are classically trained musicians and, damn it, I know you have a volume control that isn't set all the way up to eleven permanently. Look: in bar 397, we've got the strings and wind playing like billy-o at *fortissimo*.' He turned to Richard on his left, at the front of the first violins. 'And you're doing brilliantly. But, my friends in the brass, we're only at *forte*. Believe me when I say your time will come. Can you hold it in until then? Those staccato scales you've got in the third trombone and tuba, then second trombone, then first trombone – look, we're going to hear you. Save it.'

They tried again, and this time managed to control the crescendo as Eliot wished. A few bars further on, he gave the strings their head and sent them up and down their scales with such gusto that a few players fell into the half-bar rest at the end. He laughed, and stopped again.

He ran his fingers through his hair and let out a big sigh. 'I don't know how to say this and keep you all as friends. But I'm going to have to try. Strings: take your parts home and practise this last page until you can play these scales off by heart. You are all playing the same pattern: all quavers, all up, then down, then up, then down, then up a bit further, then' – he stamped his foot sharply – '*STOP*! Everybody gets a minim rest. Everyone. Not a viola who hasn't quite made it and falls over. Not a double bass who isn't watching. Not bassoon who isn't counting. I need total silence for half a bar, or this won't work. Got it? Again.'

Pete and Pearl looked nervous, and engaged their trusted bow-slightly-off-the-string technique, so they could appear to be scrubbing up and down the scales with the rest of the section, but were not in any danger of making a noise in the total silence minim rest because no part of the horsehair of their bows was in contact. Sometimes, when the conductor is being a bit scary, that is the only way. Pearl decided to slip Eliot some custard creams with his coffee at half time to calm him down.

This time, they were alert to the silences, controlled in their dynamics, and when the trumpets and then the horns tried to out-fanfare each other, the entire orchestra felt the hairs rise on the back of their necks. Eliot locked eyes with the trombones, and when the other brass fell away, he turned his whole body and pointed at them with a straight left arm and outstretched finger as if he would raise the sound with a spell if he could. Which, in a sense, he was. The wave of decibels rose from the trombone side of the hall and crashed over the rest of the orchestra, leaving Eliot feeling drenched but triumphant. He carved out the last two chords, holding the last pause with a trembling baton that asked for ever more sound until the very last cut-off.

'Not bad,' he nodded, as the players recovered. 'Not bad at all.'

* * *

Noel had bagged them a table in the pub, and was eager to hear their news as they sat beside him, setting their collection of cello and trombone cases against the wall. He raised his eyebrows at Tracie, who had joined them.

Kayla laughed. 'Yeah. Don't they grow up fast? She's having one lime and soda and then I'm sending her home. It's a school night.'

'School night for you too, Miss,' said Tracie, looking disillusioned.

'Yes. But somehow that's OK. You're right – being an adult is one long hypocritical nightmare.'

Tracie seemed oddly comforted by that admission, and nodded.

'I watched you on Saturday night, by the way,' said Noel. 'When I could fit it in at my desk – was on duty. Impressive, even on a tiny phone screen. Some of the other acts had their moments, didn't they? But I suppose live television will do that.'

'Christ, Noel, you have no idea,' said Charlie. He drank deep from his pint. 'We need some advice.'

Noel looked at him with careful assessment. 'From me?'

'You're the wisest man we know,' said Erin.

'Oh dear.'

163

'Pretty much,' Eliot said. 'I mean,' he ticked his points off on his fingers, 'you're moral, decent, polite, and know what's legal and what isn't.'

'Which is what we need advice on,' said Carl.

'We would appreciate your opinion,' said Ann.

'If you could,' said Kayla.

'Of course he could,' said Charlie. 'But will he?'

'Of course he will,' said Erin. 'Won't you?'

Noel had been drinking his pint and following the comments coming from round the table with his eyes. He replaced the glass on the table slowly. 'Will I what?'

Eliot sighed. 'It's complicated.'

Noel smiled. 'Then you'd better tell me the whole story, hadn't you?'

Chapter 27

Noel seemed very pleased to be included in Ann's general invitation round to her house on Saturday to watch the second semi-final. He arrived promptly at her suggested time, which was before anyone else turned up.

Ann opened her door wide and beckoned him inside. 'I can see this reveals the gulf between police officers and musicians. You keep strict time. We can barely do that in rehearsals, let alone life. Come in.'

Noel followed her to the kitchen and put the beers he had brought on the table. He then emptied his reusable carrier full of big bags of posh crisps next to it and stood looking round the kitchen, folding his fabric bag back into its little carrying pouch, pulling its drawstring and replacing it in his pocket. Ann smiled at him.

'The last time you were here was when we planned that sting operation – do you remember?'

'I do. Thought I'd come prepared this time. Crisp-wise.'

Ann laughed. 'These are very upper-class and will be wasted on Charlie, but I appreciate them. Thanks. There are bowls in that cupboard – d'you want to decant? Shall we go that far?'

'As long as you don't want me to make a grapefruit hedgehog with pineapple chunks and cheese. That's beyond my pay grade.'

'I've never knowingly been involved with one of those, and I'm not going to start now. There's cold beer in the fridge – do you want to start there and I'll put these in to chill?'

She opened beers for them both as the doorbell sounded, and soon her kitchen was full of people arming themselves with drinks and squabbling over crisps. Pizzas were ordered, and they went through to the sitting room to watch.

'There are officially six places to sit and seven of us,' called Ann from the back of the crowd in her hallway, 'so we'll either have to squash up on the sofa or – oh, I see Carl and Kayla have solved it. Again.'

Carl had taken up residence in his now-accustomed chair, with Kayla on his lap, as before.

'You realise if you two ever split up, we'll never be able to have these parties again,' said Charlie.

'What – purely for the seating arrangements?' said Erin. 'Not the awkwardness?'

'We could always have awkward buffets,' said Ann.

'Or not invite me,' said Noel, mildly.

'No chance, mate,' said Eliot, slapping him on the back. 'You're in the gang now. There's no escape.'

Ann put the telly on, sat down and took a long pull on her beer. 'I must say, it's nice not having to spend all afternoon at the studio. More comfortable with a beer on my own sofa.'

Erin looked at her phone, which had pinged with an incoming text. 'Alexander says they're all in position and ready to roll.' She left the phone out on the coffee table. 'His spelling is not great when he's in a hurry.'

'Maybe we should have given him that headset?' said Eliot. 'You know, to gather evidence?'

Charlie shook his head. 'I think that would be complicating it for him. I mean, I was the one who nicked it. Sorry, Noel.'

Noel shook his head and flapped his hand as if to waft Charlie's mild criminal activity away. 'Needs must.'

'Yeah,' said Erin to Charlie. 'Remember the bolt cutters.'

Noel smiled and drank more beer.

Carl nodded. 'We don't want to distract him – he's doing us a favour anyway by being our eyes and ears. He's got to perform too.'

The theme to *Pass the Baton* started, and Ann turned the volume up. 'Go Alexander! Let's see who else they've got.'

'Well, there will be those piano-playing twins from our heat, for starters,' said Eliot.

'And Gregory Knight,' said Erin. 'Who was awful but stopped us going through with Mrs Ford-Hughes, so I have a bit of conflict there.'

'Let's hope he gets kicked out this time,' said Kayla.

'Hear, hear,' murmured Noel.

'Here we go – shh!' said Ann.

Barney North was doing his welcome speech, introducing the judges and looking enraptured at everything.

'His teeth look even whiter in real life, if you can believe that,' said Charlie to Noel. 'Like, glow-in-the-dark luminous.'

'And, competing in this second semi-final, we have four superb music groups for you,' Barney was saying. The camera panned round to the performers' areas. 'Gregory Knight and his Ambient Sounds; the Honkytonk Twins; Riffraff; and The Leakey Horns!'

167

Erin's phone buzzed again. She laughed. 'Alexander says sorry again for his name. They made him choose an awful pun.'

'There he is, looking straight at the camera!' said Eliot. 'It's kind of fun being able to talk to him live.'

'He's managing to cover up his texting beautifully,' said Ann. 'Very subtle, just behind his crossed knee there.'

Gregory Knight was nodding at the audience, looking as if he hoped he was being achingly cool. The two sets of twins waved a coordinated wave, in matching outfits. The jazz group, Riffraff, waved a bit and then ignored the fuss.

The Honkytonk Twins were up first, presumably because it was easier to start the competition with two pianos on stage and then move them out of the way for the rest of the evening. They bounded into their places while Barney was introducing them, then the television feed cut to their video montage. They seemed incredibly wholesome: two brothers in one set and two sisters in the other – each set of twins dressed alike and ate identical food for the duration of the film. It was unclear if they did that all the time or whether it was for the benefit of the cameras.

Alexander used the time to text again. Erin read it out. 'Gemma super-stressed. Olive Yessel having argument with Anthony. Can't see Russell. Spying is fun.'

'Well, as long as he's enjoying himself,' said Ann.

'That man has no nerves,' said Eliot. 'Born performer. He *will* be having fun.'

Back on camera, the twins went through their act, which – while squeezing all the entertainment out of their twin gimmick – showcased their superb and undeniable talent. A furiously complicated arrangement of Liszt ensued, with two players on each piano, sometimes running round the back of their piano stool to take over at the other end of the keyboard. The audience loved it, the judges were impressed, and the screen switched to the ad break.

Alexander texted. Erin laughed but looked puzzled. 'What is he going on about? "*We're up next. Catch you on other side. Keep your clothes on.*" Keep our clothes on?'

Charlie positively bristled. 'He does know you're reading these out to us all, doesn't he?'

'Yes! I've no idea what he means. He's playing Bach, isn't he?'

'That's what he told me,' said Eliot. 'Some fugue, I think. Sounds impossible. Though if anyone can do it on the horn, he can.'

The video for Alexander's horn quartet consisted of some of their rehearsal footage, during which the camera lingered on Alexander far more than the other three, who were fine horn players but couldn't compete with Alexander on looks. The camera wants what the camera wants. They seemed to spend a lot of their rehearsals laughing, or maybe that was just a montage cut together to show Alexander moving well from all angles, like a horse at an auction.

'Christ, they love him, don't they?' said Charlie.

Ann looked at him and said quietly, 'Behave.'

Charlie rolled his eyes but said nothing more.

Back on stage live, the four horn players were standing in a semicircle behind four music stands. They wore black trousers and some rather beautiful, open-necked shirts that were patterned with what looked like autumn foliage in a vibrant gold and green. The deep gold sheen of their French horns seemed to glow in front of their shirts.

'Someone's done their costume homework,' said Kayla. 'I approve.'

As announced by Barney, they went smoothly into their arrangement of Bach's *Fugue in D minor*. Alexander's first horn part started the whole thing off as a solo with the fugue's theme, and by the time the second horn had chimed in with the same theme, Alexander was already leaping around the register, effortlessly zipping up and down arpeggios and sitting on lip trills he made look effortless but have been known to send other horn players into dark rooms to lie down.

'He is disgustingly talented,' said Eliot. 'I hope Russell decides that too and lets him go through.'

'I wouldn't worry about that,' said Erin. 'The audience will go wild. Remember how audiences do – over him?'

Eliot laughed. 'Good point. I should relax.'

The horns executed their fugue to perfection, and Alexander brought them off neatly, looking as if he had simply been playing a few scales instead of recreating what had been written for keyboard on a bit of curled up hosepipe. It shouldn't have been possible.

The audience roared into life, but Alexander raised his hand.

'One of the advantages of live television is that you can spring a surprise,' he said, smiling.

'Oh shit, what's he going to say?' said Carl. 'He won't blow our operation open now, surely?'

Noel massaged his chin with his hand, feeling for stubble. 'I doubt it. I trust him.'

Alexander was still smiling. 'We were told we could play ten minutes of music. We've used less than half that, so I thought we'd give you all a treat.'

He glanced at his fellow horn players, and undid a couple more buttons down the front of his shirt, revealing a glimpse of a ridiculously sculpted torso. The other guy in the quartet did the same, and the two women dared to undo one button each, grinning. There were immediate wolf whistles from the audience. Alexander laughed and put his horn to his lips again, looking to see if his colleagues were ready.

With a flick of his eyebrows, they launched into "The Stripper", which – even without a trombone to kick the whole thing off with a raunchy slide – managed to bring the house down as soon as the audience recognised what they were hearing. Alexander's eyebrows were working overtime, and he was positively shimmying his shoulders by the time they got to the end. The rapport he had with the audience was electric, and they loved him, rising to their feet in a standing ovation nobody was expecting.

'Fuck me,' said Carl, laughing. 'That guy has steel balls and no shame. Well played. And I say that as a trombonist whose calling card is that bloody intro.'

The judges were equally smitten, and all Barney could do was let them gush. Alexander took the top slot on the leader board, by some margin, with two acts to go. They cut to ads.

Erin was texting. 'I'm telling him how brilliant he was. Not that he needs to hear it from us.'

'Always nice to know, though,' said Eliot.

The doorbell announced the arrival of pizzas, and Charlie leapt to answer, returning with a stack of boxes. Ann got more drinks from the kitchen.

'He's still on the case,' Erin said, reading her phone. 'Gregory's up next. He says Gregory's been talking to Gemma a lot, and upsetting Arden. Dunno why.'

'Arden only looks about twelve,' said Ann. 'Some first job for work experience.'

Charlie stuffed most of a pizza slice into his mouth and talked round it. 'The big question is – will Gregory have that triangle player again?'

The ad break finished and Charlie's question was answered almost immediately, with the shot panning across the stage where Gregory Knight was standing in front of what looked like an identical band to the one he had before: alto flute, piano, bass, violin and – yes – the triangle player.

'Is he doing the same thing he did before?' asked Erin. 'I don't know if I can cope.'

'God, I hope not,' said Kayla.

'His new stuff might be just as awful,' said Eliot. 'You know, I'm really pleased Ann chucked him out of our rehearsals when she did.' Ann nodded graciously. 'As well as all the appalling behaviour, imagine if he'd come to us with a collaboration idea and we'd got sucked into doing this kind of shite.'

'We would not,' said Carl. 'Some of us would have left first.'

Noel was staring with narrowed eyes at the on-screen Gregory, who stood adjusting his microphone on its stand like he imagined a rock singer would do. The trouble with Gregory was he had neither the charisma of a great rock star nor the gravitas of a classically taught opera singer. The former can put their trust in a wall of amps behind them on stage to throw their worldview over their audience and invite them to ride along on sheer adrenaline. The latter knows that years of training means their diaphragm can push a controlled air column out of their lungs, focussed into a beam of concentrated sound that can penetrate to the far edge of a theatre like a laser. It is a remarkable power, and they rightly know their worth.

Gregory wrote doggerel and imagined it was ground-breaking literature, blaming the audience when they failed to recognise his true poetic heft 'leavened with characteristic poker-faced badinage.' He had the insular confidence of one who couldn't recognise his own mediocrity. He published himself when nobody else would, and imagined setting up a publishing company would disguise his vanity. He wrote in all caps when things didn't go his way. In short, Gregory was a nasty, talentless idiot.

'Gregory is a nasty, talentless idiot,' said Noel.

Everyone turned to stare at this unexpectedly firm opinion from their measured, careful friend.

Before they could get over their surprise, the show had moved into Gregory's intro video, which lingered over moody shots of Gregory saying things like 'zeitgeist', 'touchstone', and 'absolute truth', while nodding philosophically to members of his band who were also nodding philosophically, some with beards. Some were actually stroking their beards.

Eliot cracked first. 'Jeez. Is this for real? In Gregory's world, apparently nobody laughs at this stuff?'

'We do behind his back,' said Carl.

'I'll be happy to do it to his face,' said Charlie.

Ann snorted. 'Do you think he edited this himself?'

Erin sighed. 'You were spot on, Noel.' Her phone chirruped. 'Ooh, hang on. He says Gregory is getting annoyed with the audience who are still buzzing about the horn performance. Apparently, some of them keep looking over to Alexander and waving while Gregory is trying to get in the zone. I'll tell him to wave back, shall I?'

The video ended and Barney introduced Gregory, who stared straight down the camera lens and delivered an intense monologue that seemed to have no structural integrity with its instrumental accompaniment. The triangle player waited his turn, making everyone nervous.

The camera angle changed, leaving Gregory staring at the wrong one. He quickly scanned around and found the one currently broadcasting, latching onto it. No sooner had he done so than it changed again. The same thing happened. Everyone in Ann's living room started to giggle.

'Why is he doing this?' said Kayla. 'He looks like a newbie on *Top of the Pops*.'

'And it's pointless,' said Eliot. 'The only people with any votes are in that studio.'

'He has a higher calling – wants to communicate directly with his people,' said Ann.

Noel straightened up. 'Someone is calling those camera shots. Do you think Gregory is falling out of favour?'

Carl's muffled voice drifted out of Kayla's cleavage. 'Make it stop. I can't watch.' Kayla stroked his hair.

'Something tells me this ain't over until the triangle man tings,' said Eliot, looking proud of his joke.

'Shh – he's about to!' cried Erin, and, sure enough, Gregory's set closed with a mournful triangle tinging through what Gregory probably thought was artistic intertextual playfulness but actually just sounded as if he had choked on something and was trying to bring up a hairball.

There was a long moment of silence from the audience. Alexander told them later this was not due to a feeling of awe and reflection, but rather nobody felt like giving it a clap. The audience conductors from Quork Media had been flailing energetically in front of them for a number of seconds, holding up signs saying *CLAP!* before they elicited any sluggish response at all.

'So what's changed with this audience?' asked Charlie. 'The last lot couldn't get enough of him.'

'Remember Olive panning him?' said Erin. 'Maybe everyone else has seen the light.'

Barney broke into their analysis by starting his segment ostentatiously quietening the audience, who by that stage were hardly making any noise at all. 'Well, what an amazing reception for our groundbreaking spoken word artist and his modern classical ensemble! Anthony, give us your thoughts!'

Both Anthony and Maria were as fulsome in their praise as they had been about Gregory the last time. Between them and Barney, it sounded as if he had just raised the roof with his performance.

Erin looked at her phone. 'Alexander says the audience is looking confused. So are the other performers. He thinks they're going for another set-up.'

Olive was on screen, watching the other judges call Gregory a genius. Her mouth was pressed into a line and she shook her head slightly, pinching her nose under her glasses.

Barney took over the conversation again and spoke to camera. 'Well, my apologies Olive, but the gods of live television dictate we have no more time in this segment, so if I can ask the judges to input your scores now, and we'll see you after the break for our fourth and final contestant!' The screen flicked to ads.

'This is blatant,' said Eliot.

Noel sighed. 'I'm not au fait with broadcasting regulations. There isn't a telephone vote tonight, for instance. I'd have to look up the technicalities.'

'But there's money on the line,' said Charlie.

'Not this week,' Noel said.

'Hang on,' said Erin. 'Apparently, Gemma is looking like thunder and talking into her headset.'

'I wish we'd lent him ours,' said Erin.

'Best not, honestly,' said Charlie. 'We don't want to get him into trouble.'

'I need another beer,' said Ann, getting up to go into the kitchen. 'Anyone else?'

The final part of *Pass the Baton* started with a view of the scoreboard, which showed Alexander way out in front, and the Honkytonk Twins roughly level with Gregory. As Barney announced the interim placings, the camera went to the twins, who were looking angry and talking urgently to each other, flicking glances at Gregory. Alexander could be seen in the background typing rapidly into his phone with both thumbs.

'Ah – looks like our spy is about to report,' said Noel, smiling.

Sure enough, a second later, Erin's phone received it. She read it out. '"All kicking off. Twins furious. Audience suspicious. Olive looks about to explode which can't be good at her age." He's so considerate, even when he's reporting crime.'

The last group to play was the jazz ensemble Riffraff, who embodied all the effortless cool Gregory so desperately wanted for himself. Their drums had been moved on stage ready for them during the ads, and they slid into their set as smoothly as an otter into still water. If an otter liked jazz. Who's to say they don't?

'I like this,' said Ann, nodding along. 'Do you think they're wearing those polo necks ironically?'

'Dunno. You can't tell from their faces,' said Kayla. 'Their sax player looks good though – like *Fleabag*'s Hot Priest.'

'Ooh, you're right,' said Erin. 'He could probably wear anything.'

'Oh, for god's sake,' said Carl. 'Calm down, girls. He's Irish too – Paraic. They're not bad. That trombonist has got the chops for it. Crossed paths a bit with them. Paraic's got a great bunch of musicians together.'

'You should be on this, Carl!' said Charlie. 'You and Kayla and your band.'

Carl laughed. 'One spot on this show is enough for me, thanks. I'll stick to the clubs.'

The audience gave Riffraff an appreciatively warm round of applause, the judges liked them, and they received a healthy score, putting them second underneath Alexander. Gregory was in last place, but not by much.

'Yes!' said Erin, reading Alexander's latest. 'Gemma's gone to the junction box again. He saw her open the box, fiddle with something, shut it, and it looked like she told Russell. Just like last week.'

'Here we go,' said Eliot.

'I hope Alexander gets through – they can't change that, surely?' said Erin.

'They wouldn't dare, I don't think,' said Noel. 'Too much. Even a non-musician can tell that.'

Ann laughed. 'Pheromones are a universal language, like music, my friend.'

Noel snorted with laughter and agreed, rather ruefully.

'And so now, the moment of truth!' cried Barney. 'Audience, vote now!'

The scoreboard did its dance and settled with Alexander remaining in first place, followed by Riffraff and then Gregory. The Honkytonk Twins were fourth.

There was a huge cheer for what was clearly Alexander's popularity, and the camera panned over to him and his fellow horn players. He grinned and waved his thanks to the audience, but then straight away walked over to the twins and shook their hands. Paraic and other members of Riffraff did the same, as did some of Gregory's instrumentalists. The twins looked crestfallen but appreciative of their fellow performers' consideration. Gregory remained in his seat, the triangle player sitting rigidly beside him.

Barney wound up the programme by reminding viewers of the grand final the following week, which would be a longer programme to fit in their six finalists. And with that, the broadcast ended. Ann switched the telly off.

They looked at each other in silence for a while.

'This is beginning to stink, isn't it?' said Eliot. 'I mean, apart from Alexander being brilliant. Even they couldn't finesse him off the top spot.'

Noel scratched his chin. 'I've got some homework to do, I think. And, of course, even if they're breaking the rules, we'd need evidence. I doubt I can make this an official investigation. It's all circumstantial – however convincing.'

'More beer and lukewarm pizza while we decide what to do?' offered Ann.

It was going to be a long night.

Chapter 28

Three cameras from Quork Media turned up to the next orchestra rehearsal on Monday evening. They were waiting even before David arrived, and he was always the earliest. They pointed their black, blank eyes at him as he walked up to the doors of Sunbridge Academy.

'Hello,' he said in the general direction of all three camera operators. 'I assume you're from Quork? No Gemma or Arden this evening?'

The men agreed they were Quork, and explained they had been sent to gather footage of the orchestra members in an informal, reportage kind of way. They didn't need Gemma on site. They had been briefed.

'Ah,' said David, feeling rather outnumbered. 'Right.' He went inside. One camera followed him; the other two remained outside the door. David looked over his shoulder. 'So you're going to – um – what, follow me round?'

'Just ignore me,' said the cameraman cheerfully. 'I'll fade into the background. You won't know I'm here.'

More and more of the orchestra arrived and mostly ended up in the hall looking slightly hassled, having been followed along the road and into the school by cameras.

Some people revelled in the attention. Pearl tried to make the walk between the tube station and the school seem like a catwalk, despite the fact she was pulling her shopping basket on wheels behind her because she had been to the cash and carry and stocked up on catering-size tins of coffee, boxes of teabags and packs of biscuits. She had guessed their last rehearsal before the televised final would have media attention, and she had both dressed accordingly and laid in extra provisions. So it was that the cameramen outside the school doors were accosted by a middle-aged woman wearing a startling amount of make-up, who asked them if she might bring them out a cup of tea or coffee and a couple of digestives each. She winked at them in what she hoped was a coquettish manner and told them she could put her urn on early for them.

Max parked his van as close to the doors as possible, as he usually did, and had to ask the camera crew to move out of his way while he wheeled his four timpani, one at a time, through to the hall. As he went out to fetch the second one, he grumbled to anyone listening that they hadn't even held the doors open for him but instead filmed him struggling to open them with one hand. Max had a timp player's accurate analysis of people's willingness to help those in need. They were fewer around than one might hope.

When Eliot arrived, he stifled an internal sigh and managed to give the cameras a cheery wave as he approached. The shine had certainly worn off working with Quork Media since those heady days of meeting a producer in a coffee shop and laughing at sugar beards. He wondered whether the prize money – if they managed to get their hands on any of it – would be worth it. Maybe he was getting old and cynical.

Erin noticed Pearl fussing around the cameramen on her way in and, as she walked across the hall to put her cello at the side, she had an idea.

Charlie was looking at her approach. 'What's up? You look miles away.'

'I was thinking.' She leaned one shoulder down, put her case on the floor and glanced behind her. 'These cameras. We know their game – they'll be getting footage of us to splice together for some kind of montage, right?'

'Right. And?'

'Well, it won't just be us, will it? They'll be hanging round all the other groups in the final.'

'Yeah, probably. What's your point? We can't stop them. We kind of signed up for this.'

'Pearl is doing her best to make friends with them.'

'We can't ask her to poison their coffee.'

Erin laughed. 'No. But I wondered if I – you know, taking the spy thing to heart – if I could be extra-friendly to see if I can charm any info out of them.'

'A honeytrap!'

'Shh! I wouldn't go that far. But I can flirt a little, maybe.'

Charlie sang ABBA quietly, 'Does your mother know that you're out?'

'I haven't got the eye shadow game Pearl is bringing,' Erin admitted, 'but I could try a few Fenella hair flicks and see how far they get me. Look, I'll do a casual walk past one of them now and see if I've got what it takes.'

Charlie watched her go out of the hall to the water fountain in the foyer, returning with a small cup in one hand. She strolled up behind the cameraman just inside the hall doors and said something to make him laugh. A few more exchanges and the man lowered his camera and started talking to Erin with animation, gesturing with his free arm as if describing film shots and angles, then showing her various bits on the camera itself. Erin leaned in close, nodding and smiling, before stepping away and returning to Charlie, flicking her hair like a pro on her way.

'He's still staring at you,' he said quietly when she got close enough to hear. 'What the fuck was that? It was like watching Cleopatra working on Caesar.'

'First rule every woman learns,' said Erin. 'Talk to a bloke about the thing he likes doing and be really fascinated. It's catnip. They can't resist.'

'So all that time you claimed to be interested in beer…?'

'Oh no. I really am interested in beer.'

'You could be just saying that.'

'You'll never know. I'm that good.'

Charlie laughed. 'So, what gives? Did he tell you their master plan?'

'Not yet. It was more focal lengths and light meters, to be honest. But I have high hopes for the coffee break.'

'Aw – don't *we* get to talk to you in the break?'

'Why? Where is she going?' Ann asked, putting her case down next to theirs.

'Erin's got a dastardly plan to seduce the opposition.'

'Whoa. Hold on. I'm not Mata Hari,' said Erin.

'Let's hope not,' said Ann. 'She didn't end well.'

'I just thought it wouldn't do any harm to try to find out what they're planning,' said Erin. 'Before this weekend.'

She tried not to look directly at the cameraman as they rehearsed, but was kept up to date by Charlie about how much his camera was pointing straight at her while she played.

'A lot, mate,' he said, as Eliot brought the first half of the rehearsal to a close. 'Like, pretty much all the time. This scheme of yours might just end up with our video montage being wall-to-wall footage of you flicking your hair and no extra information.'

Erin sighed. 'Shall I try, though? Come on.'

She put her cello away and wandered off, casually asking her cameraman in passing on her way to Pearl's urn if she could get him a coffee. She brought one back to him, together with an orange Club biscuit that Pearl had retrieved from her Special Box when Erin told her the second coffee was for one of the cameramen.

'Thanks,' he said, putting the camera down to leave both hands free for coffee and orange Club. 'Very kind of you. I'm Bob, by the way.'

'You're welcome, Bob. I'm Erin. Hello.' She forced herself to giggle, trying to remember how she used to do that aged sixteen and make it look natural.

Bob was in his forties, with an expanding waist and receding hair. He patted the slight trouser overhang at the front and laughed as he unwrapped his biscuit. 'Shouldn't really.'

'Ah, you deserve it – having to work evenings. That can't be easy. But I suppose in your job there are a lot of unsocial hours. Are you on duty at the live shows on Saturday nights too?'

'No, I'm just on the – the roving brief, as it were.' He laughed at his joke. So did Erin, only more. 'Quork's got a whole load of us on this project.'

'Yes, I don't remember seeing you when we were there in the studio.'

'I would've remembered seeing *you*, if I'd been there.'

'So, come on,' said Erin, moving a bit closer to Bob and sipping her coffee in what she hoped would be a friendly yet conspiratorial manner, 'who else have you been filming? Are there any top tips you can pass on? Are they all being brilliant? They all sounded so good on the telly – so professional. I don't reckon we stand a chance.'

'You're sounding great, if this evening is anything to go by,' Bob said gallantly. 'I've never been up close to a real orchestra before. Gets quite loud, doesn't it?'

'If you think it's loud from where you are, you should try sitting in front of the trombones!'

Bob enjoyed that so much he even had to do a little 'oh dear' sigh after his laughter subsided. 'But seriously, not all the contestants are as nice as you.'

'Oh no?'

'No.' He glanced from side to side, looking for the other cameramen, who were safely mingling through the coffee break, catching members of the orchestra mid-biscuit munch and Maureen looking glum while the rest of her little knot of people laughed at something someone had just said. 'Yesterday, for instance. Me and a couple of the other guys – not this lot – had to go to some dingy warehouse space to catch that poet's rehearsal.'

'Ah yes. Gregory Knight. He's a… a one-off, isn't he?'

Bob snorted. 'That's the polite way of putting it.'

'Well, I'll let you into a secret, Bob.' It was Bob's turn to lean closer. Erin tucked some of her hair behind one ear. 'Gregory isn't popular round here. *At all*. He tried to wangle his way into our rehearsals a while back to do some "residency" or something, but we didn't get on, put it that way. So, don't hold back on my account.'

Bob drank some more coffee. 'First off, he was late starting. I mean, really late. So there's me and my mates hanging around the arse end of south London on a Sunday afternoon. No caffs open – nothing. Then when he finally gets going, he's all "Shoot me from this side" and "What are you framing for this shot?", as if he's a fuckin' director. 'Scuse my language.'

Erin frowned sympathetically and made what she hoped were appropriately shocked noises about Gregory's behaviour.

'And then,' Bob carried on, 'he insists on performing in front of a stack of his books and asking if we've got *them* in focus. And he was wearing a T-shirt with the cover of one of them on the front – and the stuff he was coming out with! I mean, I know Quork know how to work their audience. We do a lot of these kind of shows. Get the variety in, you know. Lowest common. Viewing figures up.' Erin nodded. 'And even if this guy is their dope and we're playing him for laughs – which I wouldn't mind doing, and he deserves it – but from the way he was carrying on, he looked like he was trying to play *us*, you know? We were told to get him to open up about other acts. To get him talking, but not realise we were filming, you know?'

Erin glanced at the camera on the floor and laughed nervously. 'That's not on, is it?'

'Nah. I decided not to do that to you. I mean, his stuff isn't even real music, is it? Not like yours. I like yours.'

Erin beamed at him warmly. 'Thank you. We work very hard to make it nice to hear. I know people say that classical

185

music is a broad church, but I don't think you can beat a full orchestra. I don't like tuneless, spiky stuff.' She glanced at Bob, wondering how far she dared to go. 'Did he have that triangle player with him again?'

She held Bob's gaze for a moment until she saw his lip tremble, then allowed herself to laugh. Bob joined in with relief.

'What's all that about?' he asked. 'It's just some guy hitting it at random.'

'I don't know. As I said, it's not my favourite style.'

'Anyway, long story short, it makes this evening a doddle.'

Erin finished her coffee. 'Well, I'm glad we're a bit easier than him, anyway. Shall I take your cup? I think I'd better get sorted in time for the second half. Lovely to meet you, Bob. A real pleasure.'

'Oh, right you are. Thanks.'

She took both cups through to Pearl's recycling bin in the foyer, winking at Charlie and Ann as she went past.

Chapter 29

Erin told everyone at the pub later about her conversation with Bob. 'He almost admitted that Quork is spinning this whatever way they like to boost their viewing figures. Which we kind of knew anyway. They're trying to get the acts to bitch about the others.'

'If we'd known you were going honeytrapping,' said Charlie, 'we could have asked Noel to find you a wire to wear. Do we call them wires? Or is that just in American cop shows? I've no idea.'

Eliot shook his head. 'Noel wouldn't have done that. He does have *some* boundaries.'

'Where is he, anyway?' said Carl.

'Working,' said Ann. 'Said he couldn't make it tonight. He's not our own personal police officer – nice though that would be. And anyway, he said it's a regulatory grey area because it's not a telephone vote, remember? I'm not sure it's going to be a police thing.'

'What was interesting, though,' said Erin, 'going back to Bob, was what he said about Gregory. Almost as if he was surprised at an act trying to play the same cynical game as Quork.'

'Makes me feel a fool for going in and genuinely wanting us to sound good,' said Eliot. 'Fifty thousand pounds or not.'

Kayla reached over the table for more crisps. 'It's what I have to tell the kids sometimes: even if everyone else is being cynical and trying to play the system, it's enough to know you're doing your best. To be proud of yourself. I think we can be proud of ourselves.'

'Wow, Kayla!' said Charlie. 'I didn't know you had Inspirational Guru as a side hustle.'

'Oi!' said Carl, raising his hand with a folded-up crisp packet in it.

'No, no – I meant it. Kayla, call off your boyfriend.'

'Oh, boys,' said Ann. 'Now, look, we can take the moral high road all we like, but we have to decide what we're actually going to do this Saturday if we see them trying to steal the competition from someone. Even if it isn't us.'

Eliot drank the last of his pint and set the glass on the table. 'So – to clarify – if we win, that's OK. If someone we like wins – say, Alexander, or that jazz band, or, God help us, Bożenka – then that's OK too. Basically, anyone except Gregory, is that it?'

'Sounds a bit… stark, when you put it like that,' said Erin.

Kayla nodded. 'Doesn't that make us as bad as them?'

'It wouldn't make any sense for them to have Gregory win, though,' Ann pointed out. 'It's the final. Surely controversy like that only works in the run-up?'

Charlie sat forward and put his elbows on the table. 'Well, I think we can gauge what the audience feels on the night. I mean, that was pretty obvious last time, yeah? And we have our trusty headset, though I guess we can't rely on that working again. I'll bring it anyway. Anything could have happened since then. So we might be able to find out if they're trying to fix it.'

'And we can take a quick decision on the night, depending?' said Erin.

'But what are we prepared to do?' asked Carl. 'Smash things up on live telly?'

'Easy tiger,' said Kayla.

'Um… metaphorically, yes,' said Eliot. 'Don't you think?

'Then we need to tell Alexander everything we know, before Saturday,' said Erin. 'I can, if you agree?'

Carl nodded. 'He's useful in a fight.'

'Do you think we should say anything to the other competitors?' said Eliot.

'I'm not talking to Bożenka,' said Charlie flatly. 'You can't make me.'

'Fair enough,' said Eliot. 'Though you can't argue it wouldn't be really cool to have her on our side. Imagine if she got riled with Barney. He wouldn't stand a chance. Those ice-white teeth would shatter in the frozen wastes of Bożenka's stare.'

Chapter 30

Competitors started to arrive at Quork Media's television studio on Saturday around noon and, as before, they were lanyarded and funnelled into the atrium space to wait before being called into the studio itself.

Alexander spotted some of the orchestra and strode over, smiling, bringing the oversized optimism that seemed to cocoon him and anyone nearby. 'Hi, everyone! Great to see you.' He shook hands with anyone who wanted to, and offered hugs. Eliot took both. Erin went straight in for a hug and practically disappeared into Alexander's bulk.

'We're probably not allowed to fraternise,' said Ann. 'They'll be catching us on camera so they can play it back later and accuse us of teaming up behind their backs.'

'Wouldn't be such a bad idea,' said Alexander. 'We seemed to do OK as a team over the summer.'

'Ah, but you've got your own team now,' said Eliot. 'And Quork seem very keen on divide and conquer.'

'Dunno where my team has got to. They're always bloody late.'

'What are you playing tonight?' asked Kayla.

Alexander tapped his nose. 'Aha. That's our little surprise for everyone. Even you.'

'Just keep your shirt on,' said Charlie. 'Or the rest of us will stand no chance whatsoever.'

Alexander threw his head back and laughed. 'Deal. Ah! Look – here they are.' He waved at the other three horn players just coming through security. 'I'd like you to meet Kath, Annie and Cormac. Guys, this is the Stockwell Park Orchestra – I toured with them over the summer.'

'Yeah, we saw a bit of that online,' said Annie, smiling. 'Hi. Alexander does tend to take over, doesn't he? But I guess you knew what you were getting when you booked him as soloist.'

'Not really,' said Eliot, 'but we were extremely pleased. He's a good man to have around.'

'Guys, please,' said Alexander, giving a good impression of looking embarrassed. 'Anyway, are we all set for today? All been sorted into our teams, I see.' He flicked his lanyard. 'I wonder if we're sitting next to each other.'

'But you haven't been given a colour,' said Pearl, stepping round Eliot and flapping her green lanyard at Alexander's plain white one. 'They've given us green this time. We were red before. But a leopard doesn't change its stripes.'

While the people within earshot processed yet another of Pearl's inexplicable sayings, Alexander bent down and gave her a kiss which turned Pearl pink and flustered. He smiled at Kath, Annie and Cormac. 'Everyone, this is Pearl. She runs the orchestra. Whether it's red or green. Pearl, I believe they gave us white because they ran out of coloured card. There are six groups of us this time, not four, so maybe they're having to improvise.'

'Well, you can't go wrong with a nice lavender or peach, I always say. Very classy.'

'Undoubtedly,' said Alexander gallantly, covering up the giggles starting from his colleagues behind him. He leant down to Pearl's ear-level. 'We both know your taste is vastly superior to theirs. I would have *loved* a lavender lanyard.'

Pearl was quite overcome by this alliterative compliment and retreated to calm down next to her viola case.

Even those with their backs to the lanyarding security gates could tell when Bożenka and her harps arrived because a hush fell and people tried not to make any sudden movements that might attract their notice.

Alexander leaned slowly towards Carl and whispered in his ear. 'So these are the famous Dark Harps, eh? They did look extraordinary on telly, but I've never met them in real life.'

'Yeah. Bożenka plays with us sometimes. It's always... um—'

'Unnerving,' Charlie said. He was facing away from the harps and was determined to stay that way.

'Eliot shook her hand once before rehearsal,' said Erin, 'and couldn't conduct properly for ages.'

'Snow Queen's frostbite,' said Charlie, nodding with portent.

'Great name for a band,' said Alexander cheerfully. 'Shall I go and say hello?'

Before they could stop him, he had left his horn case with them on the floor and stepped across to where Bożenka and her group had gathered in their customary circle. This time they had yellow lanyards round their necks, which against their dark clothing only made their huddle look more like a ritual, as if they were each holding a candle.

'Might I introduce myself to the mistress of The Dark Harps?' he said, in his firm Scottish baritone that carried generational memories of peat smoke and single malts.

Bożenka turned in a smooth movement that, because she was wearing a floor-length skirt, made her appear to be weightless or perhaps standing on a hidden Segway. Her eyes seemed to be level with Alexander's, which could not have been true as, though tall, she was not the same as his six foot four – but somehow, she managed it. Alexander bowed. An actual bow. From the hips.

'Maybe that's where we've been going wrong all this time,' murmured Charlie to Eliot. They were all staring in fascinated horror. 'Bowing. Of course.'

Bożenka extended her hand to Alexander, who caught it lightly with a gesture that conveyed that, if they had met at court several centuries earlier he would have naturally brought it to his lips in the most chivalrous manner possible, but modern constraints dictated it should not be thus though that would have been his utmost desire. He straightened, still holding her hand.

'Alexander Leakey, at your service.'

She blinked at him and lowered her chin infinitesimally. 'Bożenka Przybyła.'

'Honoured to make your acquaintance. All of you.' He nodded politely to the other harpists. 'I wish you the best of luck tonight. I'm sure you will play superbly.'

He bowed again, less deeply than before, and spun on his heel to return to his friends. The conversation in the room hummed up again from near silence to ordinary levels.

Alexander grinned at Eliot. 'See? I don't know what you lot were on about. You simply need to be polite.'

'Let's see your hand.'

Alexander extended his right hand and Eliot took it, prodding it gently. 'I don't understand. Did you rub Deep Heat on it earlier?'

'Maybe he's a warlock,' said Charlie.

'There's nothing supernatural about good manners,' Alexander said. 'Oh, look – here we go. They've come to get us. I'll nip ahead and switch our flags round if they haven't put us together. We can't do our spying if we have to semaphore each other.'

Charlie watched Alexander stride easily through the throng of musicians towards the studio door. 'That man has no fear. Of anything.'

'Good to know he's on our side, then, isn't it?' said Erin, leaning her shoulder into the strap on her cello case and lifting it off the floor. 'Come on.'

By the time the orchestra reached the colour-coded seating area in the studio, Alexander was already sitting in the white zone and looking relaxed. It was next door to the green pennant. Arden stood nearby, looking nervously in all directions to see if the pennant switch had been observed and whether anyone would get into trouble.

Eliot took a seat on the edge of his zone, as close as he could get to Alexander, and grinned. 'Nice work.'

'I just switched us and the yellows – it's only one chair difference so I scooted that along and swapped the flags. Bożenka won't even know. They'll be through last with their harps.'

'You've confused Arden.'

Alexander waved at Arden, who waved uncertainly back. 'Arden will be fine.'

Since the orchestra had by far the most people to seat, their zoned area was much larger than anyone else's. Riffraff's was the nearest to the door: they had been allocated black. Then came the blue zone, for Gregory Knight and his Ambient Sounds. Then there were the orchestra seats (green), and Alexander's horn quartet (white), which he had switched with the harps (yellow). Last in the line, furthest from the door and tucked into the corner by the stage area, was the red zone reserved for the tiny violinists and attendant adults of Fiddle Me This.

As the rest of the orchestra joined Eliot, found seats for themselves and arranged their instrument cases round their bags of concert clothes, small members of Fiddle Me This sprinted past in what was clearly a race to get to their seats. They screamed at each other in high spirits, falling onto their chairs at the other end as if they were playing a party game. Their careworn guardians followed at a rather more sedate pace, rolling their eyes in apology at the other musicians on their way past. They sped up when a sudden scream sounded from the red pennant area, followed by howls of either pain or a tantrum.

'I don't miss that stage of kids,' said Ann, shaking her head. 'I mean, you do it, but you're glad when it's over.'

Kayla laughed. 'You'll notice I'm not a primary school teacher. At least in secondary you can talk to them like adults. And in Tracie's case, they end up teaching *us* stuff as well, right?'

'What, like self-defence?' said Carl, winking at Tracie.

'Among other things,' said Tracie.

'Tracie will be running the country before we know it,' agreed Eliot.

They stopped talking as Bożenka wheeled her harp past, followed by the other harpists. They appeared to sustain a bubble of rarified air around them that made ordinary conversation impossible and faintly abhorrent. As she passed Alexander, she smiled and bestowed on him one of her slow-lidded blinks. He nodded in return.

Charlie leaned in to Erin's ear. '*What* is going on there? Those two are practically a power couple now.'

Behind Bożenka, Gregory walked into the studio with his musicians and found their blue seating area. Beatriz and Courtney, who were sitting on that side of the orchestra's section, immediately rose as soon as they saw him coming and found another couple of seats away from him. Ann watched them move, and kept her eye on Gregory, who looked blankly across at her as if he didn't know who she was.

'I don't care who wins,' she muttered to Eliot without moving her lips, still staring at Gregory, 'but if that little shit looks like being crowbarred into top place then count me in for any live telly swearing you want.'

'Noted,' said Eliot. 'Let's hope it won't come to that.'

The layout of the studio was the same as it had been when the orchestra were there for their heat, except the section of audience seats had been shifted over a bit to make room for the extra performers. The 'road' spaces between audience, performers, and stage remained clear to leave easy passage for cameras and the many staff of Quork Media who scurried about hither, thither, and indeed, yon. The network of thick cables that seemed to run everywhere still converged in a long box behind a screen.

Charlie took a casual stroll around the studio, hands in pockets, nodding affably at the busy stagehands moving chairs and rolls of cabling. He walked a slow loop past that screen and returned to the others. 'Looks the same as before. Loads of cables into the box and then out again. Is it visible from any of our seats in this section?'

'No,' said Eliot. 'But it probably would be from Alexander's. Hang on.'

He wandered across to the adjacent white section. 'Hi. This is me doing my spy walk. Am I doing it right?'

Alexander laughed. 'We need a password. The mongoose flies east when centipedes learn to tango.'

'That'll do. I think we're professionals.'

'What's up?'

Eliot kept his back to the main studio area. 'Behind me, do you see lots of cabling running along the side of the walkways?'

'Yeah.'

'A whole load of it comes out from underneath the audience seating area and runs together into a sort of long box behind a screen. Do you see it?'

'Yes, I can.'

'That's what Gemma was fiddling with before – we think it fixes the votes. None of us can see behind the screen from our seats this time. We were more up your way before. Can you keep an eye on it?'

'Will do. What are we going to do if they try it again?'

Eliot scratched his chin. 'Ah. We haven't quite decided that yet. Let's see what happens, shall we?'

'Right you are.'

'Oh, and by the way, your romance with Bożenka is raising all sorts of eyebrows in the green area, you know. All sorts.' Eliot wandered off again, smiling.

Chapter 31

At precisely two o'clock, Russell and Gemma came out of the glass-fronted control room together and trotted down the steps to the studio floor, coming to a halt in front of the performers. They both wore headsets, which Charlie looked at carefully. As far as he could tell, they seemed to be identical to the kind they had worn before. He looked at Erin and Eliot and nodded, leaning down to his bag and unzipping the pocket holding his stolen one.

Arden approached from the other side of the studio and hovered nearby, flicking glances at Alexander and Bożenka, but Russell and Gemma took absolutely no notice and didn't seem to know or care about the seating switch. When they weren't watching, Alexander gave Arden a quick thumbs-up, which drew a shy smile.

'Hello everyone,' called Russell, trying to get the room's attention. The raucous games continued in the red zone at the end of the row. They seemed to have developed from racing along the studio floor to some kind of obstacle course they had designed over the chairs, and had raised the noise level in the studio by a significant factor of squeaks and squeals. Apparently, no part of Fiddle Me This's existence could be expressed below a frequency of about 880Hz. No wonder their accompanying adults always had such pained expressions.

Gemma tried too. 'Ah – guys? Could we have your attention please? Violinists? Children?'

The grown-ups tried to shush them and point out they were holding things up, but if anything, the game grew more raucous.

'Wanna go and sort them out?' Carl asked Tracie, who snorted with derision.

'No chance. S'not my problem.'

At that moment, Bożenka rose from her seat next to the violinists, turned to them and stared. Within five seconds, all the children were sitting in their own seats, hands on laps, silent and attentive. Several of them seemed on the cusp of tears. Bożenka lifted her chin, turned back to her group and sat down again herself.

'Shit,' whispered Kayla. 'If you could bottle whatever she's got, all the teachers in London would pay whatever she wanted.'

'And all the child psychologists in London would wonder what hit them,' said Ann.

Russell and Gemma glanced at each other. Russell widened his eyes and nudged his head in Bożenka's direction, making it plain for anyone to understand that he wanted Gemma to thank her for intervening because he was too terrified of Bożenka to do it himself. Gemma laughed in a brittle, tinkly sort of way and carried on as if nothing had happened or, rather, as if the kids had listened to her in the first place.

'Thank you. Now, we have a busy afternoon's schedule ahead of us, and we need to keep everyone absolutely to time please. Arden will distribute a copy of our timetable to each group so you can see where you fit in – Arden, would you mind?' She handed a stack of papers to Arden, who started to pass them round to the performers.

'As you'll see,' said Russell, stepping in to lead once all danger of a wayward audience had passed, 'we're going to be doing your soundchecks and bits and bobs in the same order as you'll perform tonight, so Stockwell Park Orchestra, you're first, then Fiddle Me This, Leakey Horns, The Dark Harps, Ambient Sounds, and finally Riffraff.' He pointed at each group as he read down the list. The violins almost cheered when their name was read out, but Bożenka's head tipped slightly to one side and they thought better of it.

'We should have finished our soundchecks and floor switches by four o'clock,' Russell continued, 'then you'll all change and go through hair and make-up – you know the drill now – and be back on the studio floor ready to go live in good time.'

'Refreshments will be coming through during the afternoon,' said Gemma, 'so do help yourselves. After we're back here and ready to go live there won't be any more food. And perhaps,' she looked towards the adults in the red zone, 'you might make sure everyone has, um, visited the loo before we go on air?'

Zachary endured some pointing and giggling from his fellow violinists, but wore it more as a badge of pride than anything else. There are not many among us who can claim to have weed on live television. Even then he knew he would be using that anecdote for the rest of his life.

'Wonderful,' said Russell, clapping his hands in front of his chest in what he might have hoped was a professionally enthusiastic manner but merely made him look like a child about to be given an ice cream. 'And remember, at the end of this evening, one of you groups will be fifty thousand pounds richer!'

Gregory raised his voice through the anticipatory cheers. 'No true artist is motivated by money. We should free ourselves from the shackles of capitalism.'

'Alright, comrade, calm down,' called Carl, laughing. 'You can share it with us if you win, OK?'

Russell didn't hear any of this. 'So, let's get the orchestra set up and crack on!'

He turned to the stage area and waved the waiting army of black-clad men into motion to carry chairs and stands into the right place.

'He thinks his last name is Crowe – unleashing hell at his signal,' said Carl, sitting with his arms crossed.

Kayla laughed. 'Let's hope we all live to see the end of the day.'

Russell and Gemma talked together for a moment before Russell returned to his glass-fronted room up the stairs, leaving Gemma in charge of the studio floor.

Eliot stood up. 'Right, come on folks. Let's get going.'

In the swirl of people standing up, opening instrument cases and finding their music, Charlie walked the couple of steps over to Alexander and leaned over, handing him the headset and showing him the switch to move. 'Here. Just in case you see Gemma looking as if she's plotting our downfall or anything. Remember to switch it back off once you've finished. And don't let anyone see or – you know – *say* anything into it, or we'll all be in detention doing lines or something.'

Alexander nodded and put the headset on the floor beside his horn case. 'Gotcha. What are you playing?'

'Last movement of Brahms 2.'

'Nice.'

'Let's hope so. See you on the other side.'

Charlie hurried to join the rest of the cellos settling into position on the stage. Eliot was already at his stand.

'I don't intend to run all of this,' he said. 'Let's kick off and see how it feels. Gwynneth, if you wouldn't mind?'

As the orchestra tuned, Eliot looked round the studio. Above the empty audience chairs, he could see Russell standing on the other side of the glass, looking down at them. He gave him a cheery wave, which Russell returned rather uncertainly. On the other side of the studio, the groups of performers sat around in various stages of relaxation. The tiny violinists were still hyper, which wasn't helped by the arrival of the promised trays of sandwiches and bottles of water. Alexander fell on his group's tray with the hunger of a six-foot-four man with a long afternoon of playing ahead of him.

Eliot smiled at him, and called, 'If you eat ours too while we're rehearsing, there'll be trouble.'

'I don't know what you mean,' said Alexander, through his mouthful. 'Nobody's eating anything here.'

'Tell that to Carl,' said Eliot, laughing, and turned back to the orchestra. 'Right. Quick flick through this. If we take too long we might not have any food left. Who knows if they'll be along with more trays?'

The orchestra had rarely been more attentive in rehearsal. Eliot reflected he should use the promise of edible treats with them more often, like training a dog.

Alexander put his ear to the headset a couple of times while the orchestra was playing, but had nothing major to report when he gave it back to Charlie afterwards. 'Just some bog-standard gripes, as far as I could tell,' he said. 'Nothing about us.'

The soundchecks proceeded smoothly. Even Bożenka's group managed to play some of their piece, having rushed through their tuning regime at a dangerously cavalier speed.

The violinists continued to be in high spirits throughout the afternoon, perhaps because they knew there was going to be no horizontal floor-based choreography for them that day. Once sodden, twice dried. In the fortnight between their heat and the final, they had learned an arrangement of "Winter" from Vivaldi's *Four Seasons*, which involved their senior members (who were all of about nine years old) playing the solo part that had been divvied up between them so no one child got either all the glory or all the nerves. They flung themselves into it wholeheartedly, with additional stamps and kicks. At times, the table-tennis bats looked as if they were directing a whole cohort of baby Nigel Kennedys, minus the stubble. Some of them had even tried to emulate Nigel's spiky hair, which looked both adorable and a little unnerving, and also betrayed the average age of their adult supervisors.

Alexander's quartet gave very little away in their soundcheck – they wanted to keep their programme under wraps until it went out live. They played a bit of their previous Bach fugue to get the feel of the space again and let the camera operators know where they were going to be standing, but, apart from that, they wanted it to be a surprise.

Alexander had a quick chat with Gemma about their audio playback. 'I've had it signed off by Russell by email, and I've sent him the audio file. The opera group gave me the idea – it opened up a load of repertoire I hadn't even considered. But can you check everything's lined up for it? I don't want to play it now – it would spoil the surprise.'

'OK,' said Gemma, nodding. She walked away from him, flicked a switch on her headset and started talking fast.

Charlie had been keeping an eye on her. He reached down to where he had hidden his headset, and switched it on. Erin saw what he was doing and leaned in to listen. They heard Gemma and Russell talking, boxed-in and tinny.

Russell was mid-sentence. '– *the email and said it was fine, but the thinking is to stall it from up here tonight and let him flounder. He got far too much of the vote last time – it was obvious from space. He didn't leave us any wiggle room. We need to even it up to let us think on our feet tonight.*'

'*Gotcha. I'll keep him sweet down here then.*'

'*If you could, darling. Ciao.*'

'*Will do.*'

She turned and walked back to Alexander with a big smile on her face. 'All confirmed. Russell says we're good to go for tonight.'

'Excellent. Thanks!'

Charlie and Erin stared at each other while Alexander and the rest of his quartet came back to their seats.

Chapter 32

While Gregory and Riffraff were taking their turns to practise and let the technicians do soundchecks, caterers brought refill trays of food, telling everyone they passed that this was going to be the final food run before the show, so if they were hungry this was their last chance. People fell on them as if they had not eaten in weeks. An idle musician is always up for a free sandwich.

By deploying meaningful eyebrow lifts and subtle head-tilting, Charlie and Erin managed to convene a meeting of the Spy Ring on the border between the green and white zones. Most people were munching sandwiches. Carl, Alexander and Charlie each had three on the go at once.

'What's up?' said Eliot. He looked at the stacks of sandwiches being dispatched. 'More Checkpoint Chomping than Checkpoint Charlie. Although we do have an actual Charlie. Which makes it better, somehow.'

Ann shook her head at him kindly. One never likes to see a conductor unravel.

Charlie looked around to make sure nobody from Quork Media was within earshot and swallowed his mouthful of sandwich. 'We heard Russell tell Gemma that Alexander's audio playback won't happen this evening.'

'What?' said Alexander. 'No, she confirmed it with me. To my face.'

'Yeah,' said Erin. 'That was a lie. We'd just heard Russell tell her he was going to stop the playback to make you look stupid and so you won't get so many votes tonight.'

'Something about evening it up,' Charlie broke in. 'You were too bloody good last time and – how did he put it, Erin?'

'Wiggle room. You didn't leave them enough wiggle room. To fix the vote, if they want to, I guess.'

'Shit,' said Alexander.

There was a short silence. Several more sandwiches disappeared.

'So, now we know, can't we just march up to Russell and tell him?' said Carl. 'I'll do it.'

'Steady on,' said Eliot, 'although thank you, Carl, for the offer. Can I hold you in reserve? If we tell them we know what they're doing, we might lose any advantage we have of our eavesdropping. God, it's like we've just cracked the Enigma code.'

'And anyway,' said Ann, 'Russell could agree, now, to make it all go perfectly tonight and then renege on it. I wouldn't trust him not to. It's live. What can we do to stop him at that point?'

'He might be severely underestimating our willingness to busk it live,' said Charlie. 'I mean, he's in a job where you have to revere telly. Us… not so much. Surely that gives us an advantage.'

'If only there was a way to get round them,' said Kayla.

Charlie tapped Erin on the arm. 'Your admirer isn't here tonight, is he? That cameraman you chatted up?'

'Bob? No, haven't seen him.'

'Shame. He might have been a useful recruit.'

More silent thinking time. More sandwiches.

'What are you playing, anyway?' Eliot asked Alexander.

'Schumann's *Konzertstück*. Well, second and third movements of it. Too long to do the whole thing, which is a shame.'

'Oh, wow! Fabulous piece. And yes – shame about the first movement. I remember hearing it when I was a kid, and that very first entry of the horns made my hair stand on end.'

Alexander laughed. 'That fanfare does have a very "Hello, I've arrived!" quality, doesn't it? Even compared to what we usually get to play. Mind you, the rest of it's pretty good too.' He sighed. 'If we get to do it.'

'I don't know it,' said Kayla.

'Ah – it's great,' said Alexander. 'Four horn soloists at once, with an orchestra. Well, a recording of an orchestra in this case.'

Erin froze. 'What if…?' She stopped.

'Oh god. I know that face,' said Charlie. 'She's having one of her ideas.'

'What?' said Eliot.

Erin looked at him. 'What if we had a back-up? If the orchestra playback doesn't happen, what if we provide a real orchestra?'

Eliot snorted. 'Us?'

'Do you know the *Konzertstück*?'

'Well, to listen to, yes. I've never conducted it.'

Erin's face fell. 'Oh, but we'd need parts… maybe this is a stupid idea.'

'No, hang on,' said Charlie, turning to Alexander. 'You don't happen to have a set of parts in your case, do you?'

'Nope. Just a miniature score and the horn parts. And anyway, you can't sight-read it on live telly! Can you?'

'There are some tricky corners for the cellos,' said Ann, 'but I've played it before. I won't be the only one. We have great wind players – they can cope. It would be better than silence.'

'Well, we can't all read off one miniature score,' said Eliot. 'If we're going to do this – and I can't quite believe I'm saying this – we need parts. Even Pearl may not be able to get her hands on a full set of orchestral parts in –' he looked at his watch '– less than two hours.'

'One way to find out,' said Charlie, and went off to find Pearl, returning with her and settling her down on his chair while he knelt on the floor.

Pearl looked around at the earnest faces. 'Charlie said you needed my help. Are you still hungry? Because I have some little individual Twixes over there in my bag…' She trailed off, seeing that whatever they needed her for, a Twix wasn't going to help.

Eliot smiled and laid his hand over hers. 'No, Pearl, but thank you. We need your talent for getting your hands on orchestral parts.'

'Oh? Have we lost some of our Brahms copies?'

'No. We are going to try and save the day for Alexander. Do you have a phone number for any of your music library contacts? A mobile, perhaps?'

Pearl nodded, dug into her handbag and produced a small address book: an old-fashioned, battered hardback one with alphabetical tabs in the pages. She put her thumb on the letter L and opened it unerringly to a whole page of closely written names and numbers. 'L for library,' she said, smiling. 'They're all here.'

Alexander leaned in. 'I could kiss you, Pearl.'

'Oh!' Pearl was quite discombobulated, and got a bit fluttery.

'It hasn't worked out yet. Hang on,' said Eliot. 'Now, Pearl. This is a top secret mission. You don't need to know everything, but let's just say that things aren't as happy in this studio as we might like them to be. Could you find out if any of your librarian friends can get us a set of orchestral parts for Robert Schumann's *Konzertstück*? Please?'

'Now?'

'Right now.'

'Shouldn't we ask David? Or – oh heavens – Rafael? I mean, I don't want to order parts that will cost an arm and a leg if they haven't said it's alright.'

'You leave them to me,' said Eliot. 'The main thing is to see if we can get them.'

Pearl nodded. 'Schumann *Konzertstück*. You need them here? Before tonight?'

'If we can.'

She nodded again, and took out her phone.

The others stood up.

Alexander grinned at Erin. 'Some idea you've had! Thanks.'

'Hasn't worked yet,' Erin said nervously.

Charlie ruffled her hair, which she tried unsuccessfully to fight off. 'She's got form with ideas.'

'Right,' said Eliot. 'If Pearl can get them, I'll talk to David first. Then we need to tell the orchestra what we're planning, and hope they'll be up for it.'

'We'll be up for it,' said Kayla. 'After this summer, Alexander's one of us.'

He grinned his thanks.

'Can I have a look at your score?' Eliot asked. Alexander retrieved it from his horn case and handed it over. Eliot flicked it open to the front page where it listed the instrumentation. 'OK, OK... double wind; two trumpets; two horns but they can double up; three trombones we have; no tuba – Leroy can sit it out; timps and strings. We need a piccolo. Do you think we can get Samira here? Does anyone have her number?'

'Amber or David will have,' said Erin. 'I can ask Amber when we know if Pearl can get the parts.'

Just then, Pearl stood up, looking breathless but pleased. 'Got them! I managed to persuade my lovely friend Oonagh away from a barbeque to fetch them from her library. She's going to get a bike to courier them over to the studio here. I put your name as the contact, Eliot – I thought that would be correct? Hope so?'

'Pearl! You are a marvel!' said Eliot. 'That's absolutely fine, of course. God bless Oonagh.'

Alexander bent down to give Pearl a hug, which turned into him picking her up and kissing her on the cheek. She arrived back down on the ground looking quite pink but extremely proud.

Several orchestra members turned round to see Pearl's levitation, and laughed.

Eliot looked at his watch again. 'Right. Action stations, or whatever I'm supposed to say. I'll speak to David and Rafael. You lot get the word out to the rest of the orchestra about what's happening – and make sure you keep it subtle. I don't want Russell or Gemma getting wind of this. Tell them that when the parts arrive, we'll hand them out and they must have a look through as best they can ahead of time. Just the second and third movements. We'll get absolutely *no* rehearsal. Oh god – are we really doing this?'

'We've got this,' said Carl. 'Pearl, you're a star.' He moved off through the green zone to his fellow brass players at the far end.

Eliot exhaled like an athlete about to attempt a complicated move. 'I'll hang onto this score then, Alexander. After I've had a word with the rest of the committee I need to do some speed-reading homework myself. Crikey. It's like being back at college.'

Alexander held his hand out, and shook Eliot's firmly. 'Thank you, Eliot. This is – well, it's amazing.'

'It was Erin's idea.'

'Erin is amazing,' confirmed Alexander. 'You all are. I'll go and tell my quartet what's afoot.'

Chapter 33

One benefit of being completely distracted by plotting was that they had missed Gregory Knight's entire soundcheck, which had droned on in the background as they talked. He was not one to leaven a poetic atmosphere in the normal course of events, despite his self-belief in his "poker-faced badinage". He had long emphasised the poker face and hoped the badinage might scamper along behind. Alas, it never did. That week, however, Gregory had discovered that he had not made the shortlist of the most prestigious annual poetry prize in the country. Despite lobbying and seeding poisonous rumours about his rivals, his latest self-published collection – *Whither The Inconstant Heart?* – had been overlooked. It was yet another hammer blow to his incomprehensibly buoyant ego. Gregory felt his manufactured resentment deeply and only wished he could be allowed to persuade his fellow artists to perform similarly poignant pieces that evening.

Carl had overheard Gregory ranting to one of his musicians that the world of British poetry was blind to his talent and ran on cliques. He said that the urgency of his own sexually-charged work had been silenced by Big Verse. Carl was delighted. The story of Gregory's attention-seeking performative whingeing whipped round the orchestra in no time.

Riffraff took the stage last to rehearse, Paraic rolling his eyes to the others as he realised that later on they would have to knife their way through the leaden atmosphere Gregory would conjure, and try to inject it with a bit of different energy. Paraic was heartened to hear enthusiastic applause from the other performers when they had finished their soundcheck. Some of the tiny violinists had been improvising dance moves. Several orchestra members gave Riffraff a thumbs-up, including Carl, who had been nodding along to it very enjoyably. He went over to chat to Paraic and his mates afterwards. The whole event was beginning to feel like a real festival. Except for Gregory.

After Riffraff cleared the stage, Gemma strode across the studio floor to address all the performers. 'It's all sounding really great, folks. Fantastic! So, between now and transmission time, you can change and freshen up, then it's through hair and make-up as before, and back to your seats here by five-thirty at the latest. Any questions?'

The orchestra members darted looks between themselves, trying to look completely natural and not as if they were plotting a subversive guerrilla manoeuvre on national live television later. Some of them managed it. Some couldn't help pulling nervous faces. Pearl decided the only safe position for her while Gemma was nearby was with her hand pressed tightly over her mouth, in case she should give anything away without realising. Gemma just assumed Pearl had permanent nervous indigestion.

Amber had asked Samira to come along to the studio, wearing concert black and bringing her piccolo, and relayed to

Eliot that they would have an extra piccolo later. Eliot caught Gemma just as she had finished giving her little speech.

'Ah, Gemma – could I have a word?'

'As long as it's quick. Got a lot to do before tonight.'

'Yes, of course. One of our wind players couldn't make it to our rehearsal, but she's on her way now. Could we possibly let the front desk know to expect her? Samira. She'll be carrying a piccolo.' Eliot believed in embellishing a lie with enough truthful details to help it along.

Gemma looked at him vaguely. She had raised the point at various management meetings about *Pass the Baton* that getting a whole orchestra in as one of the groups created an unwieldy number of people to organise. This piece of news only confirmed her suspicions, but she had been overruled, and that was that. She sighed. 'Fine. I'll let security know.'

She walked away, talking into her headset. Eliot looked over at Charlie, listening in. Charlie nodded and gave a thumbs-up. Erin was sitting next to Charlie.

'Are we mad?' she said, watching Gemma go.

'Yes. But what's the alternative? Leave them to dob Alexander in the shit and do nothing?'

Erin smiled a worried sort of smile. 'When you put it like that…'

'It'll be alright. Everyone will be looking at Alexander anyway – they always do. We'll just be the backing band.'

Arden started moving everyone through to their dressing rooms, and the catering staff arrived to retrieve their trays and clear up. Several musicians made a point of thanking them for all the sandwiches they had provided, and they looked so pleased and surprised at this attention it was clear Quork Media weren't in the habit of appreciating them.

Which, given how they were about to attempt to treat the performers, was perhaps not a surprise.

As the orchestra wandered through to their dressing room, Eliot peeled off and made his way to the front doors. There were three security guards on duty.

'Hi,' he said, to none of them in particular. They all turned to look at him. 'I'm Eliot. I conduct Stockwell Park Orchestra – we're in this thing tonight.' He gestured behind him toward the studio. Three faces continued to stare impassively. 'Well, two things, really. Firstly, I think Gemma mentioned one of our wind players would be turning up. She's late. I hope she gets here soon – Samira. Could you send her through as soon as she does, please?'

One of the guards looked down a list he had on his desk and nodded. 'Yep. Got her on here.'

'Fantastic. The other thing was I'm expecting a courier delivery. We need some extra parts for tonight – left some behind, like an idiot. Can I leave you my mobile number so you can call me as soon as they get here? Then I can come and collect?'

The guard with the list nodded, clicked a pen and raised his eyebrows at Eliot, who gave his mobile number.

'Eliot Yarrow. It should be addressed to me. That's brilliant. Sorry to be a pain. Thanks very much.'

'S'alright,' said List Guard, clicking his pen closed again and slotting it into his top pocket. 'What we're here for. Good luck – tonight, like.'

Eliot grinned. 'Thanks.'

He rejoined the orchestra in the dressing room and changed into his concert clothes, then all the performers queued to get themselves signed off by hair and make-up, feeling by this stage that they were old hands at this entertainment business.

Bożenka and her fellow harpists really just went in for admiration. They didn't bother to queue: merely arrived, exchanged looks with the staff, and left. This time they were wearing black silk, floor-length gowns, again with the low-neck detail and fitted bodice that suited them all so superbly. They each wore a heavy silver torque necklace and drop earrings. Together, the effect was of a quintet of young Victorian widows intent on enjoying their newfound freedom, who may or may not have poisoned their elderly and infirm husbands whom they may or may not have married for their wealth. It was a complex look.

Eliot met Pearl as she was just leaving make-up and he was waiting to go in.

'Pearl – you look wonderful!'

She gave him a shy twirl. 'Thank you. Any news on the… delivery?'

'Not yet. I'll fetch it as soon as it arrives and distribute.'

Pearl nodded and hurried to find her seat in the studio. She had to dodge out of the way of members of Fiddle Me This, who were running wild between their dressing room and everywhere else. They had embraced their Vivaldi "Winter" theme with the enthusiasm of a primary school art collage: every small child was dressed in white tights and (disappointingly for the scientifically-inclined) identical glitter-enhanced snowflake outfits made out of stiffened lace that made it difficult for two of them to pass each other in a corridor without turning sideways. Pearl had to squeeze past a number of them before she made it back to the studio.

Charlie and Erin were already there.

'Ah, Pearl – I see you've encountered Fiddle Me This,' said Charlie. 'So did we.'

'What?'

'Your outfit,' said Erin. 'Shall I help you brush it off?'

Pearl looked down at her black concert skirt and blouse, which were liberally scattered with silver glitter. 'Oh! Yes – they have gone to town rather on their costumes, haven't they? I've got a clothes brush in my bag somewhere, hang on.'

'Of course you have,' said Charlie.

'You might have to lend it out to everyone,' said Erin. She looked down at her own clothes. 'In fact, could I borrow it, please?'

'How are they going to play?' Charlie wondered. 'I suppose their little arms can stick out of the front of the star shape.'

'Their choreography is going to be quite something. They can only see straight out in front,' said Erin, laughing.

'Here,' said Pearl, handing her brush to Erin. 'We can all use it. Charlie, you might need a spruce as well.'

By the time Eliot joined them in the green zone, there was a busy group of musicians brushing each other down, and an increasingly sparkly floor area. He had made his way back via the front door security desk, and was clutching a large brown envelope to his chest. He looked for Amber. 'Any sign of Samira yet?'

She shook her head. 'She texted. On her way.'

Eliot nodded and turned to the rest of the orchestra.

'Here we are, folks,' he said, opening the envelope and putting the stack of parts on a chair. 'Keep these safe, for god's sake. Can I have one person per section collect your music, please? Now, listen. We need to be ready to swing into action straight away. It may not happen, but we need to be prepared. It's us first, then the glittery snowflakes, then Alexander. Keep your instruments with you and ready to go. Brass – keep your mouthpieces warm. And wind – your reeds ready and licked, or whatever you do to them. We'll get no time to tune

217

or warm up or anything.' He stopped talking and grinned at his players, who were passing sheet music between them and whispering. 'We are a ninja orchestra. I know we can do this. Have a shuftie at your part – just the second and last movements – and look at any tricky bits. We'll just have to wing it. I've done a bit of homework and will come round to a couple of players now and talk through any tricky corners. Other than that, it's seat-of-our-pants time. How many of you have heard it?' Perhaps half the orchestra raised their hand. 'And anyone played it before?' Fewer hands, but still a fair number, spread through different sections. Eliot tried to remember who had played it before and who hadn't, and hoped he would be able to lead them through it.

Ann smiled at him. 'We've got this. You'll be fine.'

Eliot nodded. 'I reckon so. Well, that's all you're going to get from me. I'm not going to go all Henry the Fifth at Agincourt at you.'

'Thank god,' said Carl.

'I know you'll do your best. Now look – here comes Gemma. Be subtle.'

The entire orchestra immediately threw themselves into brushing more glitter from their clothes or tidying away their secret Schumann parts. Eliot watched Gemma approach and found himself stifling a giggle.

'Don't tell me you're not having fun,' whispered Charlie.

Eliot flicked him a glance. 'It's not boring, I'll give you that.'

As the rest of the performers came back to their zones, the studio doors were opened to allow the earliest members of the audience in. At the very front of the polite throng was a purposeful lady in a voluminous pink kaftan.

'Oh look, said Erin weakly. 'It's Mrs Ford-Hughes.'

Chapter 34

Mrs Ford-Hughes strode into the studio with the determination of one who had been in a department store sale queue all night and whose heart was set on the discounted Le Creuset. She spotted the orchestra and accelerated, waving.

'Coo-ee! Eliot, honey?'

'I don't think I've ever heard anyone from Arkansas say "coo-ee" before,' said Eliot, watching her approach.

'She's gone native,' said Charlie.

Arden tried to intercept Mrs Ford-Hughes and herd her back to the audience seating but had no idea of the sheer force that would be involved to make that remotely possible. Mrs Ford-Hughes looked at Arden absent-mindedly and carried straight on, arriving at the edge of the green zone and holding both hands out to Eliot.

'Hello, Maryanne,' he said, taking them in his own and giving them a sort of awkward double shake. 'How lovely. I didn't know you were coming! Is your husband here too?'

She half-turned and let go of one of his hands to point behind her. 'Sure – he's back there somewhere saving me a seat. I couldn't turn up without letting y'all know we were here and rooting for you!' She grasped his free hand once more and gave them both a squeeze. 'Wanted to wish you all the luck in the world for tonight. And, win or lose, we sure are proud of you.'

She finally released Eliot's hands and turned to the rest of the orchestra, spreading her arms wide. 'So proud of you all. Honestly, if I can't be here on the stage myself tonight with my gorgeous cellists,' she bestowed a special smile on Erin and the rest of the cello section, 'the very next best thing is knowing you'll be there instead.'

'Maryanne?' Alexander appeared beside Eliot from his white zone next door. 'What a wonderful surprise. How are you?'

'Oh, Alexander!' Mrs Ford-Hughes cried, and enveloped a stooping Alexander in the folds of her kaftan. 'I was hoping I'd catch you too. We're so looking forward to tonight's performances. I just know you'll knock everybody's socks off!'

Alexander exchanged looks with Eliot over Mrs Ford-Hughes's shoulder. 'Well, we'll try to. Anything can happen on live telly.'

'Oh, and here comes Gemma,' said Eliot. 'Maryanne, I think you might have to return to the audience.'

Gemma was indeed marching toward them looking furious. She batted Arden out of her way and started shouting before she had got within indoor conversation distance. 'Audience members must remain in their seating area. This is a restricted zone for performers.'

Before she turned to face Gemma, Mrs Ford-Hughes pulled a mock-frightened face at Eliot and Alexander. She swirled round, her silken folds sweeping an arc around her bosom no Quork Media employee could breach. 'Honey,

I'm Stockwell Park Orchestra's patron, and I'll wish them luck if I want to.'

Gemma came to an abrupt halt. 'Well, er—?'

'Mrs Ford-Hughes.'

'Well, Mrs Ford-Hughes, I still must insist you return to your seat.' Gemma was unsmiling.

Mrs Ford-Hughes turned back to Eliot and Alexander and leant up to kiss each of them on the cheek.

'That girl could learn some manners,' she whispered.

'You're not wrong,' Alexander whispered back. 'Keep your fingers crossed for us. Things could get interesting later.' She looked worried, so he winked at her.

'It's going to be fine,' said Eliot. 'Enjoy the show.'

Flanked by Gemma, she returned to her husband in the audience and looked back to them, still worried.

'Why did you say that?' Eliot asked Alexander. 'It's not as if she can do anything about it.'

Alexander shrugged. 'She strikes me as a very capable woman who might be useful to have on our side if it all kicks off.' He smiled. 'Am I wrong?'

'You're not wrong.'

Emboldened by Mrs Ford-Hughes, a whole row of the audience had stood up and moved across the studio floor towards the performers, calling and waving. In answer, immediate squeals shot out from Fiddle Me This in their furthest red zone. A blizzard of snowflakes ran out in front of the other performers to go and see their parents. Arden stood between the two advancing groups, arms wide in a desperate attempt to halt the oncoming avalanche, but of course it was hopeless. Excited snowflakes hopped around dropping glitter on anything within reach, and their parents tried to get close enough to their child's face to give them a kiss without having their own eye poked out by a starched lace snowflake point. The noise levels were impressive.

Russell stormed out of his glass office and came thundering down the steps, arriving at the melee on one side as Gemma arrived on the other. Between them, they separated small excitable snowflakes from taller excitable parents and sent them in opposite directions. Arden emerged from the middle and was clearly in disgrace. The rest of the audience was loving it, so Russell and Gemma looked at each other meaningfully and returned to their posts: he upstairs and she on the studio floor. Charlie reached for his headset.

'– the fuck did she think she was doing?'

'I couldn't stop her. She said she's patron of the orchestra or something. Then when I'd got her back in her seat, the rest of them just got up and yelled at their kids. Jesus.'

'Christ alive.' Russell sighed heavily. 'I know kids are popular, and I know this will play well with commissions down the line, but right now I honestly wonder if it's worth it.'

'All we have to do is prove we can produce replicable results, you said so yourself...'

'Yeah, I know, I know. They're going to be looking closely at what we deliver tonight.'

'This is just the start. Our growing pains, yeah?' Gemma looked up at the glass office. 'Eyes on the prize.'

'You're right. Fuck 'em. Let's get the judges lined up and then it's time to rock 'n' roll. And make sure Olive doesn't blow it. She's been sailing pretty close to the wind. Have a word with Barney.'

'Will do.'

Charlie stowed the headset back in his bag and looked up to find several of the others staring at him, waiting for an update.

'Same old, same old. They've got some big future thing on the line, as far as I can gather, depending on what they can produce tonight. They don't want people like Mrs Ford-Hughes getting in the way. Something about delivering replicable results, whatever that is.'

'I guess sponsors would love to be able to predict outcomes and then shift things in their favour?' Erin said. 'Reality TV is here to stay. But it's a bit too unpredictable for them.'

'Their fifty grand is buying them one big fuck-off test drive,' said Ann.

'More fool them,' said Eliot. 'I'm rubbish at driving.'

Chapter 35

Transmission time approached. The audience were settled in their seats, being schooled on what was about to happen by Quork staff and having a go on their voting panels by their chairs. Gemma was in the judges' seating area at the side of the stage, talking to the three judges and Barney North. Three Fiddle Me This snowflakes were being taken to the loo one last time: no small endeavour, given their costumes had not been designed with this function in mind.

Just as Barney was ushering the judges off the stage before the programme started, Samira came into the studio and trotted past Riffraff and Gregory to reach the orchestra, rolling her eyes in apology for being so late.

'Ah, thank goodness! Hello,' said Eliot. 'Thank you *so* much for coming. If Amber hasn't explained yet, she will. She's got your music. Don't suppose you've played picc in Schumann's *Konzertstück* before, have you?'

Samira smiled brightly. 'Yeah, I have actually. We did it at my youth orchestra. Love it.'

'Fabulous. You can just sit here while we play the Brahms, if that's OK. Try not to look as if you should be on stage or you'll get chivvied up there by someone and have to look an unemployed lemon on live telly.'

Samira nodded and went to find Amber.

The army of stagehands had set up the orchestra's seating on stage, and Arden beckoned them to take their positions before transmission started. Samira decided the best way to fade into the background was to sit on the floor among the instrument cases and not make eye contact, which proved brilliantly effective. Alexander spotted her and grinned as the orchestra tuned up.

Gemma walked along the performers' areas, checking everyone else was there and ready. She counted the number of Fiddle Me This kids and nodded, flicked a switch in her headset and spoke briefly before walking back to the centre of the studio.

Russell's voice boomed out of the overhead speakers. 'Welcome, everyone, to the grand final of *Pass the Baton*. In a moment, you'll hear the signature tune and we'll be broadcasting live. Performers, you know the drill. Audience, you've tested your voting panels and you're good to go. Do what our lovely colleagues at the front say, and remember to enjoy yourselves, as loudly as possible! We want to hear those cheers!'

They gave a great whoop of enthusiasm, and Mrs Ford-Hughes turned to the orchestra and clasped her hands above her head in support. The lights came up, the theme music played, and Barney and his teeth bounded on stage.

'Hello, and a very warm welcome to the final show of *Pass the Baton*! Our grand final!' He paused to allow the audience '*woo!*' to fill the studio, as directed by two people at the front. 'We have our six finalists: Riffraff, Gregory Knight and his Ambient Sounds, Stockwell Park Orchestra, The Leakey Horns, The Dark Harps and Fiddle Me This!' The cameras panned along the performer areas and the stage as he spoke, provoking more screaming and jumping from the snowflakes at the far end. 'And, of course, where would we be without our judges? Please welcome on stage Maria Romano, Anthony Popkin and Olive Yessel!'

Maria and Anthony came into view, Anthony almost achieving a Barney-level bound. Olive, as usual, appeared third, walking carefully and leaning on her cane. They accepted the audience applause and settled in their seats.

Barney smiled directly into the camera again. 'And so, without further ado, let's start tonight's proceedings.'

Charlie leaned closer to Erin at the front of the cello section. 'Does that man ever say anything that isn't a cliché?'

Erin stifled a giggle.

Barney hadn't quite finished. 'Before the orchestra plays the last movement of Brahms's Second Symphony, let's catch up with the musicians and relive their journey to this moment.'

Eliot quickly got the orchestra's attention and managed to convey they were to look at him, not the screen, as before. No good could come of being distracted by whatever Quork Media were going to throw their way.

The huge screen behind the judges lit up for the video montage. Interspersed with different shots of the orchestra rehearsing were clips of people walking around, overlayed with some audio. A laugh erupted from the audience at the sight of Pearl sashaying along the pavement pulling her wheeled shopping trolley and winking to the camera. They lost it completely when her voice came through the speakers offering to put her urn on early.

Pearl's mouth fell open in an anguished 'O'. Eliot locked eyes with her and mouthed 'Don't worry'. She relaxed, a little.

Then the video moved onto what looked like the offcuts of an interview with Gregory, sitting in front of a stack of his books. The camera was shaky and framed Gregory in a covert slant. 'The orchestra? Some of them are just up their own arses.' There was a gasp from the audience, and several orchestra members snapped their heads round to look at Gregory, who sat impassively in his blue zone. Eliot flicked his fingers and retrieved their attention. Gregory's voice on film continued. 'I mean, I offered one girl there a huge opportunity to work with me, and she turned it down flat. What an idiotic move. A girl like her is going to need a mover-shaker like me if she wants to get on in this business. Good luck to her without me, I say. Good luck to them all.' He laughed and the film cut back to some more orchestral rehearsal footage.

Beatriz looked incandescent. Courtney quietly moved her hand to rest it on Beatriz's knee, and Eliot put both his hands flat, palms down, pressing the air slightly, to calm her. She looked at Eliot, visibly sighed and nodded.

After what felt like an age, the video finished, and Barney handed over to Eliot to start the show.

Eliot looked round his players, making sure they were ready. He checked all the strings were up for the start and put his finger on his lips at them to remind them to play softly. He gathered his own energy – in that mysterious way conductors can make the air stretch taut over their orchestra – smiled, and nodded. They were off.

It takes skill to play quietly yet keep injecting a feeling of pace, but he had all the string players' eyes and they came with him, peeling off into their layers and recombining without losing focus or gaining dynamic. That moment, twenty-two bars later, when the whole orchestra abruptly crashed into life worked like a charm, with several people in the audience visibly jumping. The violinist snowflakes snapped to attention. Alexander grinned. Eliot took half a step backwards, put his weight on his back foot and set the engine of the orchestra running, firing off the trumpets and timpani into the mix to banish any lingering memories of shitty media companies and remind people that it only takes a few bars of this kind of pumping energy to create a feeling of total exhilaration. This is what life is all about. Brahms knew it, and could conjure it into being just by vibrating the air. Dopamine switches flipped in heads all round the studio.

After the first flush of exuberance, the movement shifted into another gear, revealing more complex textures. Beatriz played her smooth clarinet arpeggio over the rest of them as if she were a deer making an effortless leap, and Eliot flashed her an appreciative smile. Years of practice go into making a small contribution like that sound perfect, and those who knew could only marvel at how she made it sound so easy.

The strings pizzicatoed themselves into a *largamente* section that was rich and treacly, like running along a diving board on tiptoe and then slipping into warm water without a splash. Their bows slurred the notes, blurring their edges, all playing in the lowest register of their instrument until the sound was full of melting toffee. By the time the wind joined in and they had reached the triplet passages that Eliot had made them practise so much, the movement was winding itself up again. When the trumpets joined the horns in overlapping fanfares, it sounded like they were gearing up for the finish line, with the trumpets' silvery timbre cutting through the music's texture like the flash of a knife blade.

Brahms is such a tease. He diverted them again, making sure the audience knew they had to sit up and take notice when they heard the brass do that again. Meanwhile, he got the strings and wind to dance playfully for a while, putting in Scotch snaps of such infectious rhythms Eliot couldn't help jig about and conduct some side-beats with his elbows. A few more of those, and they were back to what sounded like the beginning again but – just as one cannot step into the same river twice – hearing these identical notes having just lived through what had come before made them sound different, as if you had walked around a sculpture and were viewing it from another angle. Same shape, different light.

When they reached the *Sempre più tranquillo* passage, it sounded as if they were weightless, turning slowly, before deciding which direction to take. By the third time the opening bars sounded again, they were back at the front of the statue, more firm and definite about which path they wanted. The total silence before the explosion, carelessly kicked up to by the strings with staccatos and rests, gave no warning to the uninitiated. Yet again there were startled jumps in the audience as the entire string section hunkered down to their determined quavers, thrumming the orchestra along. This time, when the trumpets joined with their silvery notes, there was no going back. By the time the first violins had been sent up five ledger lines, the audience were edging closer to the front of their seats. The violinists leaned up their fingerboards as the trombones weighed in with punchy descending notes. Then there were the famous sets of furious scales that ended in half a bar of total silence each time. Pete and Pearl had learned them off by heart and scrubbed them out, their eyes riveted on Eliot so there would be no chance of them falling into the rests. Eliot let the horns and trumpets off the leash, and when the time came for the trombone chord to power through, he stopped conducting altogether and just stood there with his right arm outstretched, releasing the essential nature of *fortissimo* trombones loose into the studio. It blew through the listeners' heads, flattening everything in its path. Eliot's left hand gathered everyone else into their final chords, and they blasted the last note in triumph.

The audience surged to their feet as one, roaring with delight, with Mrs Ford-Hughes leading the ovation, her pink kaftan all aquiver. Alexander and his quartet were standing too, as were most of the snowflake violinists (those who were not already in mid-air). Eliot clenched his fist in thanks, and nodded at the orchestra. Tracie was sitting next to Carl with a huge grin on her face, taking her earplugs out. He clapped her on the back and nodded his approval.

Barney had to wait quite some time before the audience let him speak. He turned to Olive first.

She nodded, smiling, and gave the orchestra another clap of her own. 'Bravo, my friends. Bravo. That is all I have to say to you.'

Maria Romano agreed. 'This was the perfect movement to showcase what is clearly a very talented orchestra. I can find no words of criticism at all!'

Barney turned to Anthony Popkin almost pleadingly. 'Surely Anthony, you must have a more critical eye and ear, given your profession?'

Olive snorted, which put Anthony off his answer. 'I – er – well, it's not a question of my profession giving me a critical eye. Or indeed ear.' He cleared his throat. 'There were obviously elements of this Brahms which could have been improved.' The audience started to boo. 'I mean to say, no performance is entirely perfect, but I must give credit where credit is due: yes, this was a fine rendition of *Herr Brahms*.' His dive into a sudden heavy German accent for Brahms's name was inexplicable.

And that was that. The judges gave their scores – perfect tens from Olive and Maria, and a nine from Anthony – and they went into the first ad break.

The orchestra was hurried off the stage area by the ninja stagehands swooping in to remove their chairs and stands in readiness for Fiddle Me This. They carried their instruments back to the green zone and put them away in cases, but didn't clip them shut. Brass players kept their mouthpieces in their pockets. Wind players kept hold of their reeds. Max kept a watchful eye on where his timps were being rolled to offstage.

Eliot walked through his players, congratulating and slapping backs. He whispered to Beatriz that he would be happy to help deal retribution out to Gregory, but not until after their possible next performance, if she didn't mind. She smiled and nodded. Alexander gave them a personal round of applause as they came to sit back down.

'Superb, guys. Really, really good. I'm feeling guilty now you might not be able to take the rest of the evening off.'

'Oh, don't worry about that,' said Ann. 'It was only one movement. We're used to doing whole symphonies, you know.'

The snowflakes were handed their pre-tuned violins and herded onto the stage, leaving a faint trail of glitter as they went. Gemma announced the imminent end of the commercial break, and they were live once more.

Chapter 36

Barney introduced the montage for Fiddle Me This, who had apparently not attracted Gregory's ire. It consisted of clips of their rehearsals where they marched round learning their choreography to Vivaldi's "Winter", which quite often degenerated into a game of tag, so they then had to be regrouped by increasingly hassled table-tennis bat wielders.

The video playback finished, lights on the stage turned suitably wintery, and the entire row of Fiddle Me This parents in the audience added to the atmosphere by shouting 'Come on, Zachary!' and similar, as if they were at Wimbledon just before a big serve. Eventually, they had to be shushed by the umpire in the form of furiously waving Quork staff.

The snowflake costumes, though striking, did have a rather limiting effect on the children's field of vision. It was OK while they were mainly stationary, but when they came to weave in and out of each other's lines there was a certain amount of jostling for position compounded by the fact that not being able to use their peripheral vision meant the leaders didn't know where anyone else was. Competitive spirit being what it is, as the music got more energised, so did their movement, until their performance was basically a race round the stage to see who would lead the pack. A few of the stragglers clashed snowflake spokes as they tried to overtake, became entangled and were forced to duet for the remainder of the piece.

Despite everything, they managed to land the ending of the music and bow to the audience, several of them still locked together. They were herded off-stage by the table-tennis bats, and the judges delivered their verdicts through broad smiles.

As the second ad break started, half a dozen men with brooms swept Vivaldi glitter off the stage and others brought four stands out for the horn players. Alexander, Kath, Annie and Cormac blew through their horns to keep them warm and zipped up and down a few arpeggios. Pearl took her bag over to the little violinists and, while the table-tennis bat adults weren't looking, handed out all her spare individually-wrapped Twixes as prizes. She thought someone should get them that evening. Pretty soon there was glittery chocolate all over the white lace.

At Eliot's signal, the orchestra surreptitiously began to get their instruments ready.

Charlie was leaning down with one ear next to his headset, listening intently. Eliot sat down next to him. There was nothing they could do but wait. Erin tightened Charlie's bow for him and rosined it.

Ann looked over at the judges. 'They're relaxed. Whatever happens, it doesn't look like they're in on it – this bit of whatever "it" is, at least. Or they're really good actors.'

The judges were still smiling from the Fiddle Me This episode, leaning back in their chairs and chatting with Barney. Gemma was standing between them and the audience, clearly speaking into her microphone.

Charlie looked up at Eliot, indicating he should listen in. They both leaned close to the headset. A thin version of Russell's voice drifted out.

'Yeah, the violins will have a chunk of the audience in their pocket anyway – there's that whole row of bloody parents. The orchestra was OK but remember what happened after Leakey played before? Off the fucking scale. We won't be able to reel that back. Stick to the plan.'

'Even after Anthony said he would drag the horn players?'

'Darling, we both know Anthony has a high opinion of himself. I don't think he's got as much clout with the voting public as he likes to think.'

'Maybe.'

'Right, so I'll cut the feed from up here and you can just get them to play their bit on their own, OK? They'll be fine doing that. Leakey has form with impromptu performances. Remember how we found him.'

'You're right. OK.'

'Cool. Ciao.'

Charlie flicked the headset switch off and replaced it in his bag. Eliot went to talk to Alexander.

'Right, we're on. Russell's going to cut your music feed from the control room. We'll be ready to go on your nod.'

Alexander sighed. 'I guess I'll have to look surprised at first and see if they have a change of heart. But we won't keep you waiting long. We've prepared a little surprise for you.' He smiled. 'Thanks for having my back, Eliot. And here's us supposed to be competing against each other.'

'They picked the wrong musicians for that,' said Eliot, touching Alexander's shoulder briefly in solidarity. 'Don't take any notice of anything they throw at you in that stupid pre-performance video – they'll try to put you off, if ours was anything to go by. Good luck. Hope I don't balls it up for you.'

Alexander and the others went on stage and Eliot returned to sit next to Charlie again. He retrieved the miniature score and his baton from his bag. The lights changed, and as the intro music started again, Barney came to life and faced the camera.

'Welcome back! It's time for our third group to play: The Leakey Horns! Let's take a look at what they've been up to.'

The montage video about the horns had been heavily edited to show split notes and other mistakes in their rehearsals, with liberal bleeped-out swears. Then it cut to Gregory, again sitting in front of his books in what was clearly the same situation, but this time he was being filmed from a different angle. The camerawork was shonky, betraying its covert nature. This was someone dragging the unvarnished dirt out of Gregory without him filtering it for public consumption.

'Leakey? That guy is nothing but a social media whore. Look at him chasing views and likes from that ridiculous summer flash mob thing. A true artist is deeper than his good looks. We'll see who lasts.'

This section was cut into more rehearsal bloopers, which covered up the audience's absolute silence. Several looked over at Gregory, who again was sitting impassively.

As the camera switched to the stage and Barney announced they would be playing part of Robert Schumann's *Konzertstück*, the audience gave Alexander a warm round of applause. It was going to take more than a disgruntled poet to put them off their favourite horn player.

Alexander grinned and raised a hand to acknowledge their support. He looked at the other three in his quartet,

235

waggled his eyebrows and put his horn near his lips, waiting for their entry that would come after four bars of orchestral introduction at the start of the slow second movement.

There was silence. It hung, then stretched out ever thinner, forming a skin over the adrenaline that flooded everyone, even those who knew what was coming. Alexander looked around the studio for Gemma, who made a great show of putting her hand to one ear and nodding, as if receiving instructions via her headset. The audience shuffled uncomfortably and looked at each other. They started to whisper.

Alexander tucked his horn under his arm and walked to the edge of the stage area towards Gemma, who had no option but to meet him there.

'What's going on?' he asked.

'They're having playback problems in the control room,' she said, managing to look genuinely worried. 'I don't think it's going to work – I'm so sorry. Can you do your bit without it?'

'Without the playback?'

'Yes?'

'There's no chance we can try it again and see?'

She relayed this question into her microphone but shook her head. 'I'm so sorry.'

The cameras switched between Alexander talking to Gemma, the other three horn players on stage, the judges talking worriedly to Barney, and the other performers looking shocked.

'Well,' said Alexander, 'tell you what. I've got a better idea.' He turned to the audience and smiled. 'Sorry folks, I'm told our planned orchestral accompaniment can't happen because of – what did you say it was, Gemma? – technical reasons, yes.'

Gemma carried on looking contrite. 'Sorry.'

'The good news is we have an emergency backup orchestra! Eliot, you're on. Guys?' He turned to the small army of stagehands who were scattered around off-camera. 'Any chance you can get the orchestra seats and stands back on stage, pronto?'

Gemma turned to Russell's glass control room in horror, one hand going to her headset. 'What do you expect me to do?' she hissed through clenched teeth. 'I can't exactly— OK, OK. I'll try.' She hurried after Alexander, who had gone back to the stage and was speaking rapidly to his other three horn players. They suddenly turned to face the oncoming orchestra piling onto the stage, and ripped through the opening fanfare of the very start of *Konzertstück*, which they weren't scheduled to play but thought it was the least they could do to celebrate the orchestra's arrival. This fanfare is the best razzy flourish anyone has ever written for the horn, managing to compress the impression of all four Musketeers swinging in on unexpected ropes to save a desperate situation, dismounting from them with triple somersaults, suave perfect landings and showbiz smiles.

It was all over in a couple of seconds, but Eliot cracked up laughing even as he was directing where his musicians should sit.

Russell was clearly yelling instructions into Barney's earpiece too, because he left the judges and stepped over to Alexander. 'Sorry – I don't think you can do this. We are on live television, after all.' He beamed into the nearest camera lens, hoping a spotlight might twinkle off a tooth, and turned back to Alexander. 'This will take too long. Please play your entry straight away or, well, I'm told we may have to disqualify you.'

'But we're pretty much ready,' said Alexander, gesturing to a nearly full orchestra settling in behind him. Eliot waved cheerily.

'You can't!' added Gemma from the floor.

'I'll tell you what you can't do!' shouted a familiar voice from the audience. Mrs Ford-Hughes rose from her seat. 'You can't stop my orchestra helping fellow musicians in need. My wonderful Stockwell Park Orchestra!' She flung her arms towards the players, and the audience burst into spontaneous applause. 'You should be thanking them for being willing to try and keep this show on the road.' More applause.

Eliot saluted her from his place, and Alexander grinned. She sat down.

Barney and Gemma looked at each other in silence.

The horns had shuffled their stands over to make room for the orchestra, which was now in place.

Eliot looked at Alexander. 'Shall we?'

Alexander looked at Barney and Gemma. 'May we?'

Barney smiled, shaking his head and shrugging, taking no responsibility for what might be about to happen, and spoke directly to the camera. 'So here we have, slightly later than planned, for which I apologise: The Leakey Horns – *and* Stockwell Park Orchestra – playing the second and third movements of Schumann's *Konzertstück*.' He backed off the stage, leading another burst of applause. Gemma ran up the stairs to the control room.

Chapter 37

Eliot pressed his borrowed miniature score – the size of a large paperback book – flat on his stand. He had already thoroughly broken its spine, for which he would apologise to Alexander later, but he wasn't about to handicap himself with a score that needed one hand on it to stay open. Conducting something for the first time usually went wrong somewhere. He didn't want the main thing to go wrong on live television to be a recalcitrant score that wanted to rest like a butterfly when he would rather it were a moth.

He looked around the orchestra. Every pair of eyes was drilling into his: he had never felt this level of crackling attention from them before. He nodded slightly, smiled to convey a confidence he wasn't going to admit to them he wasn't entirely feeling, and gave a whole bar of slow three to indicate the speed to the violins before they came in on their upbeat. Conducting is about trust. He knew they would follow him if they believed.

The strings' soft phrase curled out of them beautifully, Richard leading with exaggerated body movements that radiated his surefootedness: he knew Eliot could do with all the help he could to steady the players' nerves. Gwynneth joined them at the end of the phrase with a plaintiveness only an oboe in a minor key can convey. Eliot turned his head slightly to catch the eyes of Alexander and Kath and bring them in. This movement started with just the first and second horns of the quartet playing a melancholy refrain and the orchestra quietly following them. Eliot was careful to watch Alexander's body language to check constantly if he was going at the right speed for them, hoping if he had to adjust that the orchestra would come with him. He needn't have worried. They were glued to his baton and made micro-shifts in tempo if he merely thought them. He felt as if he was driving a racing car with a fluttering accelerator after their more relaxed rehearsal vibe of a loaded truck that laboured uphill. Annie and Cormac came in to round off the phrase and cement the sound of a full horn quartet in people's minds, foreshadowing what would come.

It was difficult playing only a partial section of this piece. Usually when an audience heard this slow middle movement, it had come after the explosive first one with its pyrotechnic acrobatics, especially from the first horn part. Robert Schumann wrote it in 1849 when he was in a creative frenzy – that year his *Konzertstück* was just one of more than forty works he produced. He deliberately used it to show off the virtuosic capabilities of the fashionable new valve horn, which was becoming much more popular than the old hand horn. The piece was famously so difficult that some people thought it unplayable, and even now it is rarely performed because of the difficulties of getting four technically brilliant soloists together at once.

Alexander and the other horn players created a stillness that drew the audience in, despite not having had the springboard of the first movement to use. It was Eliot's job to keep the orchestra in the background, which allowed them to shake out some of their nerves by playing slow *pianissimo* notes that were relatively easy. When the cellos came to a semiquaver section that bloomed out of the texture, Ann loomed from her seat at the back, giving them all confidence to go with her. The speed of the piece was slow enough that even sight-reading semiquavers was perfectly possible, and they coordinated like pros.

A few bars before this calm idyll was due to end, Eliot looked at the trumpets, who had been counting their rests. He gave them the unmistakable signal that he was going to need them imminently. He had already had a quiet word while they were all looking through their parts that this entry was going to need all the nerve they could muster, since it involved trumpets playing a sudden *fortissimo* over the top of the rest of the accompanying orchestra still at *pianissimo*. The trumpet line was the harbinger of the approaching third movement, which Schumann layered in during the final four bars of the second.

The horn soloists weren't playing at this point, so Eliot managed to thread the trumpet's little hiccupped demisemiquavers into the texture while keeping the rest of them quiet, simultaneously telegraphing that, at any minute, things were going to get exciting.

The third movement was attacca – following straight on from the second with no break – and they managed to negotiate the boundary together, which involved going from three-in-a-bar to two-in-a-bar, getting faster all the time, until they had settled into a quicker speed. Under normal circumstances, a tricky corner like that would have taken many attempts, with several players taking turns to fall off before everyone got it right. They didn't have that luxury. Eliot kept one eye on the orchestra, one eye on his score, and another eye he didn't know he had on the horn players, watching for the tempo they wanted to take for the last movement.

Schumann had put the entire orchestra on horseback for this one, with a rhythm of galloping hooves scattered liberally between the soloists and the rest of the instruments. The chase was on. Alexander led his horn players in a breathtaking display of skill, making frankly impossible leaps and careless filigree phrases sound off the cuff, when many a horn player would plod through them at half speed and still not make the jumps to the high notes.

Alexander, the born performer, was enjoying himself enough after their first phrase to grin at the orchestra when they had a few bars on their own, nodding along with the infectious rhythm they were giving him. He came in first after that section, leaning into another riff and bringing his other horn players with him. Some of the strings got a little ragged round the edges of their rat-a-tat rhythms, but they were trying so hard their sound kept its integrity. They swooped in and out with their dynamics as Eliot asked, and when the orchestra dropped out suddenly to leave three of the horns running up a semiquaver section marked *mit Bravour*, they simply sounded like one instrument, the synchronicity was so tight. Deservedly, the horns got a few bars rest after that, and all of them turned to appreciate the orchestra, who by that stage were daring to enjoy themselves. Samira's piccolo shrilled out over the top, Max's timpani were driving the rhythm from below, and Richard led the violins through a thicket of accidental-strewn semiquavers without letting them baulk or lose energy. Eliot tucked them back inside the horn texture in time to hear Alexander drift out a throwaway arpeggio starting on a note so high it had no right to be played by a horn at all. He made it look like an aside. Eliot shook his head in disbelief and carried on, smiling.

The orchestra could smell the finish line, and weighed into their *fortissimos* with such gusto Eliot had to remind them to shut up when the horns came in and they were supposed to be delicate accompanists. When they reached twenty-six bars from the end, marked *mit Bravour bis zum Schluss* (with brilliance until the end), there was a frisson of extra adrenaline. Everyone's notes had accents or staccato marks, everyone was crescendoing to *fortissimo*, and the entire thing hurtled into the final jubilant chords with triumphant gusto.

Alexander turned and wrapped Eliot in a bear hug as the applause exploded. They were both grinning hugely. Releasing Eliot so Kath, Annie and Cormac could receive their conductor's congratulations, Alexander held his horn aloft towards the orchestra in heartfelt thanks, before turning to acknowledge the audience, who were on their feet. Mrs Ford-Hughes could be seen in the centre: a vibrating pink kaftan having the time of her life.

Barney and all three judges were on their feet too, even Anthony Popkin, who seemed to have forgotten any instructions he may have previously received from the control room. Barney eventually calmed the audience down enough to speak.

'Well, that was quite simply the most extraordinary performance I've seen anywhere, let alone on live television.

Thank you. We are running a bit late now, so I must ask the judges to score that, if they can, in double quick time.'

'That's easy,' said Olive, smiling.

Maria nodded. 'I think we are all in agreement, aren't we, Anthony?'

Anthony looked momentarily nervous, but then also nodded. 'Nobody could mark that performance down, under these extraordinary circumstances. Bravo.'

So they went into the commercial break with a perfect score of ten from each judge. The cameras stopped rolling, and Russell and Gemma descended the steps from the control room together.

Chapter 38

The orchestra and horns were hurrying off-stage to let the chair-movers whisk away any sign they had been there at all and set up for Bożenka and her harps who were on next. As Alexander reached the white zone and was cleaning his horn before putting it away, Bożenka leaned across from her adjacent yellow zone and put a hand on his arm.

'Alexander,' she said, low and soft. He turned at her touch. 'An exquisite performance.'

'Thank you, Bożenka. You are most kind. And I wish you the very best with yours.' He bowed his head. She bestowed on him a calm smile before gathering her fellow harpists to go on stage.

Carl and Charlie were staring.

'Fuck me,' said Charlie. 'He's made actual friends with her. How?'

'I'd say he cowed her into submission with his height,' said Carl, 'but it's never worked for me, so he has to have something else going on.'

'Oh, watch out,' said Charlie, ducking to buckle his cello in its case. 'Gemma and Russell. Warpath. Incoming.'

'Eliot!' called Russell, looking slightly purple round his edges, 'what was the meaning of barging on stage? Wanted to hog the limelight? Wasn't a standing ovation for your own piece enough? Do you not realise you wouldn't be here at all if I hadn't invited you?'

Gemma scuttled up after him, nodding angrily like a cross pigeon pecking at grain. 'We are running behind schedule on a live show. What selfish behaviour to the acts coming after you. Are you deliberately trying to scupper their chances?'

Alexander wandered over, in the middle of emptying his valves. 'Ah, hello you two.' He shook a U-bend of horn tubing towards the floor, and some of the water flung itself over Russell's feet. 'Oh, sorry. Did that get you? It's only water. Look – don't tell Eliot off. He was helping me out after your "technical breakdown" and I think you should thank him.'

Everyone had heard the quotation marks Alexander had put in.

Russell was looking with distaste at the damp spotting pattern on his suede boots. He had opened his mouth to reply, when Carl stepped over and stood next to Alexander, and he thought better of it and closed it again.

Gemma glared at Eliot, not yet willing to back down. 'And you just happened to have parts for Alexander's piece in your bag, is that it?'

Eliot looked at her steadily. 'What are you suggesting, Gemma? That, somehow, we got wind of a crazy plot to throw Alexander off his stride, and within a couple of hours we had not only worked out a way to solve his problem but managed to lay our hands on a set of orchestral parts and get them here? On a Saturday afternoon?'

He let his questions float around in the air. After a while they seemed to realise they were not going to get answered, and slipped away into the air conditioning vents. Gemma swallowed, looked at her watch, then at Russell, and they both retreated: he to his upstairs eyrie and she to her accustomed place in the centre of the studio floor.

Eliot let out a long breath.

'Nice one,' murmured Alexander, and went to sit down in his own zone.

The lights went up again, and Barney smoothly introduced The Dark Harps, who shimmered blackly under the glare, their golden harps adding to the lustre. They wove their usual spell of absolute silence and stillness before opening with Chopin's *Nocturne Opus 9 No. 2*. After the fireworks people had experienced just moments before, they filled the studio with a calm waltz, with Bożenka herself adding embellishments almost as incidental brushwork. They lulled people into soporific appreciation, and came to rest gently. Before the audience had a chance to wonder if that was that and if they should applaud, Bozenka's eyes flashed at her fellow harpists as she led them straight into more Chopin: this time his *Etude Opus 10 No. 4*, also known as the "Torrent". They fell into it at a furious pace, fingers flying over their strings at incomprehensible speeds. Five harps playing at full tilt was quite the spectacle: pedals being shifted around under the black folds of their dresses, eyes locked with each other as they slotted themselves into the sparkling geometry of the piece, arriving as a whole at the final cadence.

This time the audience were in no doubt of the finish, and applauded the sheer technical skill they had just witnessed. Bożenka and the others stood and bowed, accepting their due.

'That really was impressive,' said Erin to Ann, joining in the applause.

'She must have a beating heart in there somewhere, to be able to play like that,' agreed Ann. 'But please don't ever leave me alone with her.'

Another set of judging, another commercial break, and the harps had been replaced on stage by Ambient Sounds.

Charlie turned away from the stage and pulled a face. 'You can't make me look. I might have to listen, but you can't make me look.'

Gregory seemed to have disassociated himself from the comments he had been filmed saying. Maybe he had simply disassociated himself from normal life. He stood behind his tall microphone stand, again holding it like he thought a rock star would. One can only assume he was wearing sunglasses in his imagination. Behind him were his usual ragtag of musical associates: piano, bass, violin, trusty alto flute, and – yes – the triangle player.

He looked straight into a camera to speak. It happened not to be the camera actually transmitting at that point, but he was not to know and nobody in the control room switched.

'Tonight, we have heard various musicians share with you what they thought was important to share. It's not up to me to proscribe laughter. I had prepared another of my compositions, melding what I believe is the essence of life with the transcendental flowering of music. However, since learning this week of yet another example of individual creativity being crushed under the boot of tedious so-called quote commercial acceptability unquote, I have decided to dedicate my performance tonight to those of us who are talent's lodestar. If you choose not to stand in solidarity with me, that is your destiny. But not mine.' He clenched his fist against his heart. 'Not mine. My band –' he waved behind him without looking '– will play around my thoughts. We will weave together as one and wend our way into the wonder of words.'

About halfway through this speech, Erin and Charlie had got the giggles, which quickly spread through the orchestra. By the time Gregory had finished, Ann was wiping her eyes and Eliot had his entire face in both hands, his shoulders shaking. Barney was staring at Gregory, open-mouthed, with two fingers pressed against one ear, clearly receiving more instructions from Russell. Olive's lips were twitching, and Anthony and Maria were openly smiling.

Gregory, unperturbed, waved again at his band, who started up a cod-jazz rhythmic vibe. The members of Riffraff immediately turned to each other and rolled their eyes, Paraic quite clearly swearing fluently. Gregory leaned into his microphone, closed his eyes and started to speak.

Nobody was quite sure, afterwards, how long he had been allowed to go on. Viewers at home were treated to perhaps a minute or two of Gregory droning on about how poetry would anneal his soul, accompanied by a singularly inappropriate perky triangle ting every now and then, until the camera cut to Barney apologising that because of the overrun owing to previous technical difficulties, they were going to have to go to a break now and he would catch them on the other side. The shot that framed him happily did not include the three judges just off to his right who were by then doubled up with silent laughter.

When they were off-air, the stage managers crept closer to the musicians until their presence was off-putting enough to affect their playing, and they paused, at which point Gregory opened his eyes and stopped talking. Barney took that opportunity to lead enthusiastic applause, walking out to Gregory on stage and explaining quietly that they had been forced to go to a commercial break but jolly well done and he was sorry for his travails. Gregory and his band were hurried back to their zone, and Riffraff took their place on the stage. The judges meanwhile gave their scores quietly, and their mediocre totals for Gregory joined the others on the leader board without fanfare.

After such an episode, the audience welcomed Riffraff's set with audible pleasure, and they were soon nodding along with a superb arrangement of "My Funny Valentine".

Carl leaned back in his chair, put his hands behind his head and sighed happily. 'This is more like it. Paraic knows what he's doing.'

His chair was right next to Gregory's, on the border between the green and blue zones, and if Carl's elbow happened to hit the back of Gregory's head as he stretched, it was certainly an accident.

Ten minutes of great music had perked everyone up by the end of Riffraff's performance, and there was warm applause greeting them as they finished. Barney thanked them, and asked the judges for their thoughts one final time.

Once their scores had been recorded, the rankings showed Alexander (with impromptu orchestra) was top with a perfect score, the orchestra being non-impromptu was only one point behind themselves, and Bożenka, Riffraff and Fiddle Me This were all within a few points of each other close behind. Trailing by tens of points was Gregory, who was by this stage refusing even to look at the board, muttering to anyone who would listen that art transcended opinion and also that his opinion was the only one that mattered. He had his laptop open and was typing furiously: whether it was a new poetic masterpiece, his next blog post or simply an angry email was uncertain. People who looked over his shoulder reported there was a lot of caps lock work going on.

Barney looked to camera. 'Now, don't go away, because on the other side of this break we'll find out who has won fifty thousand pounds…' he paused to let the audience let out a scripted *woo!* as encouraged by the staff waving in front of them, 'as winner of the grand final of *Pass The Baton*!'

Chapter 39

While the cameras weren't rolling, Gemma was having her regular conversation into the headset. Charlie held his set near his ear, surrounded by a crowd of players including Eliot, Erin, Charlie, Ann, Kayla, Carl and Alexander. They couldn't all hear properly, and relied on Charlie's face to relay the salient points.

'What do we do if they try it again?' whispered Kayla from near the back.

'Flatten 'em,' suggested Carl.

'Shh,' said Eliot, flapping his hand.

Charlie put his finger to his lips and turned the volume up as much as he could.

'*I think we should give it to the harps,*' said Russell. '*I've always said, those dresses are stunning. We could use them going forward.*'

'*But they're not the easiest people to work with, Russell. Come on.*'

'*I can't let Leakey go through. The sponsors need to know who's in charge, and if it's between me and this audience, it's gonna fucking be me. He ruined my boots.*'

'*The orchestra, then?*'

'*After what they did? No fucking way. And how did they know anyway? Are we bugged? Shit.*'

'*What? No way – they can't.*' Gemma looked round to the performers' area, and saw the crowd of people around Charlie. '*What the fuck? Are you listening to us?*'

Charlie, who had his back to Gemma, again put his finger to his lips and motioned for everyone to remain absolutely still.

Russell's voice sounded impatient. '*Forget it. They're just talking, from what I can see from here. Leakey's there too. Look – it'll have to be Riffraff then, yeah? We can't give it to the kids.*'

'*What? Yeah, maybe. Obviously not Gregory.*'

'*Obviously. Though he was useful. But no.*'

Gemma looked at her watch. '*Right. Riffraff it is. You prime Barney.*'

She flicked her headset switch, glanced over at the orchestra's zone, and walked quickly to the junction box behind the screen. Charlie switched off his set, stowed it safely away in his bag and followed her with his gaze.

'So what do we do?' he asked the crowd around him, without taking his eyes off her.

'Can I flatten 'em?' asked Carl.

'Tempting,' said Alexander.

Erin smiled. 'No.'

'We've got about thirty seconds to decide,' said Eliot. 'The adverts will be over soon.'

Ann put her hand on Carl's arm. 'Right, listen. You go and tell that guy you know in Riffraff what's going on. He doesn't have to do anything, but it's only fair they know. And I'll have a word with Olive Yessel.'

Without waiting for any reply, Ann half-walked, half-ran over to the judges.

253

'Bloody hell,' said Charlie. 'I've never seen her move so fast.'

Carl made his way equally quickly to Paraic, and immediately started talking to him quietly. Olive looked startled when she saw Ann approaching, and Barney tried to direct her back to her zone, but Ann was not to be diverted. Barney was left loitering uncertainly in front of the judges' chairs. He looked at his watch.

Eliot nodded. 'Barney's learning the hard way. You've got no chance, mate, when Ann's on a mission.'

Ann leaned down beside Olive, on the other side from the other two judges, and could be seen speaking urgently into her ear. Olive's face, always relatively serious, did not move. Her eyes flicked over to the orchestra, where she saw most of them looking directly at her. Ann straightened up and walked back to them, and reached the green zone just as Carl returned from speaking to Paraic.

'Barney was no match for you,' said Erin.

'I told him I just wanted to thank Olive for being a judge – from one string player to another, kind of thing.' Ann chuckled. 'I think he bought it.'

'Nice one,' said Carl. 'Message delivered to my mate Paraic – and the others. They didn't know if they should do anything. I said I didn't know either, but knowledge is power, or something. Fuck knows. Told them we were just telling Olive too.'

At that moment, the lights changed and the theme intro started up. Gemma reappeared from behind the screen, looked up to Russell and nodded.

'Right, everybody,' said Eliot. 'Let's sit down and see what shakes out. And Ann, by the way – you are a bloody marvel, no matter what happens.'

'Hear hear,' said Alexander, smiling and going back to his own seat. 'Didn't want the poxy money anyway.'

Barney took his place facing the camera.

'Here we go. Oh god,' said Erin, moving her hand over to Charlie's lap and clutching his hand without looking. Charlie turned to look at her for a moment, but as she didn't turn to him, he squeezed her hand and went back to watching Barney.

'Aaaaaand we're back!' cried Barney. 'All that remains of this very first final of *Pass The Baton* is to ask our wonderful audience here to vote. Those votes will be added to our judges' scores to decide who will win that fifty thousand pounds!'

The wonderful audience dutifully clapped. The entire row of Fiddle Me This parents got up to do a coordinated cheerleading routine, but forgot they were British parents and so, when it came to doing it in public, what actually transpired were some half-hearted wiggles and a few embarrassed waves. The cheerleading cheerleaders, who had clearly choreographed the whole thing, made up for this by whooping as they gyrated, which only made the half-hearted lot even more embarrassed.

'Oh god,' said Kayla. 'If their kids don't win it'll be mayhem. I know a few parents like that at school.'

Barney was trying to ignore the parents who were now attempting a Mexican wave but didn't know how to reverse it along their row, so they ended up looking like a very confused wave tank someone had tipped on its side and had sprung a leak. He rallied, and engaged the judges in one last conversation before the results came through.

'So, Anthony, tell me your highlight from the series.'

Anthony leaned back in his chair and crossed his legs. 'Well, Barney, I must say I had a soft spot for those xylophone players in skeleton suits!' He performed a performative laugh and waited for the audience to join in and then subside. 'But seriously though, the standard has been incredibly high throughout the series, I think you'll agree. All the musicians who have made it to this final tonight deserve our praise.'

Barney looked at the audience and winked. 'Anthony there, sitting on the fence. And how about you, Maria? What stands out in your memory from what you've seen over the series?'

Maria Romano straightened her back and smiled. 'It would have to be those talented singers of Arioso, if I'm being completely honest, Barney. I can't believe they didn't get through to the final. Not,' she looked over at the performers quickly, 'not that I begrudge a single one of you your place here. All thoroughly deserved! But I have to confess a little professional preference creeping in there.' She laughed.

'Shall we tell her they were part of the stitch-up?' whispered Charlie.

'Let's get the first lot of revelations out of the way,' said Erin. 'If there are going to be any.'

Barney turned to Olive Yessel. 'And you, Olive? Has anything tickled your fancy?'

Olive turned to look directly at Ann. 'I have found so much truth in many performances I have listened to from my seat here. Many people have worked hard and risked much. I am in awe of their dedication.'

Barney cleared his throat, and smiled. 'Well, a sincere and heartening analysis there from one of our most eminent violinists. Brava. But now, the time is upon us! No further ado will be done!'

'Oh for fuck's sake get on with it,' muttered Ann.

'Audience – are you ready?'

The audience cheered.

'OK! Three – two – one – VOTE!'

An energised version of the theme tune played over the speakers. Coloured spotlights roved round the studio. The leader board dissolved into dancing stars. Paraic turned to look at Carl. Olive continued to stare at Ann, who returned her gaze. Eliot shared a shrug with Alexander. Erin gripped Charlie's hand even tighter. Another of the tiny violinists wet themselves in the excitement but nobody noticed until later, when they marvelled at the absorbency of a snowflake costume.

The scoreboard settled, focused, and revealed Riffraff flashing alone in the middle of the board, surrounded by images of exploding fireworks. No other placings were given.

The audience burst into a round of applause, but it was more of a muted sound and, if any of them had been asked, they might have questioned the choice of 'burst' as a verb at all. Even the dancing parents were somehow not utterly convinced. Mrs Ford-Hughes clapped steadfastly, nodding, blinking tears of disappointment back into her eyes. She would rather have died than have anyone think her a bad loser.

Barney meanwhile had beckoned all of Riffraff to join him to receive the oversized fifty thousand pound cheque which at that very moment was entering stage left, carried by two black-clad members of staff. Paraic led his band on stage and stood in front of the judges, who had got to their feet. Anthony and Maria were clapping and smiling. Olive leaned on her stick.

'It's a good job we haven't won,' said Carl. 'Imagine trying to pay that thing into your bank.'

The clapping died down as Barney held a microphone out to Paraic, saying 'Congratulations! Riffraff are our winners! What are you going to do with fifty thousand pounds?'

Paraic took the mic out of Barney's hand, smiling nervously. 'It's – it's a great honour. Thank you. And thank you to the audience for voting for us.'

'Oh shit. He's bottled it,' said Charlie.

'Hang on,' said Erin. 'Look.'

Paraic hadn't finished. 'I'm sure a lot of you did vote for us. We *were* good!' He laughed at the clap that provoked. 'But I think there's a mistake somewhere.'

Gemma jerked her head round to the control room and looked panic-stricken.

'I don't think the votes were counted properly,' Paraic went on. 'I mean, come on!' He gestured to Alexander and the orchestra, and a whoop of genuine delight went round the audience, making it perfectly clear who had truly won the vote. 'Now, I'm not a computer expert, and I'm not going to pretend to understand this. Let's just say that I don't feel fifty thousand pounds better than those guys over there.'

Everyone laughed. Gemma started walking towards Paraic, but he put his hand up to stop her.

Olive stepped forward and stopped next to Paraic, looking at him and nodding. 'I too wonder if there might have been some error in the voting mechanism. Now, I'm old enough to remember steam travel, so I can't claim any specialist knowledge. But I know the difference between right and wrong.'

Paraic smiled at her. 'I've an idea.'

Russell himself burst out of the door at the top of the steps and ran down them in little, tippy-tappy steps that sounded loud in the studio silence. 'I'm sorry, but this has gone rather off-script, wouldn't you say? We are out of time. Riffraff, congratulations.' He turned to the audience and tried to get them to start another round of applause, but they just sat there staring at him.

'My idea,' continued Paraic, turning to the audience and other performers, 'is to share the prize. How about ten grand each, guys?'

The performers erupted into cheers. Even Gregory raised his head and looked interested.

Olive leaned in to Paraic. 'There are six groups, dear. That doesn't add up.'

Paraic laughed and looked at the audience. He was an experienced performer, and knew he had them in the palm of his hand. 'Gregory said he didn't want the money – something about capitalism being shite. Nobody wants us to split this six ways, do you? We're not sharing it with him, are we?'

'NO!' yelled the audience, delighted with the way this was turning out.

Russell and Gemma were forced to stand on the studio floor and watch their careful plans go horribly awry. More pressingly, Russell thought about the bollocking he was about to get from his superiors for allowing the word 'shite' to go out live on early Saturday evening telly – even if it was said in the most affable Irish accent and might be able to be passed off as a local dialect.

Olive smiled and nodded, and shook Paraic by the hand. 'Well done, young man.'

Paraic beckoned to the rest of the performers. The tiny violinists raced up to the stage and got there first (of course), followed by the orchestra and Alexander's horn quartet, and even Bożenka and her harpists walked quietly to join them at the side of the stage. Gregory slammed his laptop shut, grabbed his bag and walked out of the studio towards the atrium. The rest of his band looked bemused.

The noise level in the studio was now truly enthusiastic, with all the stagehands joining in, whooping and clapping above their heads. Alexander kissed Bożenka's hand and went over to lift Eliot up in a hug. Mrs Ford-Hughes, unable to contain herself, made her way to the stage area and was enveloped by members of the orchestra. The last thing viewers at home saw was Barney trying to say goodbye to them over the heads of yelling performers and just as excitable audience members.

When the cameras had stopped rolling, Olive walked up to Ann and shook her hand.

'Thank you, Olive,' Ann said, smiling. 'I knew you were the right person to tell.'

'Don't thank me. That brave young man over there is the one. Brave, and generous.' Olive's eyes twinkled. 'What are you going to do with ten thousand pounds?'

'Well,' said Eliot, catching the last of this conversation, 'it might cover the cost of hiring those Schumann parts, eh Pearl?'

Pearl turned round. 'I think it might stretch to a little more than that, Eliot.'

'Posh biscuits for a year!' yelled Charlie.

'You loon,' said Erin, laughing. 'You're so predictable.'

'Am I?' said Charlie. He stepped toward her, leaned close and – since she didn't back away – slowly began to kiss her. A cheer, led by Carl and Kayla, spread through the whole orchestra as she wrapped her arms round his neck and kissed him back.

Olive looked at Ann, smiling. 'I see orchestras haven't changed much.'

'You wouldn't believe how little,' said Ann. 'Nobody learns anything.'

'Hey, Olive,' said Alexander. 'Would you like to come to the pub with us to celebrate? I think we're all going for a drink.'

Acknowledgements

As always, my first thank you is to Abbie Headon: original commissioning editor of the series and tireless supporter of my work, without whom the Stockwell Park Orchestra would never have played in public. The conversations we have in the editing mark-up margins are a pure joy.

Thanks also to copy editor Caroline Goldsmith, proof reader Lynne Walker, Danny Lyle and everyone at Farrago. Their careful reading saved me from more than one embarrassing blooper.

Clare Stacey at Head Design again produced the wonderful cover: her imagination has been a joy to work with throughout this series.

Ben Blackman has been relegated back to the acknowledgements page after the previous book, because the fictional Ben didn't reappear this time. We all know he's itching to get back in.

Finally, I'm certainly not going to thank, but must acknowledge, Covid. *The Prize Racket* is the second novel I've written, delivered and edited during this global pandemic, and trying to keep on being funny is difficult to sustain while so many people are going through hell. I felt a fraud a lot of the time. But, in the end, I decided to carry on pigheadedly doing my job: a professional amuser of people. I can't suddenly be a doctor, but I can help distract us for a while. I deliberately don't let Covid into these books. We deserve some time off. I hope it helps.

About the Author

Isabel Rogers writes poetry and fiction, but never on the same day. She won the 2014 Cardiff International Poetry Competition, was Hampshire Poet Laureate 2016, and her debut collection, *Don't Ask*, came out in 2017 (Eyewear). *Life, Death and Cellos* was her first novel to be published.

She had a proper City job before a decade in the Scottish Highlands, writing and working in the NHS. She now lives in Hampshire, laughs a lot and neglects her cello. She is on Twitter @Isabelwriter.

Also available

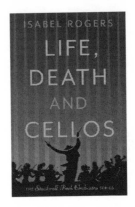

Classical music can be a dangerous pastime...

What with love affairs, their conductor dropping dead, a stolen cello and no money, Stockwell Park Orchestra is having a fraught season.

After Mrs Ford-Hughes is squashed and injured by a dying guest conductor mid-concert, she and her husband withdraw their generous financial backing, leaving the orchestra broke and unsure of its future.

Cellist Erin suggests a recovery plan, but since it involves their unreliable leader, Fenella, playing a priceless Stradivari cello which then goes missing, it's not a fool-proof one. Joshua, the regular conductor, can't decide which affair to commit to, while manager David's nervous tic returns at every doom-laden report from the orchestra's treasurer.

There is one way to survive, but is letting a tone-deaf diva sing Strauss too high a price to pay? And will Stockwell Park Orchestra live to play another season?

Also available

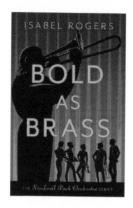

**Community music projects always spread harmony...
don't they?**

When players in Stockwell Park Orchestra fear they may
be getting out of touch with the community, they invite
children from two nearby schools to join them for a season.

Supercilious, rich Oakdean College pupils have never mixed
with the rough Sunbridge Academy kids, and when things
go missing and rumours spread, the situation threatens to
turn ugly. DCI Noel Osmar has to tread carefully: after all,
he's off duty. Step forward, Carl the trombonist.

Can music heal social rifts? Who has been stealing and why?
And will the orchestra's newly-composed fanfare turn out to
be fantastic... or farcical?

The Stockwell Park Orchestra Series, Volume Two

OUT NOW

Note from the Publisher

To receive updates on new releases in the Stockwell Park Orchestra Series – plus special offers and news of other humorous fiction series to make you smile – sign up now to the Farrago mailing list at farragobooks.com/sign-up.